# LUCKY LEAP DAY

## ANN MARIE WALKER

sourcebooks
casablanca

Copyright © 2022 by Ann Marie Walker
Cover and internal design © 2022 by Sourcebooks
Cover art by Elizabeth Turner Stokes

Sourcebooks and the colophon are registered trademarks of Sourcebooks.

Published by Sourcebooks Casablanca, an imprint of Sourcebooks
P.O. Box 4410, Naperville, Illinois 60567-4410
(630) 961-3900
sourcebooks.com

Cataloging-in-Publication Data is on file with the Library of Congress.

Printed and bound in Canada.
MBP 10 9 8 7 6 5 4 3 2 1

*For Maggie*

# CHAPTER 1

IT WAS OFFICIAL: WHISKEY WAS the devil. Not in a blue dress but an amber bottle. It didn't matter whether it was mixed with a fruity punch or poured straight into a shot glass. Although, to be fair, the shot glasses were definitely a bad idea. So, so bad. The thought alone had Cara squeezing her eyes shut tighter. Not that it was any use. The bright morning sun still felt like fire even with her eyes closed.

What had she been thinking? She was a lightweight when it came to drinking alcohol. Why in the world had she thought she could handle Irish whiskey? Was it because her grandmother had been known to end each day with a "wee nip"? Or because a bartender with a brogue so thick, it was hard to believe he was still speaking English had charmed her into trying his famous whiskey punch? Or maybe, just maybe, it was because she'd spent most of her time in Dublin—a whopping three days—thinking about how she was supposed to be in Ireland with her now ex-boyfriend?

Either way, the end result was the same. Which was why opening her eyes, much less standing up, would have to wait until the bed stopped spinning. It wasn't as though she'd set out to get completely "stocious" as the locals liked to say. In fact, the first drink was way more punch than whiskey, and there was no denying it went down smoothly. After that, it was a slippery slope that led to one too many shots, which led to...what exactly?

Cara had a nagging feeling in the pit of her stomach that she'd done something stupid. Then again, maybe the uneasiness she felt in her gut was just a whole lot of undigested alcohol.

She drew a slow breath through her nose and thought back... A band playing to a crowded dance floor. The guitar player winking at her from the stage. *What was his name? Finn...Maguire?* A dog nudging her thigh. *A dog in a pub?* No, that was later. *But where?* Putting her glass on the bar when the set ended. Weaving through the crowd...*and then?*

*Ah, yes.* The kiss.

While on a scale of one to ten, kissing a relative stranger probably ranked a minus two when it came to bad decisions made in a bar, Cara Kennedy was not that kind of girl. Back home, she was definitely more wallflower than femme fatale. But in Ireland, Cara could be any version of herself she wanted, and apparently what she wanted was to kiss the cute guitar player. She'd marched right up to Finn and kissed him. And not some shy little peck either. At first, he'd been startled, probably caught off guard by the awkward woman who now grabbed him and kissed him with whiskey-fueled confidence, but it only took half a heartbeat for his arms to come around her waist as he deepened their kiss. Then all bets were off.

"I don't know what brought this on, lass, but I'm here for

it," he'd whispered in her ear. And then his teeth nipped her earlobe just before his lips began leaving a trail of openmouthed kisses along her neck—stopping to gently suck on the spot that never failed to drive her wild before dragging his tongue back up the column of her throat—just like he was doing now in her semiconscious dream. Cara squirmed. While she couldn't deny the pleasure her memories brought, her head hurt so badly that any sudden movements might have resulted in some form of aneurysm. Fantasy Finn, guitar player and kisser extraordinaire, seemed to suffer no such plight. He was relentless, licking her neck, then moving lower to lick her arm before nudging his snout under the palm of her hand and whimpering.

*What?*

Cara forced her eyes open to find a black-furred canine prodding her hand for a pat. Wait. She knew that face. She knew that white streak across its nose. Oscar Wilde. No, no, not Oscar Wilde. Oscar the dog, named after Oscar Wilde. Finn's dog.

What was Finn's dog doing in her hotel room?

*Oh no...*

Cara's brain finally caught up to her reality as she slowly took in her surroundings: navy-blue walls covered with posters advertising a local band, a small, wooden desk holding a pile of books and a few empty beer bottles, a guitar case propped against the far corner, and green-and-blue-striped curtains that were askew and doing a crappy job blocking even a fraction of the sunlight. The room was far from that of a luxury hotel chain, because it wasn't a hotel room at all. It was a bedroom.

It was Finn's bedroom.

She turned her head—slowly, so as not to crank up the volume on the distorted drum solo of "Everlong" currently playing behind her eyeballs—to find the man himself fast asleep on the pillow beside her. Even hungover as hell, Cara couldn't help but appreciate the sight of him. Everything from the impossibly long lashes that fanned out over his cheeks, to the stubble that covered his strong jaw, to the smattering of dark-brown hair in the center of his otherwise bare chest...

*Bare chest...*

A moment of clarity filtered through her hangover, and as it did, Cara realized Finn's wasn't the only bare chest in the room. She glanced down at the hunter-green sheet draped across her body, covering one boob while exposing the other in some sort of half-assed version of a toga. She was absolutely naked beneath, something that should've occurred to her the minute she woke up, but to be fair, she wasn't exactly operating on all cylinders.

She closed her eyes again, then pressed the heels of her hands against the lids in a pathetic attempt to quiet the pounding long enough to piece together the string of events. One: she'd had far too much to drink. Two: she'd kissed Finn at the pub. Three: she was naked in his bed.

Didn't take a rocket scientist to figure that one out. And while points one and two weren't exactly her finest moments, if Cara were honest with herself, they weren't what was causing the queasy feeling deep inside her. It was the fact that she'd spent the night with Mr. Sexy Brogue, and yet she had absolutely no recollection of actually having had sex with him.

She could practically hear her friend Julia's reaction. *Way to go, Cara. Only you would finally have a vacation fling and yet somehow manage to come home without any memories as a souvenir.*

Oscar whimpered in what sounded like empathy but in reality was just a plea for affection. *I hear ya, buddy,* Cara thought. *I just can't quite lift my arm yet.* Or speak words out loud, which was just as well seeing as how she wanted to collect her wits, not to mention her clothes, before Finn woke up.

"Morning," a groggy voice next to her said. So much for making herself somewhat presentable before he saw her.

Cara lifted her hands off her face and opened her eyes. Finn was staring at her from across the pillow, looking about a thousand percent better than she felt. Not only were his green eyes clear and bright, but he was actually smiling. She really shouldn't have been surprised. Finn Maguire had been smiling pretty much since the moment they'd met. "Morning."

"You're naked," he said as his gaze drifted over her body.

She let out a small laugh that nearly split her brain in two. "I noticed." Not that she did it often, but when she did, waking up next to a guy who was looking at her the way Finn was would have been the start of something that would have ended hot and sweaty. At the moment, the only sweat in her immediate future was the cold, clammy variety she felt misting on her brow.

She needed water. And a bathroom. And for both, she would prefer to be dressed. But as Cara scanned the room, she didn't see any of her clothes. Not on the chair or the dresser. Not even dangling off a lampshade.

She pulled the sheet higher and attempted to sit up, only to quickly lie back down. *Whoa.* Neither the stomach nor the head liked that too much. She was, however, upright long enough to see that the floor was bare. "Do you happen to know where my clothes are?"

Finn nodded. "I think they're in the living room. And maybe the kitchen," he said. "I'm afraid they're a bit scattered about."

Cara assumed her clothes were "scattered about" because Finn had been removing them one piece at a time as they made their way to the bedroom. She'd no sooner had the thought than a fuzzy image popped into her head. "Did I…"

"Do a little striptease?"

Unable to speak, she merely nodded.

Finn's answering grin was the only confirmation she needed.

"Oh god," she said, closing her eyes again. If only squeezing them tight enough could actually make her disappear.

"Aww, no need to be embarrassed."

She opened one eye. "Seriously, on a scale of one to ten, how bad was it?"

"Bad? It was bloody fantastic."

"Good to know," she said. But that wasn't actually what she needed to know. Cara took a deep breath and asked the question that had been weighing on her mind since the moment she realized she was naked.

"Did we use a condom?" *Please say yes. Please say yes.*

"No."

*No?* How drunk had she been to have had unprotected sex with a guy she barely knew? She didn't even have unprotected sex with her ex-boyfriend. Then again, in the end, it turned out she barely knew him either.

"It's okay, luv. Don't panic. We didn't actually have sex."

"Are you sure?"

He chuckled. "I'm fairly certain."

"How certain?"

"On a scale of one to ten," he said, quoting her earlier guide, "I'd say ten out of ten we didn't have sex."

"Really?"

"Yes, really." Finn lifted the sheet to reveal that he was fully dressed from the waist down. "Unless after making love to you, I decided to put my jeans, belt, and boots back on before falling asleep."

The relief Cara felt over finding out she hadn't had unprotected sex with a virtual stranger was fleeting, and the satisfaction she might have felt over hearing Finn use the words *making love* as supposed to oh, say, *banging you*, was nonexistent because the thought hammering away at the forefront of her mind was, *I stripped for the man, and then he didn't even want to have sex with me.*

"Not that I didn't want to, mind," Finn said as if reading her thoughts. "In fact, we were definitely on our way to. One moment we were, and then the next…" Finn cracked a lopsided grin. "Well, here we are." He rubbed the stubble on his chin. "Guess we can chalk it up to too much whiskey."

"Guess so," Cara agreed, then on a nervous laugh, she added, "At least we didn't do anything stupid." She meant what she said, and yet she couldn't deny the twinge of disappointment that twisted through her belly. Not that she would have wanted to have had sex in the state she'd been in the night before, but it still felt like a lost opportunity. When else in her life was she going to have the opportunity to take a page out of someone else's script and have a passionate, no-strings-attached fling with a sexy Irishman? Never, that was when. Because even though it looked like Finn was sporting some serious morning wood under those jeans, Cara was in no condition to even attempt slow and easy, let alone hot and heavy. There was also the fact that she knew she looked even worse than she felt, and that wasn't taking into account her dragon breath. Yep, the opportunity for a vacation fling had definitely flung.

Oscar whimpered again, and this time, even though her arm felt like lead, Cara somehow managed to place her hand on his head if for no other reason than to stop him from making a noise that sounded like a trumpet blaring in her already pounding head.

*Ah, yes.* Peace and quiet.

Her eyes drifted shut.

"We should probably talk about what happened at the pub," Finn said.

So much for peace and quiet.

Cara braced herself for the embarrassing details of the night before that Finn was undoubtedly about to share, but when he spoke, all he said was, "You know, the Leap Day stuff."

*Leap Day?* What the heck did Leap Day have to do with anything? Sure, she'd gone to the pub on the twenty-ninth of February, but only because that was the night Finn's band was playing, not because it was Leap Day. Wait. The band had been playing *because* it was Leap Day. That was right. Something about St. Brigid and gloves and women taking control of their destiny and...

*Holy hell.*

Cara opened her eyes, and as she did, a cloud shifted outside the window and a beam of sunlight streamed into the room, catching on a band of silver foil twisted around the ring finger of her left hand. She blinked, then blinked again as flecks of sun glinted off the makeshift ring.

The last words she'd spoken—*at least we didn't do anything stupid*—ricocheted around her head.

*No.*

*It had to be some kind of joke.*

Her gaze darted to Finn's face. He didn't look shocked or even surprised—and he certainly didn't look like they were about to share a laugh—but he did look confused. A million questions formed on her lips, but none could make their way out of her mouth. She reached across the bed and grabbed his left hand. His ring finger was sporting a band of twisted foil that matched her own.

And just like that, the word dam burst.

"Tell me this is a joke. How did this happen? What did we do? What were we thinking? No. We didn't, did we? I mean, no one would have let us, right?"

Finn reached for her, but Cara was already in motion. She rolled out of the bed, taking the sheet with her. "This can't be happening."

Finn's brows rose. "You honestly don't remember?"

"Do I look like I remember?" Cara knew her voice was several octaves too high, but there wasn't much she could do about it. At the moment, it was taking every bit of concentration to keep from emptying the contents of her stomach all over the hardwood floors.

Oscar stood at the edge of the mattress and barked.

Finn climbed out of bed. "Let me run him out really quick, and then we can talk."

Cara took full advantage of the reprieve, stumbling to the bathroom on trembling legs. She might not have been able to remember all the events of the previous night, but one thing was certain: her life was a huge mess. There was no telling what it was going to take to sort it all out, but first things first. Right now, she had a pressing need for a toilet and a toothbrush. She knew she wouldn't have the luxury of the latter, but surely Finn wouldn't mind if she stole a little of his toothpaste to swipe across her gums. Least he could do, seeing as how he was apparently her husband.

*Her husband!*

The word echoed in her head as she gulped cold water straight from the faucet. After splashing some on her face, she straightened to face the mirror. The raccoon-eyed reflection staring back at her was a judgmental bitch, and rightfully so, but beating herself up would have to wait. Her *husband* would be back in a few minutes. Maybe if she tried really hard, she could salvage a shred of dignity by piecing together a few of her own memories before asking him to fill in the gaps.

Cara dropped to the floor. The cool tile felt like heaven against her overheated skin, and before she even realized what she was doing, she'd stretched out with her cheek pressed against the floor. *That's nice.* Maybe if she rewound her thoughts to the moment when she first met Mr. Sexy Brogue, she'd be able to figure out how three days later, she was Mrs. Finn Maguire.

# CHAPTER 2

EVERYTHING HAD SEEMED SO SIMPLE when she flew to Dublin. But that was before Cara drank her weight in whiskey. Before she decided to act on impulse. Before she woke up married.

On the plane, she'd been full of hope that her time in Ireland was going to be just what she needed to recharge not only her body but her soul. Despite never having been to the birthplace of her great-grandmother, seeing the lush, green landscape from the airplane's window—laid out below her like a patchwork quilt dotted with thatched roofs and flocks of sheep—had felt like coming home. Even the flight attendant had looked as though she could have been Cara's sister, having the same brown hair and blue eyes as all the women in the Kennedy family. Cara could even see a hint of freckles beneath the woman's makeup that nearly matched her own. For a moment, she'd wondered if everyone she passed on the streets of Dublin would look like a long-lost relative. That feeling—combined with the fact that the seat next to hers was empty and the wine was free—had Cara convinced that her trip to Ireland might turn out to be the best decision she ever made.

Even a lost suitcase wasn't enough to dampen her optimism. Besides, it wasn't *really* lost. The airline knew where it was— London, to be exact—and promised it would be delivered to the hotel as soon as it arrived. Sure, it meant she'd have to spend her first day in Dublin dressed in the same yoga pants and oversize sweatshirt she'd worn on the plane, but still, she was in Dublin— *Dublin!*—and she had the passport stamp to prove it.

Unlike most of her friends, Cara had made it to the age of twenty-seven without ever using the little blue booklet that held the promise of adventure in faraway lands. She couldn't afford to study abroad when she was in college, and since then, her life had been consumed with work, work, and more work. But not for the next three days. For the next three days, she was going to explore Dublin's cobblestone streets by day, drink dark beer in cozy pubs by night, and, most importantly, pretend she didn't have a care in the world.

But as she stepped out of the terminal, it didn't feel like she was in Dublin. In fact, it didn't feel like she was in Europe at all. It wasn't like she was expecting a man dressed in a tweed hat and a wool sweater to greet her on the sidewalk with a pint of Guinness, but she *did* expect to hear a few Irish brogues as she made her way through the throngs of passengers dragging suitcases, waiting for buses, or hailing cabs. Instead, what she heard was mostly other Americans with a few Eastern Europeans sprinkled in here and there. Walking along the wet pavement, Cara felt like she could have been in any city in the northern United States. At least it wasn't raining anymore, because from the looks of the swimming-pool-size puddles, it had been coming down in sheets.

When Cara reached the rideshare platform, she opened the app. Her request was picked up almost immediately. Devin would arrive in a black Toyota in four minutes.

As she waited, her mind wandered to thoughts of hot water and cool sheets. She might have had to wear day-old clothes, but at least she could enjoy a shower and a short nap before launching into full tourist mode. Her entire body felt heavy and sore, and while a soaking tub was an unlikely luxury given the reputation European hotel rooms had for being small and efficient, if she were lucky, maybe they'd installed one those oversize rain shower heads. Cara's eyes began to close. She could almost feel the cascade of water...

...sloshing up from the curb.

*What the...?* Cara's eyes flew open as a black Toyota swerved back into traffic. *Devin?* She looked down at the screen of her soaking-wet phone. Sure enough, her ride had been canceled. Guess her driver realized dousing his passenger with a tidal wave of murky water was going to earn him one star and had decided to cut his losses.

Cara pushed aside the hair that was now plastered to her face and called for another ride. Once again, her request was picked up in seconds. Now all she had to do was hope her new driver—she glanced at her phone again—some guy named Finn, didn't mind a waterlogged rider, because at the moment, she was drenched clear to her underwear.

A rather beat-up Volkswagen Golf arrived a few minutes later. This was her five-star ride?

Cara shook the excess water from her hand and reached

for the door handle. If she hadn't been so cold, she would have taken a moment to remind herself yet again of career goal number seventeen—earning enough to order Uber Black—but she had bigger concerns than the fact that her driver's car had likely rolled off the assembly line the same year she'd graduated from middle school. At the top of that list was him being okay with a wet back seat, followed by her room being ready when she arrived so she wasn't forced to drip-dry in the lobby. Of course, her suitcase's miraculous arrival wouldn't hurt either.

"Are you Cara?" the driver asked as she leaned into the back seat, and as he did, all thoughts of her soggy panties and matted hair left her, because, holy guacamole, she'd just hit the Irish brogue jackpot. Then he turned and flashed her a lopsided grin, and not only did his perfect rating suddenly make sense, but for the first time in her life, Cara understood what people meant when they said their heart skipped a beat. Her breath caught, and for a split second, it felt as though the entire world stood still.

"Cara?" he asked again.

"Umm, yeah," she finally replied as though she'd forgotten her own name. And who knows, maybe she had. Because not only did her Uber driver have a bona fide Irish accent, but he was hands down the cutest guy she'd seen in…well, ever. And that was saying a lot given the people she met in LA. Just last week, she'd been in the same room as Tom Holland. Granted, it was a conference room at the agency where she worked, and he'd been there to meet with her boss, but still.

Her driver didn't say another word. Instead, he began pushing buttons on the app as though it were every day that he picked up a passenger who looked like she'd just climbed out of a swamp.

"You sure you don't mind…?"

He glanced up, and she gestured to her dripping clothes.

"Not at all," he said, his words all rolling together into one. *Notattall.* The grin was back, and this time, an undeniable mischief lit his green eyes. Cara couldn't tell if it was because he found her charming or ridiculous, but judging by the fact that she'd only spoken five words to him so far, her money was on the latter. Not that a longer conversation would have changed much. Cara was the queen of awkward small talk, at least in her personal life where she usually found herself either tongue-tied or oversharing. There was no middle ground, and honestly, she wasn't sure which one was worse. Shame they didn't give out medals for such an undesirable skill, because if there was a foot to be inserted into a mouth or a misinterpreted comment to be paired with an uncomfortable laugh, Cara could pretty much count on sticking the landing.

Thankfully, her embarrassing tendencies didn't apply to the work environment. Maybe because everything there was transactional. Or maybe because she felt confident in her role as an assistant, as mundane as it might be. There was no risk in preparing a contract, nothing personal about making a lunch reservation, and no emotion involved with walking her boss's pampered poodle. But with a man? And a hot one, no less? Forget about it; she was toast.

"Looks like you've had a rough welcome to our fair city," her driver said as Cara slid into the back seat. "Can't very well leave you on the pavement." A small frown creased his brow. "No cases?"

"None in this country." She'd no sooner closed the car door than the charcoal sky released what could only be described as buckets of rain. Cara had never seen anything like it, but her driver was as unfazed by the sudden downpour as he was by her soggy clothes.

He turned to face the road, but then his eyes met hers in the rearview mirror, setting off a flurry of butterflies somewhere deep inside her. "I'm Finn, by the way." Cara couldn't see his mouth, but from the way his eyes crinkled at the corners, she knew he was smiling again. "Guess you already knew that from the app."

With that, he merged into the steady traffic. Finn's focus might have been on the road, but Cara never took her eyes off his reflection in the mirror. It was as though she couldn't look away. Normally, she paid little to no attention to a taxi or rideshare driver. Not that she meant to be rude, more that a few minutes alone in the back seat of a car meant a few minutes to catch up on the bajillion emails and texts she dealt with on a daily basis. Maybe it was the jet lag or the sexy brogue, but whatever the reason, she couldn't seem to tear her gaze away from Five-Star Finn.

While the rearview mirror offered a limited view of his face, this new angle did afford her an opportunity to admire his hair. Aside from his eyes, a guy's hair was the first thing she noticed. In Cara's opinion, the way he styled it and the amount of product he used said a lot about a man. Mr. Sexy Irish Brogue's dark-brown hair checked all the right boxes: well kept on the sides and back, but a little too long on top with just the right amount of dishevel-ment. Her own personal kryptonite. It looked soft too, not gunked up with products, and for a moment, it was all she could do not to reach out and touch it. *Right*, she thought, because that was what a normal woman would do. She could only imagine the story about the creepy American he'd tell his friends at the pub later that night. Not that she knew he'd go to a pub, but between his green eyes, his sexy accent, and his cream cable-knit sweater, the guy looked like he'd stepped out of an Irish tourism ad. Made sense he'd clock out and head to the local pub for a pint.

The car rolled to a stop at a red light, and a dog popped its head in the space between the two front seats. He was black and sort of like a Lab but with longer, wavier hair and a white streak across his nose. He looked nice enough, and judging by the way his tail was wagging, he was friendly enough—which already made him a far cry from her boss's uptight poodle—but historically, animals and Cara were a bad mix. Didn't matter if it were a dog, a cat, or a guinea pig, for some reason, she seemed to repel them all equally. And after her recent string of bad luck when it came to matters of the heart, she'd have been lying if she said she wasn't starting to wonder if her invisible force field now applied to men as well.

Once again, Finn's eyes met hers in the rearview mirror. "Hope you don't mind dogs."

Cara was just about to tell him that it was usually the dogs who weren't necessarily fans when the pup jumped into the back seat and began licking the side of her face.

*Okay, then...*

"Oscar!" Finn said. "That's no way to treat a lady."

Oscar looked at his owner for all of two seconds then came back to lick the one spot he'd apparently missed.

"Sorry 'bout that. He's not usually such a needy buck." Finn glanced over his shoulder and cocked a lopsided grin. "Guess he likes you."

"Guess so," Cara said. Oscar nudged his head under her hand for a stroke. The irony of the situation—or maybe the jet lag—nearly had her laughing out loud. Instead of realizing her fantasy of running her fingers through Finn's unruly hair, she was petting his dog. Then again, given the way her life was going these days, that sounded about right.

"First time in Dublin?"

Cara nodded even though she knew his eyes were on the road. "Yes."

"Well, then, on behalf of the nation, *céad míle fáilte*." He met her gaze in the rearview mirror once again. "It's Gaeilge. Means a hundred thousand welcomes."

"Thanks." A shiver rushed across Cara's damp skin. She'd have liked to think it was due to the nip in the air, but if she were honest, it probably had a little something to do with sexy accent guy switching to his country's native tongue. Oh, who was she kidding? It had everything to do with that. Forget dirty talk, this guy could read the dictionary and she'd melt in his hands.

Finn stole another glance over his shoulder. "Sorry," he said. "The heat doesn't work." Then, to his canine companion, he added, "Don't just sit there, Oscar. Warm her up." Cara wasn't sure if Oscar understood his owner's command or merely wanted a better angle for his back rub, but either way, he draped himself across Cara's lap.

"Pleasure-seeker?" Finn asked.

"Excuse me?" Cara croaked.

Finn laughed. "Your trip. Are you here for business or pleasure?"

"Oh, pleasure." In reality, it was neither, but seeing as how "nursing a broken heart" wasn't one of the choices, Cara decided to go with option B.

"Brilliant. Meeting friends at the hotel, then?"

"Nope. It's just me." Solo. Single. Unaccompanied. Alone. Cara would have probably spent the rest of the ride running through synonyms if her driver hadn't asked a question that brought her thesaurus recitation to an abrupt halt.

"If you don't mind my asking, what's a pretty lass like yourself doing traveling alone?"

If she were more like her boss—a woman who had no problem with confrontation—Cara would have taken a moment to explain how a recent study revealed that nearly 60 percent of travelers take at least one solo trip a year and that statistics like that weren't affected by being "pretty" much less a "lass." But Cara wasn't Hollywood's top-grossing agent. She was merely her assistant by day—second chair at that—and a fledgling screenwriter by night. And she certainly didn't have Samantha Sherwood's ability to wither a man with one hard stare. Of course, all of that was irrelevant because if Cara were *really* honest with herself, she had zero desire to chastise her driver because she was far too busy enjoying the compliment portion of his question.

"I was supposed to go with..." Cara paused. If someone in LA had asked that question, she might have told them the whole sordid tale if for no other reason than to have the validation of a total stranger's righteous indignation. But in Dublin, in the back seat of a car driven by the best-looking Uber driver she'd ever seen, regardless of the country, Cara found herself wanting to avoid the rabbit hole she'd been tunneling through the past two weeks. "...a friend," she finally said. "I decided to come anyway because..." There were so many ways she could finished that sentence...

*Because I've never left the United States.*

*Because I've never been anywhere on my own.*

*Because I want a different life, and this is as close to that as I can get.*

*Because I hate the fact that I let myself fall for a man and then he crumpled me up like a piece of paper and tossed me in the trash.*

*Whoa!* That last one took Cara by surprise seeing as how it sounded a bit like a Taylor Swift lyric. And not from the ass-kicking *Reputation* album either, but more like something from the early years when there were a lot of teardrops falling on her guitar.

"Because I deserve to have some fun." She said the words with a surprising amount of conviction. And why not? It was true, and there was no time like the present to start acting like it. After all, it was a new day in a new country, which, she decided then and there, meant a brand-new Cara as well. Besides, the flight was already paid for, so...

"I'll drink to that." Finn's eyes crinkled at the corners again. "Or I would if we were having a pint of Gat."

"Gat?"

"Guinness."

Now, that would be a nice way to start her trip, sitting next to Finn at the bar of a dimly lit pub—make that a booth by a fireplace—sipping a pint of Guinness. Or even better, a bone-warming glass of Irish whiskey. Not that she ever drank whiskey, but when in Rome and all that.

"Where in the States are you from?" Finn asked.

"California."

His eyes met hers in the mirror. "Really? North or South?"

"South. Malibu actually."

Finn's brows shot up. It was a common reaction when she told people where she lived. Usually she was quick to follow the news with the revelation that it wasn't actually her beach house, but rather it belonged to former silver-screen star Penelope Parker, one of her grandmother's oldest friends. If she were really being forthcoming, she'd mention that she didn't actually live in the house at all but rather the pool house. And that she wouldn't even be able to afford *that* if it weren't for the fact that her surrogate grandma let her live in the tiny bungalow rent free. But for some reason, she didn't want to share those details with her handsome-as-hell Uber driver. She was enjoying the look of awe the news had put in his eyes, and considering how she was currently soaked in gutter water, Cara could use whatever advantage she could get.

"Bloody hell, that sounds lethal."

Cara wasn't entirely sure what he meant by *lethal*, but judging by his tone, she assumed it meant something along the lines of *"awesome"* because in truth, that was exactly what it was. There wasn't a day that went by when Cara didn't pinch herself as she sipped coffee on a deck overlooking the Pacific Ocean. She was about to describe it to him, but when she opened her mouth, her teeth began to chatter.

"Sorry again about the heat." Finn frowned. "I'll have you to your hotel in two shakes of a lamb's tail."

The news wasn't as welcome as it should have been, because despite being in desperate need of a hot shower, Cara couldn't help but wish her destination was a bit farther if for no other reason than to listen to Finn a little while longer.

She'd no sooner had the thought than her phone pinged with a text from the hotel informing her that they were unable to accommodate her request for an early check-in.

"No rush," she said on a quiet groan. "My room won't be ready for an hour."

"That's shite," Finn said, and Oscar whimpered in agreement. At least that was what it sounded like. "Sorry, luv."

*Luv?* No doubt about it, she could really get used to being around Irish men.

"It's fine. My mom always said things happen in threes—lost luggage, a cascade of street water, and now this." She attempted a shrug, but instead her shoulders merely shook. "Maybe this means everything else will go smoothly."

Her optimism didn't last long.

As they rounded the corner, Cara spotted her ex coming out of the hotel. *Dammit.* She knew running into him was a possibility seeing as how they were staying at the same hotel, but it wasn't like she'd had much choice since it was the only one in Dublin where she could use points. Still, never in her wildest dreams—or more appropriately, worst nightmares—did she imagine seeing Kyle Banfield for the first time since their breakup after being doused in muddy water. No way she was going to let that happen. "Actually, can you stop here?"

"It's lashing rain, yeah," Finn said. "Don't you want me to get you closer?"

"No, this will be fine," she said then forced a laugh in an attempt to make the whole thing seem normal. Fat chance of that. "Don't think I can get much wetter. Even my panties are soaked…I mean my clothes…I'll be fine once I take them off." Jesus, if only her mouth came with an emergency shutoff valve.

Kyle turned in their direction, causing Cara to duck down in her seat. No doubt her behavior seemed ridiculous, but as much as she hated looking like a weirdo in front of the sexy Irishman, it was better than looking like a drowned rat in front of the asshole American.

She peeked between the passenger seat and its headrest, watching as the doorman hailed a cab for Kyle, and only sat back up once the taillights had disappeared around the corner. A quick glance to the rearview mirror let her know Finn was watching her, although he hadn't said a word.

"Um, sorry about that." She knew from the warmth on her cheeks that they were bright red.

Finn turned, draping one arm over the back of the same passenger seat she'd just been hiding behind. "No need to apologize, luv. I got nowhere to be." His kind words and crooked smile were nearly enough to wipe the image of Kyle out of her mind.

"I'm sure you'd have another fare by now if it weren't for my—" The words were already spilling out of her mouth when it dawned on her that there was no good way to end that sentence.

"It's fine," Finn interrupted with what again sounded like one word. *Tisfine.* "I only make a few airport runs on the weekend." He grinned. "Bit of pub money."

Cara was about to thank him for the ride when he startled her by clapping his hands together. "Right then, how 'bout we take a little drive?"

"A drive?" Cara frowned. "Isn't that what we just did?"

Finn shook his head. "That was a lift. A fare. This would be…" He paused to consider his words. "A bit of a tour."

"You're going to take me on tour?"

"Of sorts."

"Of what exactly?"

He shrugged. "We'll take a spin around the city center while you wait for your room to be ready. No sense in hanging about in the lobby." The mischief in his eyes was back, only this time, she wasn't sure if what she saw was amusement or pity. He was right about the hotel situation. Cara couldn't think of anything worse than having to kill an hour in the lobby of a swanky hotel while looking and feeling like the Creature from the Black Lagoon, with or without the possibility of running into her ex. And it wasn't as though strolling around was an option. It was a mild February, even by Ireland's standards, but far too cold when your clothes were wet. Was that what this was about, saving her from near certain pneumonia? She'd been told Ireland was a hospitable nation, but still, how many guys would offer to take a complete stranger for a "spin around the city" just to keep her warm? Unless…was he *flirting* with her? Nothing had ever sounded so enticing and preposterous all at once. Despite the fact that every cell in her body was screaming *yes*, the ones in her brain were reminding her that she barely knew this man. Then again, she *had* been in his car for the past fifteen minutes.

"Hmm." She narrowed her eyes at him. "Not sure I how I feel about accepting a ride from a stranger."

Finn's expression faltered, but then Cara watched as he realized she was playing. Mostly. He stuck his arm into the back seat. "Finn Maguire."

"Cara Kennedy." She placed her hand in his. His skin was warm against the chill of hers, and the sensation spread as though she'd broken into a molten cake.

"There, we're not strangers anymore." He winked. "Plus, you've been in my car for a while now," he said, echoing the thought that had occurred to her as well.

"That was different. It was a professional transaction."

"I could charge you if it would make you feel better." Cara could tell by the way his lips twitched at the corner of his mouth that he was enjoying their banter.

"And how much would that set me back?"

"Aaah, the price is steep. Would have to be at least ten, maybe twelve smiles."

That wouldn't be a problem seeing as how she was already grinning from ear to ear despite trying her best to maintain a straight face for the sake of their negotiation. "That *is* steep," she said. There was no denying the fact that she was also enjoying their little game—and that spending an hour with Mr. Sexy Brogue beat the hell out of waiting alone in the hotel lobby—but despite his charming introduction, he was still a stranger, at least in the relevant sense of the word.

"I promise not to kill ya and dump your body in the woods," he said as if reading her mind.

"Isn't that exactly what a killer would say?"

"Fair point," he said. "I could call my mam. She'd vouch for me."

Cara considered his offer. He *did* work as a driver, which meant he'd been through some sort of screening process, right? And if nothing else, he had a "mam" he claimed would vouch for him, which also meant he wouldn't want to let her down. Oh, who was she kidding? The gorgeous Irishman in front of her was offering her an adventure, even if only for an hour. Old Cara would have said no, but New Cara was definitely going to say yes.

"For twelve smiles, I'd need the car to have heat. Ten is all I'm willing to offer."

"What if I throw in a sweater?"

"Eleven. That's my final offer."

"You drive a hard bargain, Miss Kennedy, but you have yourself a deal." Finn reached for the hem of his sweater and pulled it over his head, leaving him in only a T-shirt. "Here," he said. "Will be a tad big for you, but it ought to warm you up."

"Thanks."

His gaze dropped to her chest. "Might want to take that wet one off first."

He was right, of course, but it wasn't like she had a private place to change. They sat in awkward silence for a beat before Cara finally clued him in. "I'm not wearing a shirt under this, so if you don't mind…"

"Oh, yeah, sure," Finn said. He turned to face forward, but before he did, Cara caught a glimpse of a grin tugging at the corner of his mouth.

"No peeking in the rearview either."

He chuckled as he flipped the mirror up in a gentlemanly gesture. "Your virtue is safe with me," he said, then added, "although they say body heat is the best way to warm up. Skin to skin."

Cara laughed. "This will be good enough."

"Ah, but as my mam always says, 'tis the quality of the life that makes it worth living."

His words conjured an image of a sweet, gray-haired woman cross-stitching that expression on a pillow while soda bread baked in the oven. "I doubt she meant for you to use that to sneak a peek at my boobs," Cara said as she crouched down in the back seat and wiggled out of her mud-splattered sweatshirt. As she did, the thought of Finn joining her in the back seat for a bit of that skin-to-skin contact he'd just mentioned popped into her jet-lagged mind, and before she knew it, her imagination had them reenacting the steamy car scene from *Titanic*.

"I don't know about that," Finn said, yanking her out of her fantasy. "Mam and Pop had twelve kids, including my mum. I'd say she'd fully support a little boob action."

So Mam was his grandmother, not his mother, and she was the one going to vouch for Finn. Cara wasn't sure if that made her feel better or worse about her decision. Grandmothers were notorious for only seeing the good. Then again, Finn's grandmother sounded like a straight shooter, so maybe...

"Almost done?" he asked, pulling her from her internal debate. "Will be hard to see the sights after the sun sets."

Cara rolled her eyes, knowing full well he couldn't see her. It was barely two o'clock. "One sec." She poked her head through the neck of Finn's sweater. It smelled like him—a mix of laundry detergent and a woodsy cologne—and she would have been lying if she said she hadn't inhaled a deep breath. "All set."

Finn was still smiling as he turned around, but at the sight of her, his expression morphed into something Cara couldn't quite place.

"Everything okay?"

"Yeah, of course." He cleared his throat. "Looks good on you, that's all." Then his nearly ever-present grin returned. "Let's roll."

# CHAPTER 3

THE FIRST THING CARA LEARNED from her self-appointed tour guide was that to *really* experience Ireland, she needed to get out of the city.

"No time for that," she told him when he suggested a few days in Galway or a day trip to the Cliffs of Mohr. "I'd hoped to get down to Glendalough, but I don't think I can even squeeze that in."

His mouth turned up in a smile that was more of a smirk. "Let me guess, because that's where *P.S. I Love You* was filmed?"

Yes. "No," she said.

Finn shot her a look that made it clear he wasn't buying what she was selling.

"Okay, fine," she admitted, laughing at his satisfied grin. "But not just that, *Braveheart* as well."

"How long are you here?" he asked as he took a roundabout with practiced ease.

"Only three days. I fly home Monday."

"You came all the way to Dublin for a long weekend?" He looked about as surprised as Cara's family had been. But that was what happened when you booked a trip that revolved around a speech your then boyfriend was giving at a conference and you hadn't accrued much vacation at your job.

"Afraid so."

"Next time, then," he said with a decisive nod.

A twinge of disappointment rolled through her belly. It wasn't surprising, really. Had time allowed, she would have loved to have explored the Wicklow Mountains or headed west to trace the branches of her family tree. No doubt her father could have even given her the names of a few distant relatives to look up if she made it all the way to Dingle. But somewhere in the back of her mind, Cara knew the regret she was feeling wasn't only over a missed opportunity to connect with Irish kin but that if and when she did return to explore the west coast of the Emerald Isle, Finn Maguire wouldn't be her tour guide.

"What's on for Dublin?"

Cara took her phone out of her pocket and opened the notes app. "Let me see."

He glanced over his shoulder and laughed. "You have an actual list?"

Oscar lifted his head from the seat, then cocked it to one side. *Everyone's a critic*, she thought.

"Of course I have a list," she told them both. "What self-respecting tourist wouldn't have a list of sights they wanted to see?" Then again, Cara had a list for just about everything in her life. Finn Maguire didn't know her well enough to know that little tidbit, although he'd learn about it soon enough if he spent a little time with her. *What?* The jet lag must have been kicking in, because that was the most ridiculous thought she'd ever had. Scratch that. The one about getting busy with Finn in the back seat of his car definitely topped this one, but still.

"Cara?" he said, pulling her back into their conversation.

She met his gaze in the mirror. "Hmm?"

"Your list?"

"Oh, um, the usual, I suppose."

"You can't expect me to believe you have a file on your phone that says, 'To do: the usual.' Tell me. Perhaps I can steer you away from a few that aren't worth your time."

"Definitely going to hit Jameson. And Guinness of course."

"See, right there. That's what I'm talking about. Do yourself a favor and just take a picture in front of the gates then head down the street to a charming little pub called Arthur's."

"After Arthur Guinness?"

"The girl's done her research."

"I'm thorough, if nothing else."

"What good is a list if it's not comprehensive?" he asked with a straight face.

"Exactly!" Cara agreed. But then she saw the smile tugging at the corner of his mouth. "You're teasing me, aren't you?"

"Aye, but here we call that *taking the piss*."

"That conjures an entirely different image."

He chuckled. "Don't look at me, luv. I didn't invent it. But as for Guinness, the entire place is one big museum."

"They don't brew it there?"

Finn shook his head. "Not anymore. The beer tastes just as fine down the street, and you'll save yourself thirty quid. Jameson is the same only worse because the whole place glows green. It's like the bloody *Wizard of Oz*."

"More Emerald City than Emerald Isle?"

"That was terrible," he deadpanned.

Cara opened her mouth to disagree but couldn't. "You're right. It was."

"If it's Irish whiskey you're after, you can't do better than Teeling, and they have a tour as well."

"I'll keep that in mind."

"What else do you have on that list of yours?"

"Trinity College."

Now Finn was the one who rolled his eyes. "Predictable."

"*What?* Can't very well come to Dublin without taking a picture in their library."

"If it doesn't appear on Instagram, did it ever really happen?"

"You're pissing again."

He smiled and shook his head. "Something like that. What else?"

Cara shrugged. "St. Patrick's Cathedral. Oh, and I'll probably grab lunch at the Brazen Head."

"Where all you'll see are other Americans."

"At Ireland's oldest pub?"

Finn's eyes darted to the mirror again, and if his pointed stare hadn't told her everything she needed to know, Oscar's yawn certainly did.

"Okay, fine. What do you suggest?"

"You can't do any better than Kilmainham Gaol."

"Oh no, no, no. I toured Alcatraz, and that was one jail too many for me."

"While I'm sure a boat ride out to an Al Capone gift shop wasn't the highlight of a trip to San Francisco, this will be quite different." He narrowed his eyes. "Do you know much about the Irish rebellion?"

Cara shook her head. Despite her heritage, she was embarrassed to admit how little she knew about the history of her great-grandmother's homeland.

"The men who led the Easter Rising of 1916 were held at Kilmainham," Finn said as they waited at a red light. "Until they were executed by firing squad, one by one."

"What was the Easter Rising?"

"Ah, for that, you'll have to take the tour."

"Tease."

His eyes met hers again, only this time his gaze was darker and more intense. "I never tease unless I'm willing to deliver."

Cara swallowed the lump that had formed in her throat.

"You might fancy the Writers Museum," Finn continued, apparently unfazed by his innuendo. "Dublin's literary history is rich. Yeats, Joyce, Beckett. And, of course, Oscar's namesake."

"You named your dog after Oscar Wilde?"

Her canine companion barked at the sound of his full name.

Cara laughed. "I'll take that as a yes."

"To live is the rarest thing in the world," Finn said, quoting the poet. "That's my mam's favorite. Beautiful, innit?"

"Do you have a favorite?" Surely, he did seeing as how he'd named his dog after the man.

"The truth is rarely pure and never simple," Finn said, quoting the poet and confirming her suspicion.

They chatted a while longer—about nothing and everything all at once—until Finn eased the car alongside the curb. When he did, Cara realized they were back at her hotel.

"That wasn't much of a tour, I'm afraid," Finn said as he shifted the car into park. He was right. Finn had driven her around town for nearly an hour without pointing out a single landmark. Not that she was complaining.

"It's all good." And it was. Cara had three days of sightseeing ahead of her. Spending an hour with a sexy guy who had an even sexier accent wasn't on her to-do list, but she already knew it was going to be hard to beat.

Finn turned in his seat and grinned. "Here at Finn Maguire Tours, we pride ourselves on one hundred percent customer satisfaction."

"Don't worry. I'll still give you five stars." *Just like every other woman you've charmed in the back seat of this car.* And just like that, they were back on the *Titanic*, her hand pressed against the steamy windows as...

Cara gave her head a hard shake. Was this what sleep deprivation did to her? She needed to get out of there before she said or did anything stupid. "You're great...I mean, you're a great ride...I mean, the ride was great."

So much for not saying anything stupid.

Cara reached for the handle and cracked the door open so her dignity could fly right out.

But Finn didn't laugh at her. In fact, the way he was looking at her gave Cara the distinct impression she wasn't the only one having thoughts of getting her out of the rest of her wet clothes. Then again, it was probably just her imagination.

"Happy to be of service," he said. His voice had dropped to a low rasp, and that, combined with the way the words rolled off his tongue, had her shifting in her seat. "Can I do ya for anything else?"

Okay, so maybe *not* her imagination.

Julia would have given him her number right then and there. Scratch that. Her best friend would have probably invited him up to her room. But Cara wasn't Julia, which was why instead of propositioning Finn before climbing out of the car, all she did was leave him with a smile and a simple, "I'm good, thanks."

The cold air hit her like one hell of a wake-up call, but it wasn't until Cara staggered into the hotel's lobby that she realized she was still wearing Finn's sweater. She spun through the brass-framed revolving doors until she was back on the sidewalk, but while there were several cars parked on the street, none of them was a rusty, green Volkswagen.

Damn her jet-lagged brain. Returning his sweater would have been the perfect excuse to invite him in. He could have waited in the lobby while she changed, and then she could have offered to buy him a drink at the hotel's bar. A pint with Finn would have been the perfect way to spend her first afternoon in Dublin.

The wind kicked up, and a shudder rippled through Cara's body. She knew it was silly to feel so disappointed about a missed opportunity with a man she'd only known for an hour. Catching pneumonia because she was standing on the sidewalk looking for him was even worse. Besides, if it was meant to be, she'd see him again. Maybe he'd pick her up the next time she called for a car? Cara snorted quietly to herself because, let's be honest, that against-all-odds type of thing only happened in movies. It was just as well. After the Kyle debacle, a man was probably the last thing Cara needed in her life, even for a few hours. Of course, that didn't stop her from glancing over her shoulder one last time as she made her way back through the revolving door.

....................................................

"That was *absolutely* what you needed!" Cara's best friend shouted as only a best friend could.

Cara held the phone away from her ear. Julia was a bit louder than most during a normal conversation—one of the many traits she blamed on her Italian heritage—but after listening to Cara recount the events of the previous day, she was downright deafening. It didn't help matters that while it was Saturday morning in Dublin, it was just after midnight on Friday in California and Julia had been to a happy hour that had only just ended.

"It was a moment of weakness," Cara said. "But it would have been a mistake. After Kyle...I'm just not ready for a man in my life."

"It's not like you were going to bring him home to LA with you, Car. Just up to your room."

"I'm not ready for a man in my bed either," Cara said. "Not right now anyways."

"Look, not every man is an asshole like your ex." Her volume had returned to a normal decibel, but Cara knew darn well that Kyle Banfield was a topic Julia felt worthy of a few screams and shouts. She hadn't liked him from the start, deeming him uptight and judgmental—and those were the kinder adjectives—within an hour of meeting him. Not that she'd shared any of her opinions with Cara. For some reason, the always outspoken Julia Moretti had decided to keep her opinions to herself for once. It was an experiment Cara made her promise never to repeat, something she was already beginning to regret.

"And I'm not saying you had to sleep with him. In fact, given the way you've been feeling lately, it probably wouldn't have been a good idea." That was an understatement if she'd ever heard one. Cara had never been one to master the idea of casual sex. No matter how hard she tried to fight it, having sex with a man brought an emotional attachment that nearly always messed with her head when things ended, at least when she wasn't the one doing the ending. "But he might have been a nice distraction from Lord Voldemort."

"Well, it's too late now," Cara said. "Unless he picks up my next ride—which, let's face it, has about the same odds as winning the EuroMillions jackpot—that was the one and only time I will see him." Actually, the odds were even worse than the lottery seeing as how Finn told her he only made a few airport runs, and even those were just on the weekend.

"Fine." Julia exhaled into the phone. "But promise me that if another opportunity presents itself, you won't pass it up."

"I promise." Cara knew darn well it wasn't likely she'd meet another man who made her toes curl with nothing more than a little rearview mirror eye contact—and that it was even less likely she'd do anything about it—but she needed to wrap things up or she was never going to get through the day's agenda. "Call you tomorrow."

"Wait," Julia said. "What are you wearing?"

"Pervert."

Julia snorted. "Be that as it may, you know what I mean."

Cara looked down at her outfit. "Yoga pants, a sweatshirt the hotel gave me, and my Adidas." Her phone lit up with a message that Julia Moretti wanted to FaceTime. Cara hit the green button, and her friend appeared on the screen. Her long, dark curls were piled into a knot on top of her head, and she was wearing an oversize Backstreet Boys T-shirt Cara had seen her sleep in at least a hundred times.

"I need to approve the sweatshirt," Julia said matter-of-factly.

"Says the woman wearing a ratty shirt she's had since high school."

"I'm going to bed. You're going out."

"Amazing I somehow manage to dress myself every day without your help." The sarcasm in her voice was impossible to miss, but Julia was undeterred.

"This is different. You're in Ireland, where men with sexy accents are on every corner."

Cara laughed. "You make it sound like they're all gigolos."

Julia ignored her lame joke. "Hold your phone out so I can see."

Cara humored her friend, although for the life of her, she didn't know why. It wasn't like she'd had a lot to choose from, because not only had her luggage not been in her room when she arrived, as of seven a.m., it had somehow made its way north instead of west and was currently on a flight departing Scotland. If the desk clerk hadn't taken pity on her, she would have been stuck wearing either the muddy sweatshirt she'd worn on the plane or Finn's sweater, both of which were currently draped across a chair by the radiator.

At the sight of it, Julia's mouth formed the perfect O. "What in the world?"

"Give me a break," Cara sad. "I told you my luggage isn't here yet."

"Don't they have stores in Dublin?"

Cara rolled her eyes. "Yes, but my budget is tight enough as it is." Which was why she couldn't really afford to turn down the front desk manager when he offered her a sweatshirt with the hotel's name and logo printed across the front in silver glitter.

"At least it's blue," Julia said. It was the one silver lining of the silver glitter considering the way the color matched Cara's eyes. "If you do meet a guy, maybe he will be too mesmerized by your eyes to notice the billboard across your boobs."

"Hey, before I go, everything okay at work?"

"I'm not going to talk to you about work while you're on vacation."

"I just feel bad that I left you on your own with Samantha."

"She bugged out early yesterday for her weekend in Palm Springs, so it was pretty quiet. Doubt I'll hear much from her before Monday, which means I can spend the whole weekend trying out recipes." Julia was always coming up with a new plan to become an influencer. The way she figured, she spent half her free time scrolling through social media anyways, might as well get paid for it. Her latest idea was an Italian cooking account featuring recipes that had been in her family for generations. It was actually one of the best ideas she'd ever had—certainly better than the one dedicated to photoshopped images of male models with household items as various body parts—especially since Cara usually scored a meal or, at the very least, a tasty dessert from her efforts.

"Don't make the ricotta gnocchi until I'm back." That was one Cara definitely didn't want to miss.

"Wouldn't dream of it. Now, go kiss a dude named Barney Stone."

"It's not a dude. And it's *Blarney* Stone."

"Yeah, I know," Julia said with a wink. "But my idea sounds so much better."

# CHAPTER 4

CARA SPENT THE NEXT TWO days in all-out tourist mode. On Saturday, she fed the ducks at St. Stephen's Green, toured Dublin Castle, and had dinner at a pub that was nearly as old as the city itself. She also discovered that the Temple Bar area was apparently *the* spot to celebrate a "stag night." At least that was what she assumed based on the number of groups weaving through the cobblestone streets with one of the members of their entourage dressed in some sort of costume ranging from Thor to a ballerina all while wearing a sash and crown.

Sunday began with a visit to St. Patrick's Cathedral, followed by an afternoon at Trinity College, where she spent far too long wandering the stacks of their often-Instagrammed library before wrapping up her day with a tour and tasting at the whiskey distillery Finn had recommended. The days were long—especially the afternoons when the jet lag seemed to sneak up out of nowhere—but productive. So much so that on her last day, the only thing she had left on her list was the Writers Museum.

She wasn't sure why exactly—especially since her luggage had been delivered the day before—but as Cara set out to enjoy her last full day in Dublin, she did so dressed in the same sweater she'd worn on the first. Finn's sweater. Maybe it was because the cream-colored cable knit made her feel like less of a tourist and more like a native Dubliner as she strolled the banks of the River Liffey. Oh, who was she kidding? She wore the sweater because it not only reminded her of her handsome Uber driver, but it still smelled like him as well and, as ridiculous as it might have sounded, made her feel like she wasn't alone in a city she had intended to explore with her boyfriend. In a strange way, it felt like Finn was standing beside her as she wandered through the eighteenth-century townhome that housed everything from Oscar Wilde's most famous plays' programs to a first edition of Bram Stoker's *Dracula*, which was probably why she spent more time there than she had anyplace else.

It was two o'clock when she finally stepped out into the February sun. Far too early to call it a day—not when she had so few—which was why she dug her phone out of her bag and began scrolling through a site that promised inside scoop on "The Ten Best Things to Do in Dublin."

Number four: Kilmainham Gaol.

*What the hell*, she thought. It couldn't be worse than Alcatraz, and at least she didn't have to take a boat to get there.

When she arrived, she passed through iron gates, then entered the building through a nondescript door. According to the woman at the ticket counter, it was the same one the prisoners passed through upon their arrival. There was one important distinction. Those men and women weren't greeted by someone they knew.

Well, kinda knew. At least she was pretty sure it was him. He had his back to her, but then again, that was the same view she'd had the other night...

"Finn?" The word had no sooner left her lips than she regretted opening her mouth at all. She was probably one of dozens of rides he'd picked up at the airport that month. Would he really remember her? Then again, how many of them had been drenched from head to toe with gutter water? *Ugh.* Not exactly how she wanted to stand out. Which was why Cara found herself wishing she could rewind the past three minutes and stop herself from blurting out his name.

But then he turned, and instead of confusion crossing Finn's face, it was realization that slid across his features and a smile that played on the corner of his lips. "American Cara."

"You remembered."

He drew closer. "So did you." If possible, he was even better looking than she remembered, something she hadn't thought possible. But in the dim light of the car, she hadn't been able to see the gold flecks in his green eyes or notice the dimple that flirted with making an appearance when he cracked half a grin. And she certainly hadn't realized how tall he was or how broad his shoulders were. But all of that was secondary to something more, something intangible, a presence that drew her forward while at the same time left her feeling as though she'd stumbled backward into a free fall.

Cara cleared her throat. "Well, I don't have many friends in Dublin." *Crap.* Why did she say that? Finn wasn't her friend. He wasn't even an acquaintance. Although, to be fair, the way he'd looked at her the other day, right before she got out of the car, had definitely given her the impression that was something he'd like to change. It wasn't entirely unlike the look he was giving her right now. "I mean, I don't know many people...haven't met that many, that is...since I got here and..."

She felt her cheeks heat. Whether it was due to the intensity of Finn's stare or her awkward reply, she couldn't be sure. Either way, a little blush wasn't a bad thing considering her pale complexion and utter lack of makeup. Damn it. Why hadn't she taken the time to put on makeup that morning? *Because you didn't expect to see Mr. Sexy Brogue today.* Or any day, for that matter. It was true. She hadn't expected to see him there, dressed in a light-green oxford that did crazy things to his eyes and a pair of faded jeans that made Cara want to do crazy things like grab his ass. And while she probably should have expected his seemingly ever-present smile, she certainly didn't expect him to press a kiss to her cheek when he said hello.

*Don't overthink it*, she told herself. *It's a European thing.*

"I knew what you meant," Finn said as he stepped back. Then with a tilt of his head, he added, "You made an impression on me as well."

Cara cringed. "Guess it's not every day you pick up a soaking-wet passenger."

"That's not what made you memorable." His voice had dropped. It was low and rough and exactly how she imagined it would sound if he were whispering naughty intentions in her ear. "In fact, I was hoping I'd see you again."

*Okay, so maybe that kiss wasn't merely a custom.*

"You were?" If her face hadn't been red before, it certainly was now.

He nodded. "And it seems fate obliged."

The news that she hadn't been the only one who had hoped fate, or a well-timed Uber request, would result in a second encounter had that passing thought of whispered intentions taking root as a full-on fantasy. Her mind immediately went to the thoughts she'd had the first time they met. She and Finn in the back seat of his car, revving each other up before...

*Wait.*

The light caught a name tag pinned to his shirt, pulling Cara from her daydream just when it was getting good. "Fate, huh?"

The mischief in his eyes matched his grin. "Exactly."

She raised one brow. "Wouldn't have had anything to do with the fact that you recommended this place and you also happen to work here?"

Finn chuckled. "To be fair, I wasn't positive you'd buy a ticket."

He had her there. "And here I was thinking you were only a tour guide for me," she teased. "Guess I don't feel so special anymore."

He moved closer. "While 'tis true I may give tours to many here in the jail." His gaze dropped to her mouth, and for a moment, she actually thought he might kiss her—on the lips this time—right there in the lobby of a two-hundred-year-old jail. "When it comes to our spin around town," he said, "you're my one and only."

Holy guacamole, he was good at this. But still, Cara needed to get a grip. Finn wasn't going to kiss her at his job. He probably wasn't going to kiss her at all. Ever. But she had to admit she was enjoying their banter.

"So, a first?" she said, trying to give as good as she got.

He nodded slowly. "A first."

They stood there, his innuendo hanging in the air between them until a woman approached. "Your next tour is ready," she told him. Cara realized it was the same woman who had sold her a ticket when she arrived.

Finn held out his hand. "After you," he said, then as she passed by added, "Nice sweater."

*Shit.* How had she not thought of that? She wanted to say something, to apologize, assure him she wasn't a sweater thief, and offer to return it to him somehow—*Oh, there's an idea! Over drinks maybe?*—but there was no time. Before she could reply, Finn was on the job.

"Welcome to Kilmainham," he said as he weaved his way through the group. "To many, this building represents great suffering. And while that's true, it is also a memorial to those who fought for Ireland's independence."

The group followed Finn as he led them down narrow stone passageways, up caged staircases, and across metal catwalks that ran alongside rows of heavy wooden doors. And while she imagined any guide would command the presence of a group of tourists as they learned about one of the bleakest chapters in Irish history, Cara knew it was much more than the austere setting and the sobering details that captivated Finn's audience. It was him. What Finn had was more than mere charm, it was a charisma beyond any script or setting paired with passion and genuine emotion. They weren't just listening to a tour guide; they were watching one hell of a performance.

"Men, women, and children were held here, often as many as ten to a cell," he said as they walked single file across a grate to yet another row of doors. The damp air wafted up from below them, bringing with it the smell of must and metal. "One candle was meant to provide both heat and light, but since each was expected to last for two weeks, most of their time was spent in cold and darkness."

Once they'd gathered on the other side of the gangway, Cara peeked through a small hole in one of the doors. The cell was nothing more than a concrete room with one tiny window. Hardly enough space for two people, let alone ten. Cara couldn't imagine how they slept in those conditions, and she didn't want to even think about the bathroom arrangements.

"Most had been charged with minor offenses, but the more notable prisoners were jailed for their convictions rather than their crimes." Finn let his words settle over the group before asking them to follow him to the Stonebreaker's Yard.

The warm sunlight should have been inviting after nearly an hour spent in the cold, dark jail, but instead the bright light was harsh and jarring. Cara shielded her eyes as she scanned the courtyard.

"As was typical for the Victorian regime, most prisoners were sentenced to hard labor that usually consisted of breaking stones, which were later sold." Gravel crunched beneath Finn's shoes as he stepped to the center of the courtyard and nodded to a small, black cross that had been hammered into the ground a few feet in front of the courtyard's back wall. "But this is also where fourteen of the men who led the Easter Rising of 1916 were executed over a span of nine days."

Standing with a group of tourists holding brochures and cameras, it should have been hard to imagine what it must have been like for those fourteen men—emerging from the door behind her, into the last place they would see on earth—but Finn painted a sobering picture with his words.

"The men were brought out at dawn to face a firing squad of twelve British soldiers." He took three long strides, then raised his arm. "Who took aim from here." There was an audible gasp from someone in the crowd. "Other prisoners later recounted hearing the volley of shots ringing from within these stone walls, knowing another soul had passed on from this world."

Silence settled over the courtyard, interrupted only by the sound of a passing car, until a young boy asked why a cross had been placed at the other end as well.

"Good question," Finn told him. Then, to the mesmerized crowd, he explained how one of the prisoners had been so badly injured that he'd had to be brought to his execution by ambulance. He pointed to a pair of large wooden doors at the far end. "The ambulance pulled in right there, and Mr. Connolly sat about where that second cross has been placed."

A murmur rippled through the small group.

"That's the end of our tour, ladies and gentlemen, but I'll stick around in case you have any questions." Finn waited while the members of his tour walked reverently across what amounted to some of Ireland's most sacred ground, then patiently answered each and every question they posed.

Cara walked along the stone wall. She slid her hand along the jagged rocks, silently wondering if some of the smaller holes had been made by bullets intended for one of those fourteen men.

"Hard to imagine, innit?"

She turned to find Finn standing behind her. "Actually, it's quite easy to imagine thanks to your description. The hard part is imagining how they must have felt. How their loved ones felt."

He cocked his head to one side. "Do you have a few minutes?"

"Sure. Why?"

"That was my last tour of the day, but there's something I'd like to show you."

# CHAPTER 5

FINN LED CARA BACK INTO the jail and through a maze of winding stone corridors before stopping in front of a set of carved wood doors. "This is usually part of the tour, but since it's currently being renovated, I couldn't take the group back here." He swung the doors open to reveal a two-story room with plank floors and arched windows. "This was the chapel."

They stepped into the nearly dark room, taking care to avoid the scaffolding and paint cans. Unlike other places of worship in Ireland, this room was bare-bones minimum. The only indication the space held any religious significance at all was the lone cross sitting atop a simple wooden altar that sat against the back wall. There was a pair of candlesticks as well, but they were far from ornate. Even the windows were stark. Instead of intricate stained glass overlooking a courtyard or garden, the panes were frosted, something Cara assumed was designed to hide the somber reality that there was, in fact, no view.

"Believe it or not, this chapel was the site of many weddings," Finn said.

"Really?" Cara couldn't think of a less romantic location for a wedding. "Why would anyone want to get married in a jail?"

"For someone who worked here, this might have been their parish. Or a female prisoner might have wanted to marry the father's child before the baby was born so it wouldn't be a bastard."

Imagining a wedding in a prison chapel was bad enough, but giving birth in the building sounded even worse.

"The most famous wedding to take place here was that of Joseph Plunkett and Grace Gifford."

"Plunkett?" Cara asked. "Wasn't that one of the men from the Easter Rising?"

Finn smiled. "I see someone was paying attention during the tour."

More like hung on his every word. "It wasn't exactly a cheap ticket. Of course I paid attention."

"And here I thought it might've been your captivating guide."

It had definitely been her guide, but she wasn't about to admit it. "Tell me about Grace and Joseph."

"Ah, yes, well, they had planned to marry anyway. On Easter Sunday, as a matter of fact."

"Guess those plans got put on the back burner." Not that an armed insurrection wasn't a good reason to postpone your wedding, but it also spoke volumes as to the dedication these two had to their cause.

Finn nodded. "Plunkett was essential to the military council affairs going on that day, so he had no choice but to cancel the wedding."

Cara's thoughts were so focused on the simplistic nature of the wedding they must've planned—a wedding that could've been canceled the same day, as opposed to, say, the over-the-top ceremonies couples often spent a year or more planning—that the reality of Joseph and Grace's situation didn't hit her until Finn reminded her why their wedding ultimately took place in the Kilmainham chapel.

"They agreed ahead of time that if he were to be arrested, she would marry him in prison."

But he wasn't just arrested. He was executed in the stone yard they'd been in not ten minutes ago.

"According to her sister's recounting of that night," Finn continued. "Grace was brought to the jail on the evening of May third, where she spent two hours alone in the prison yard while Joe waited in his cell."

A knot formed in the pit of Cara's stomach at the thought of a woman who not only had to be married in the building where her husband would spend his last days but also had to spend the hours before the ceremony pacing the very ground where he was to be executed.

"At eight o'clock, she was brought to this chapel." Finn's tone was somber, and his voice hushed. "Joseph was escorted by soldiers carrying bayonets. It was those same soldiers who served as the witnesses to their wedding that took place right there." He pointed to the simple altar. "The gas supply to the prison had failed that night, leaving the chaplain to read the service by the light of a single candle."

Finn moved closer to the spot where Cara assumed the tragic

couple had said their vows. She followed until they were standing side by side in front of the altar.

"Oh, Grace, just hold me in your arms and let this moment linger. They'll take me out at dawn, and I will die. With all my love, I place this wedding ring upon your finger. There won't be time to share our love, for we must say goodbye."

It was a moment before Cara could speak, and when she did, her voice was thick with unshed tears. "That was beautiful."

"It's from a ballad written to commemorate that night." Finn turned to face her. "But truth be told, they never had any time alone."

"She wasn't allowed to stay with him?" Up until that point, Cara hadn't really stopped to consider the reality of a wedding night spent inside a jail. There was little doubt it would be far from romantic, but denying them that time together seemed beyond cruel. "They were going to execute her husband in the morning. Least they could have done was let her spend her wedding night with him, even if it was only in a cell."

"They were separated the moment the service was over."

Cara's eyes grew wide. "And that was it?"

Finn shook his head. "They saw each other one more time. The chaplain had made arrangements for Grace to stay nearby. That's where she went after Joe was taken to his cell. She was brought back to the jail the next day in the early morning hours, but she was only allowed to spend ten minutes speaking to her husband, all while twenty soldiers with bayonets guarded the corridor. According to reports, one stood by with a stopwatch in his hand."

"Then what happened?" She knew the answer to the question, and yet she asked it anyways. It was ridiculous, really, because it wasn't as though her hopes for the tragic couple would somehow change history.

"He was taken away and executed later that same day."

A shiver raced across Cara's skin. "And she never saw him again." This time, Cara's words weren't a question but a fact.

Finn nodded. "Could you imagine what it must have been like, to know it was the last ten minutes you'd ever have together and not even be allowed to touch?"

His words heightened their proximity, and the air between them became charged, but with what, she couldn't say. It was as though some outside force were pulling them together. Finn's eyes searched hers, and in that moment, she was sure he felt it too.

"The chapel is said to be haunted," he said. "Some have even said they've seen the ghost of Grace Gifford, wandering the halls in search of her true love, longing for the final kiss she was denied."

Once again, Finn's gaze dropped to Cara's lips. Only this time, there was no question as to his intentions. He was definitely going to kiss her. Right there. In the same chapel where two star-crossed lovers were denied that simple pleasure.

Finn reached up, cupping her jaw, and even that small contact felt intimate and vital while, at the same time, forbidden. The combination was exhilarating. Her heart pounded, then, for a split second, stopped. Her breath caught in her throat as he leaned forward and brushed his lips ever so slightly against hers. It was soft and gentle, reverent even, and yet every nerve in her body sprang to life and all thoughts left her but one. *More.*

Then a door slammed somewhere in the distance, and the moment, just like their kiss, was broken.

Cara startled.

Finn stepped back.

"Sounds like they're locking up."

Her eyes grew wide. "Not exactly what you want to hear someone say in a jail."

He chuckled. "No, I reckon not."

"I should get going." Except in truth that was the last thing she wanted.

Finn pushed the door of the chapel open, then led her to the exit. "Let me grab my coat, and I'll walk with you for a bit, if you'd like?"

Yes. Yes. And oh, yeah, yes. But instead of blurting out the answer that was bouncing around her head, Cara Kennedy tried her best to play it cool. "Sure, I'll meet you outside."

A few minutes later, Finn joined her on the sidewalk.

"Where's Oscar?" So much for playing it cool. Cara had no sooner asked the question when she realized how ridiculous it sounded. Of course he didn't bring his dog to work. Not to the jail, at least. Having Oscar ride along in the car while he shuttled someone from the airport was one thing; bringing him to a historic landmark was quite another. How had she managed to get off on the wrong foot with only a two-word question? "Not that I expected him to be here—of course you wouldn't bring him to a museum—I meant, where is he when he's not with you, home with your mam—not that I assume you still live at home—although there wouldn't be anything wrong with it if you did." Holy cow.

Even for Cara, that was a *lot*. It was going to be a long walk if she didn't get it together. But Finn seemed unfazed, watching her with the same amused expression that had been on his face two days before.

"With my mate." Finn winked. "He'll be gutted to have missed a chance to snog with his best girl."

Cara wasn't exactly sure what snogging was, but she was quite certain she'd rather do it with Finn than his dog.

"Shall we?" he asked.

"Snog?"

Finn laughed. "Start walking."

*Oh*. Crap. That wasn't embarrassing at all. She needed to change the subject. "You have a ladybug on you," she said. *Ladybug?* She should have stuck with asking him to snog.

Finn looked down. "My lucky day," he said, carefully removing the insect from his shirt. "First, I got to see you again, and now a ladybug wish." He closed his eyes briefly, then set the little lady free.

"You were right," Cara said as they finally began to walk.

"Of course I was." He flashed her a wide grin. "But about what?"

She laughed. "About the jail. I never knew, well, any of that."

"I'm glad you enjoyed it," he said. "And now you know about *both* my jobs. How about you?"

"Me?"

"Aye, what is it you do back in Los Angeles?"

"I write screenplays."

It wasn't a lie. Cara *was* a screenwriter. She just didn't pay her bills by writing scripts. That fact made it more of a hobby than a career, but Finn hadn't asked how she earned a living. He'd asked what she did. To be fair, she wouldn't really call her position at CTA a career either. Sure, she worked for the most successful female agent in Hollywood but basically as a glorified intern. At times, she rubbed elbows with celebrities, usually by bumping into them on the red carpet of some event—accidentally and awkwardly—while rushing to bring something to her boss. And yes, she had been in the room with some of the town's power players, although only to serve coffee or distribute copies of contracts. But that was Cara Kennedy, the Los Angeles edition. In Dublin, Cara could be the best version of herself, even if that version was only based on half the pertinent information. What was the harm in letting herself bask in the life she hoped to live? She wasn't hurting anyone. Besides, it wasn't like she was ever going to see Finn Maguire again.

The thought plucked at a chord somewhere deep inside her, but Cara pushed the sensation aside, choosing instead to enjoy the moment. She took a deep breath of the crisp air, then stepped across a large puddle to the safety of a smooth bit of pavement. She was about to give herself a mental high five for gracefully avoiding the murky mixture when—

"Careful," Finn began to say just before she lost her footing. "It's a little slick."

That was an understatement if she'd ever heard one. The dark section of sidewalk was as slippery as a river stone. Cara's arms flailed as her foot skidded across the concrete, but there was nothing to grab, no way to save herself from the inevitable fall.

Then Finn's arms were around her, one circling her waist and the other catching under her knees. "I've got you," he said, cradling her against his chest.

Did he ever.

Cara's breath came in short, quick bursts that had far more to do with Finn holding her as though about to carry her over a threshold than the fact that she almost had another run-in with muddy water, only this time by falling squarely on her ass.

"Thank you," she managed to say. "At the rate I'm going, I'll be naked by the end of the trip." *Oh boy.* "I mean, I keep ruining my clothes and—"

Finn's laugh vibrated against her. "I knew what you meant."

Cara didn't need a mirror to know her cheeks were flaming. "You can set me down now."

"Are you sure? For the sake of your wardrobe—and my sweater—I might need to carry you the rest of the way."

*Now, there's an idea.* "I think I can manage."

Finn set Cara on her feet. "I'm sorry I forgot to give it back," she began, intending to broach the subject of returning his sweater. But after taking a few steps, she realized he hadn't followed. She turned to find him right where she'd left him, watching her as though he was thinking everything and nothing all at the same time.

Cara ran her fingers through her windblown hair. "What?"

"The sweater suits you," he said. "You should keep it."

She wasn't sure what answer she'd been expecting, but that certainly wasn't it. She glanced down to where the cream wool hung halfway down her thighs. "It's a little big."

"Yes, but it's Irish, and so are you from the looks of ya."

"Is that so?"

He nodded. "Your eyes are as blue as the sea, and your face holds the key to the heavens."

Cara bit back a nervous laugh. "Does that line usually work?" she asked, wondering if he could tell that it already was.

"It's not a line at all." She loved the ways his words ran together. *Tis notta line attall.* "Legend has it that the gods feared the Gaels would forget about the stars and the heavens because it was too difficult to see them through the mist that covered their small island. So they sprinkled a fine dust over the Irish people that covered them in freckles to remind them of the stars and the heavens."

Cara had always hated her freckles growing up, and as an adult, she tried to cover them with makeup. But the way Finn looked at her as he explained that the Irish word for freckles was *bricini*—which according to him meant "little stars"—had her rethinking her position on the matter.

"So you see," he said. "You fit right in 'round here." Then he flashed her a crooked grin. "As long as you don't open yer mouth."

Cara's jaw dropped open, and Finn's head fell back on a laugh.

"I meant yer accent, luv." His voice grew softer as he moved even closer. Close enough for her to see the darkening of his green eyes and to hear the quickening of his breath. "All I'm saying is that you sure look like a local." He reached up to tuck her hair behind her ear. "And a beautiful one at that."

His thumb brushed her cheek, and his gaze dropped to her

mouth, setting a flurry of butterflies loose deep inside her. Then Finn dipped his head and Cara's lips parted and...

...and then words tumbled out of her mouth.

"I'm told I'm the spitting image of my great-grandmother. She was born here. Well, in Ireland. Not here exactly. Kerry."

*Gah!* What was wrong with her? Cara spent most of her life tongue-tied, and then the one time all she needed to do was just shut up and let the cute boy kiss her, she had to ruin the moment with a bunch of unnecessary details about her family history.

"All the more reason to keep it, then. An Irish lass needs an Irish sweater."

What the Irish lass needed was a kiss from an Irish lad. And not just a faint brushing of his lips against hers but a full, uninterrupted kiss that made her toes curl. "Oh, yes."

*Crap.* She hadn't meant to say that out loud. Thankfully Finn assumed she was talking about the sweater and not the sidewalk make-out session that was playing through her mind.

"Good, it's settled then." They walked a few more blocks—Finn's small talk pairing with Cara's often inane replies—and before long, they were standing in front of her hotel.

"You didn't have to walk me all the way home." Except it wasn't a home. It was a hotel. One she'd be checking out of in the morning.

"Swanky place," he said. Cara followed his gaze through the widows of the hotel's lobby bar. It was fairly typical for large hotel chains: white marble floors, taupe leather chairs, oversize brushed-gold light fixtures. Nothing terribly "Irish" about it, but even from the sidewalk, Cara could see they had a decent selection of beer on tap. *Invite him in!* The voice inside her head might have been her own, but it sure as hell sounded like Julia.

Finn glanced at his phone. "Shit. It's later than I thought," he said as he frowned at the screen. "I need to crack on."

She should have known he had somewhere to be. Boys who looked like Finn Maguire always did.

"It's my mam's birthday, and my mum will give out if I'm late for tea."

Cara shook her head and smiled. "You've said so many words I don't understand."

Finn chuckled. "My mum is my mother. My mam is her mother."

That much Cara had already figured out.

"Tea isn't just something to drink in the afternoon," he explained. "It's also what we sometimes call our evening meal. As for *giving out*, that means she's going to scold me like I'm a young lad."

Cara didn't know if she'd ever get used to Irish colloquialisms, but one thing she knew for sure: she was definitely not ready to say goodbye.

"What would you say to a proper pint in a proper pub?" he asked. "There's this big Leap Day thing at the Hole in the Wall, and my mates and I will be there around eight. I mean, unless you already have plans?"

The words *I'd love to* were on the tip of her tongue when the refrain from Meredith Brooks's "Bitch" began blasting from her phone.

Finn flashed her a curious expression.

"Ringtone for my boss."

"Boss?" He frowned. "I thought you were a screenwriter?"

"I mean the director. Must need a last-minute rewrite or something." God, she was a terrible liar.

The call rolled to voicemail, then almost immediately the song began to play again. Something must have been horribly wrong if Samantha was calling Cara. Her usual go-to was Julia, not to mention that in LA it was only—Cara glanced at the phone screen—nine a.m. *on a Sunday.* Samantha Sherwood might have given life her all six days a week, but she never did anything before noon on Sunday. It was the one time even Julia could count on a quiet phone. Whatever had her calling now—all the way to Ireland, no less—had to be bad.

"I need to take this," Cara said, already backing away.

The look of disappointment on Finn's face should have been enough to have Cara pitching her cell phone into the nearest trash can, but she'd invested three years of her life at CTA, first in the mail room and then two years as an assistant. It was only a matter of time until she either moved further up the agency ladder or, even better, caught a break with one of her screenplays. She wasn't about to blow that on anything or anyone, not even a cuter-than-he-has-a-right-to-be Irishman.

"Oh, okay," he said. "Will I see you later?"

"Yes. Maybe." Her brain was short-circuiting. "I hope so," she added before dashing into the hotel lobby to deal with whatever emergency had erupted back home.

# CHAPTER 6

IT WASN'T AN EMERGENCY THAT had Samantha calling Cara in Dublin. It was her ridiculous dog, a high-strung poodle that needed to see a therapist nearly as often as her owner did.

On this occasion, Coco was melting down because she had misplaced her favorite stuffed toy, an equally ridiculous ice cream cone. Not that ice cream was ridiculous per se, but when it featured four smiling scoops piled atop a gold lamé waffle cone, it was. And apparently only Cara knew which overpriced pet boutique kept replacements in stock or how to have one messengered to Samantha's home in Palm Springs.

Ah, her glamorous Hollywood life. And thanks to her so-called career, her conversation with Finn had been cut short before he could even finish asking her out. Wait. He was asking her out, wasn't he? Maybe he was just inviting her to hang out with him and his mates. *Don't be an idiot.* The voice in her head was back, and this time, there was no mistaking it for her own. This time, it was all Julia.

Cara shoved her phone back in her bag, and as she did, she

realized she had a bigger problem than an interrupted conversation because, abrupt or not, there was one thing worse than saying goodbye to Finn. Saying hello to Kyle.

He came through the revolving door all swagger and smiles. He was wearing his "power suit," a navy-blue Tom Ford he'd bought for a meeting at Microsoft, something Cara was well aware of considering his penchant for dropping both names and labels. Bring it on, she thought, because unlike the first night—when she'd looked and felt like a drowned rat—Cara felt more like her normal self. Scratch that, she felt better than normal. Granted, she might have only been wearing jeans and a sweater that was much too big, but the cream wool that was rolled three times at her wrists was far more than a souvenir, it was a metaphor for her entire trip. Despite the rocky start, she'd ended up having a great time sightseeing alone in Dublin—the flirtatious moments with Finn hadn't hurt either—reminding her once again that some of the best things in life happen not only when you least expect them but when you aren't looking for them at all.

She felt happy and hopeful, and more than anything, she knew with absolute certainty that whatever fate had in store for her next, it would be infinitely better without Kyle Banfield.

She was about to walk up and tell him as much when a woman followed him through the revolving door. She was stunning. Her blond hair fell in soft waves on her shoulders, her makeup was flawless without being overdone, and her dress, a simple black number that hit just above the knee, was undoubtedly designer. She was the kind of woman that every man—and probably most women—noticed, so it wasn't too surprising when Kyle approached her the moment she stepped into the lobby. If anything, it was downright predictable. What *was* surprising was the fact that he placed his hand on the small of her back as he began to guide her toward the elevators.

*What the hell?* Had he invited someone else to join him on a trip that, up until two weeks ago, they were supposed to be taking together? That would be pretty low—not to mention quick—even by Kyle's standards. Maybe he'd met someone after he arrived. Scenarios began bouncing through Cara's head, but she didn't have much time to consider the options, because thanks to a sudden change in direction, Kyle and the blond were heading her way. It wasn't intentional, that was for sure, because even in the dimly lit lobby, Cara could see the color drain out of Kyle's face when he saw her.

"Cara?" he said.

The blond looked at Kyle. "You know each other?" Her accent was American, so presumably she wasn't a local.

Kyle nodded. There was a smile plastered across his lips, but his eyes were shooting daggers. "What are you doing here?"

Cara was about to fumble through some totally awkward explanation that provided far more detail than necessary when the blond jumped in. "Crazy running into a friend when we're so far from home."

Cara's eyes locked with Kyle's.

"Totally crazy," he said. And just like that, the confidence she'd felt five minutes ago vanished.

"Small world though, am I right?" the woman said.

"Absolutely," Cara said. Then, since it was becoming obvious

Kyle wasn't going to make any introductions, added, "Sorry, and you are?"

The woman beamed up at Kyle like he was Thor, Loki, and Cap all rolled into one. "His girlfriend," she said.

The words hit Cara like a physical blow. *His girlfriend?* Until thirteen days ago, that had been Cara's title. When the hell had these two started?

Kyle tensed, but the blond either didn't notice or didn't care. "Guess I shouldn't say that too loudly." She glanced around, then leaned in to whisper, "We haven't made it official with HR yet."

"HR?" Cara asked.

The woman nodded. "Since Kyle and I both work for the same company—although in different cities—there's paperwork we have to complete before we can take our relationship public." The blond rolled her eyes. "It's all rather silly, mostly to protect them from litigation, but it hasn't been all bad." She looked up at Kyle. "It's been rather fun sneaking around the past few months."

*Months?*

Kyle's eyes darted back to Cara's. Her face felt hot, too hot, and a tightness spread from her belly to her chest. All around her, guests were enjoying their night. Music played, silverware clinked, and laughter rose above the hum of conversation. But everything in Cara's world narrowed to the sound of her pulse beating in her ears.

"So you're not from LA?" Cara managed to ask. She tried her best to sound nonchalant, but there was little doubt her surprise, not to mention her humiliation, was visible for all to see. Or at least those who knew the full story. Cara hated that she wore her emotions not only on her sleeve but all over her face as well. That was why she knew better than to ever play poker, and it was also why in a hotel lobby in Dublin, she knew her ex-boyfriend could see exactly how this newsflash had affected her.

"No, I'm based in San Francisco," the blond said.

Images of Kyle—packing his overnight bag for a quick business trip to San Francisco—played through Cara's head like a montage in a movie. He wore a different suit in each one but had the same stupid grin on his face as he walked out the door, and now she knew why.

"We make the long-distance thing work," she said. "But I'm sure you can imagine how happy I was when I found out the company was sending me to this conference as well."

Guess that explained the need for the eleventh-hour breakup. Couldn't very well bring girlfriend number one on a business trip that included girlfriend number two. Or was she number one, and this woman was number two? Probably depended on whether the rankings were based on time or importance. Not that it mattered. The bottom line was pretty simple: Kyle had been hedging his bets by keeping things going with Cara as a backup plan while he started something new.

"I'm sure you were thrilled," Cara said. "I know I was. To be going to Dublin, I mean."

It was impossible to miss the way the muscle in Kyle's jaw twitched. At the rate he was grinding those molars, the guy was going to need an emergency visit to the dentist before he ever made it back to California.

"So, do you live in LA too?"

Cara nodded. "Malibu, actually."

"Nice! Next time I visit, we should totally invite ourselves over."

*What?* Cara stiffened, but then she looked at the woman beaming up at Kyle with a smile brighter than the sconces in the lobby, and instead of anger, she felt solidarity. It wasn't her fault Kyle was two-timing both of them. Cara's problem wasn't with the beautiful woman standing in front of her. It was with the toad they both hoped might turn into a prince.

"Yeah, maybe," were the words that came out of the toad's mouth, but the look on his face was screaming *"I'm about to puke."* Cara managed to take a bit of satisfaction from that. And why not? She might've been the idiot ex-girlfriend who was having her blind faith served up to her on a silver platter of humiliation, but she was also the ex-girlfriend who had the ability to bring Kyle's world crumbling down around him with a few simple words. It was obvious the new love of his life had no idea she'd been sharing him, at least for a while, and something about the possessive arm she had linked through Kyle's told Cara that little tidbit of information wouldn't go over very well. Of course, there was also the matter of human resources. Cara knew—and more importantly Kyle knew—she had the ability to cause trouble for him in more ways than one. Not that she would've ever done anything like that since, in the immortal words of Destiny's Child, her momma raised her better than that. But still.

The blond turned her attention back to their little dysfunctional group.

"Oh! We should get together while we're all in Dublin," the new girlfriend said. "Grab breakfast or something one morning?"

That was never going to happen, but since torturing Kyle a bit was the only thing keeping Cara from dissolving into tears, she decided to play along. "That would be great."

"I'm sure Cara has better things to do in Ireland besides dine with other Americans," Kyle said.

"I do have a rather full schedule."

"Well, if you change your mind…" The blond looked up at Kyle, seeming to finally clue in to his discomfort. A tiny crease formed between her perfectly sculpted brows as she looked back and forth between him and Cara. "I'm sorry, how did you say you know Kyle?"

The panic vibrating through Kyle's frame was practically visible. Clearly, he was terrified that she would blow his cover, potentially ending the relationship, although Cara assumed his more immediate concern was that she would say something that would end his night. Either way, it would have been the perfect opportunity for the big redemption moment in any good rom-com.

Cara opened her mouth, then closed it again.

"We go to the same gym," Kyle blurted out. It wasn't a lie. He just left out everything else from the past six months. Like how he'd pursued her, pushing for more right from the start. How he'd always taken things one step faster, making plans that implied a commitment far greater than not only any she'd ever had before but at a pace that she now realized should have been a major red flag. Or how he'd ended things in an email, an act of cowardice topped only by the time Berger broke up with Carrie via a Post-it note on *Sex and the City*.

An all-too-familiar lump formed in Cara's throat. She cleared it with a cough, but when she spoke, the sound that came out of her mouth still sounded more like a choking frog. "I better get going," she said, glancing at her bare wrist as though a watch had magically appeared. "Can't be late."

The elevator behind her opened on a soft ping, and Cara stepped inside. "Nice to meet you," she managed. *Nice to meet you?* What was wrong with her? Then again, it could have been worse. At least she hadn't said *"I'm sorry."*

The elevator door closed, and Cara collapsed against the wall. As she did, she was flooded with thoughts of everything she *should* have said. If only she could have taken a moment to write it down first. The characters in Cara's screenplays never stumbled over their words. They never said the wrong thing, and they never made fools of themselves in front of an ex-boyfriend. But written dialogue paired with slug lines and parentheticals was one thing. Actual spontaneous human interactions were another. When she was writing, she had time to edit, delete, and rewrite. Reality afforded no such luxury. Cara often thought how much easier life would be if it came with a few crucial keyboard functions. Or even better, if her brain could somehow format everything as a screenplay *before* words came flying out of her mouth. But life didn't come with a delete button, and there were no rewrites, on set or anywhere else. Still, sometimes she caught herself narrating her life in hindsight—a wishful do-over of sorts—as though she were reading from a script. Like at the Academy Awards, when they announce the screenplay nominees using a clip from the film paired with a voice-over of the script.

## INT: HOTEL LOBBY. EARLY EVENING.

**BLOND**
(looking confused)
I'm sorry, how did you say you know Kyle?

**CARA**
I didn't.

BLOND looks up at KYLE, who looks as though he's
about to poop his pants.

**KYLE**
(sweating)
Cara is—

**CARA**
(interrupting)
The one you were really hiding from, not HR.

**BLOND**
(even more confused)
I don't understand.

**CARA**
I'm sure Kyle will be happy to explain.
Actually, maybe not. You might just get
an email.

Boom. Done. Sweet and simple. But real life was more of a novel than a screenplay, and Cara wasn't Julia Roberts. She wasn't even Sandra Bullock or Meg Ryan. No, Cara was more Renée Zellweger, and not in *Jerry Maguire* but *Bridget Jones*. Which was why, as her gaze fell to the bed in the middle of her hotel room—and more importantly to where the staff had turned down the duvet and placed a piece of chocolate on each of the two pillows—Cara already knew her night was going to include belting out a pajama-clad version of "All by Myself."

At least she didn't have to share her candy.

Cara snatched up both the foil squares and flopped onto the bed. She'd just shoved the first piece into her mouth when her phone rang with a call from Julia.

"Hello," she said around a mouthful of chocolate.

"What are you doing?"

"Lying on my bed eating candy."

"So basically the same thing you do in LA."

"Pretty much." And wasn't that a sad statement. "What about you?"

"Just starting a batch of cornetti al cioccolato."

Cara might not have spoken Italian, but even she knew that last word was chocolate, and since she had just polished off her last piece…

"Talk dirty to me."

Julia laughed. "Dark chocolate layers of flaky brioche wrapped around a succulent ribbon of hazelnut cream with a sprinkle of—"

"Stop, you're killing me."

"Don't worry. I'll save one for you."

"One?" Cara gave a harsh laugh. "Better save at least five."

"Five chocolate croissants?" Julia asked, but her tone quickly went from teasing to concern. "What happened?"

Tears pricked Cara's eyes as she rolled onto her side. "I saw Kyle."

"I'm sorry, Car. But you knew that was a possibility."

"I know, and you tried to warn me." Repeatedly. "But it's for the best."

"This I gotta hear."

Cara drew a deep breath through her nose. "Because if I hadn't run into him in the lobby, then I wouldn't have met his new girlfriend. Except she's not new." *Do not cry.* "He's been seeing her for a few months."

There was a beat of silence on the other end of the line. "What?"

"Yep. She works for his company. In the San Francisco office."

"So all those trips…?"

"…were to see her."

"Shit. I'm sorry, Car. That must have been awkward as hell." Julia didn't bother to ask how the conversation went. She already knew Cara didn't have the type of brain-to-mouth coordination it would take to come up with a fist pump scene five minutes after finding out her turd of an ex-boyfriend was even more of a shit than she first thought.

There was a rustling followed by the sound of a door shutting. "Listen, you might not want to hear this, but in a way, he's done you a favor. There's no going back after finding out something like that."

"I know."

"Say it like you mean it."

"I KNOW!" Cara practically shouted.

Julia laughed. "That's better. Now, tell me something good. What did you do on your last day?"

"Let's see." Cara rolled onto her back, her eyes tracing a crack in the plaster ceiling that stretched from a crystal light fixture in the center of the room to the corner where beige drapes spilled from a gold rod into a puddle on the floor. "Went to Trinity. The library is even more amazing than it looks in all the memes. Saw the harp. It was a little underwhelming. Had steak and Guinness stew again. Excellent, again. Found out what was actually in the black pudding served with my breakfast. Not so excellent. Kissed Finn."

"You did *what*?"

"I kissed Finn," she repeated. "Well, technically he kissed me, and it was really more a touching of lips than a kiss, but still."

"Way to bury the lede there, Kennedy. Start from the beginning." Julia Moretti was a talker, but she was also a thorough listener. According to her, the highlight reel wouldn't cut it. She wanted a story to "start from hello." And if possible, it needed to be told face-to-face. Julia had once told Cara that in college, if the story was really good, she and her roommate would get up, turn on the lights, and put on their glasses. It was something Cara never quite understood—although she suspected it was tied to the whole "Italians talk with their hands" thing—but Julia insisted some stories needed to be seen and not merely heard. Which is why Cara wasn't at all surprised when her phone screen switched to a FaceTime request.

Cara wiped her eyes, then accepted the call. "What if I'd been naked?"

Julia snorted. "You and I both know the only embarrassing situation I could have caught you in was chocolate smeared on your face." She wiggled her eyebrows. "But it sounds like you might have a chance to smear chocolate on a hunky Irishman before this trip ends."

"It was barely a kiss, Jules. Kind of a big jump to go from there to chocolate body paint."

"Sometimes it's better to leap before you look."

"That's not how the expression goes. Besides, I'm flying home tomorrow."

"I know. You'll have to up your game."

Game? What game? "Julia, if I had game, I wouldn't be lying in a king-size bed alone, eating chocolate meant for two."

"Be that as it may, there's no time for your usual pace."

Well, that was true. While most of Cara's friends followed the "third date's the charm" rule, Cara moved a lot slower when it came to sex. She'd learned early on that one-night stands weren't for her. No matter how hard she tried to keep it simple, sex with a guy tended to elevate the meaningless to meaningful and caused her to see someone as special when nine times out of ten, they were anything but. Basically, she imprinted on a guy like a puppy the moment they were naked. Which was why she tried to avoid putting the cart before the horse and stick to developing an emotional connection *before* taking off her clothes.

"You're going to have to speed things up a bit if you have

any hope of quality time with this guy before your flight, and by quality time, I mean—"

"I know what you mean." Cara cut her off. "But you know how I get."

"This will be different," Julia said without the slightest bit of doubt in her voice.

"How can you be so sure?"

"Because hel-lo, this dude lives in Ireland. It's not like you two will run into each other and decide to have another go. Now, back to this kiss," Julia prompted. "I feel like Netflix skipped an episode or something. Back up. Where did you see him?"

"The jail."

Julia's eyes nearly popped out of her head. "He was in jail?"

Cara laughed. "No, he works there. Kilmainham Gaol. It's a museum now."

"I don't remember any prisons on your spreadsheet," Julia teased.

Cara rolled her eyes. "I made a list, not a spreadsheet. And it wasn't. Finn suggested it the other day. But he didn't tell me he was a tour guide. He just said he had hoped fate would bring us together."

"I think I have to agree with the handsome brogue on this one. Fate definitely brought you two together."

When it came to matters of the heart, Cara didn't believe in things like fate and destiny, because if she did, then how could she explain all the crappy stuff that happened to perfectly nice people? "It wasn't fate. He works there, and he's the one who suggested I go."

"Yes, but he didn't know if you would actually turn up.

And you didn't know he was going to be there. And he didn't know if you would know he worked there."

"They don't know that we know that they know," Cara said, teasing Julia by quoting one of her favorite *Friends* episodes.

"I'm serious, Car. I'm assuming it's a fairly large place. You could have arrived while he was out with another group and never even crossed paths." The screen grayed out, and the word *paused* replaced Julia's face.

"What are you doing?"

"Looking up this jail," she said. "Oh! I know that place. It's where they filmed *Paddington 2*." Cara wasn't at all surprised by that random tidbit of knowledge. With sixteen nieces and nephews, her friend watched a lot of kid movies. But if Julia kept interrupting her, they were never going to get to the good stuff.

"Do you want to hear what happened or not?"

Julia's face returned to the screen. "Yes," she said. "But start from hello." After that, she listened quietly—well, quietly for her at least—as Cara recounted the events at the jail, everything from the courtyard to the chapel.

"So what you're telling me is he kissed you in a wedding chapel? At the altar."

"To be fair, it wasn't a wedding chapel per se. It's just a chapel where weddings took place."

"Correction. It's a chapel where possibly the most tragically romantic wedding *ever* took place."

Well, when she put it that way...

"I'm sorry," Julia said. "Killing her husband was bad enough, but not letting them at least consummate the marriage?"

"*That's* what I said!"

"And here I thought Catholics were all about procreation back then."

"Guess they didn't want her bringing a future insurgent into the world."

"Hmm," Julia hummed, a surefire sign she was thinking. "What happened to her after he died?"

"I don't know actually." Cara grabbed her laptop off the nightstand and after a few keystrokes had the answer to Julia's question. "It says here that Grace Gifford Plunkett was an artist and cartoonist active in the Republican movement." Her mouth popped open as she read the next section. "You'll love this, Jules. On her marriage certificate, she was listed as a spinster. She was twenty-eight!"

"Better hurry up and find a husband, Cara. You've only got one more year till spinsterhood."

"You realize you're older than I am, don't you?"

"I embraced my inner spinster a long time ago," Julia said with a laugh. "Did Grace ever get remarried?"

Cara scanned the rest of the web page. "It doesn't look like it. In fact, it sounds like she followed in her late husband's footsteps, using her art to promote the left-wing Irish political party."

"Okay, enough with the history lesson. Back to the Irish sex god."

"It. Was. One. Kiss."

"Yeah, but it must have been a pretty good one for you to be drowning your libido with chocolate."

"I don't have to be horny to eat chocolate."

"Ah, so you admit you're horny?"

"You're impossible." Although she was right. Problem was, Cara wasn't feeling particularly desirable after her lobby run-in with Kyle.

"Why didn't you suggest going out tonight?"

"He did, actually," Cara said. "Invited me to some Leap Day thing at a pub."

"What kind of Leap Day thing?"

"No clue. Probably just an excuse to drink. He said something about a proper pint in a proper pub."

"Then why are you in bed alone?" Julia was almost shouting.

"He had to go to some family dinner first."

"Please tell me you said you'd meet him later."

"Sort of."

"*Sort of?*" This time, there was nothing "almost" about the shouting.

"I'm pretty sure I said *maybe*. I don't know. I was rushing to take Samantha's call."

"Shit." Julia groaned. "Sorry 'bout that. I didn't even have a text from her today."

"It was about a toy for Coco. I'm sure she didn't even try you." As far as Samantha was concerned, personal emergencies, especially those pertaining to her pampered pooch, fell to her second assistant. No way Julia could have intercepted that one.

"It's your last night in Dublin. Hell if you should spend it in your hotel room. I mean, seriously, you just told me about a woman who kept going after she lost everything. Surely you can go out for a beer after only losing Kyle, who, it turns out, wasn't that great to begin with."

When she put it like that...

"Wipe the chocolate off your face, put on those jeans that make your butt look ah-mazing, and go find the Irish sex god." Julia grinned. "And when you do, ask him if he has a brother. Preferably a twin."

Cara couldn't help but laugh. "First, you don't even know what he looks like, so how do you know that you'd even want a twin?"

"I know your type. Pretty boy with great eyes, even better hair, and a nice ass."

She was right, but still.

"Second, you can hardly call him a sex god."

"Why not?" Julia asked.

"Because at this point, we don't know."

"You sound like Bernie in the opening of *About Last Night*."

"Bingeing eighties movies again?" One of the stars of that era had come to the office for a meeting a few weeks back, prompting Julia to take to Netflix in search of his early work. Since then, she'd developed what could only be described as a near obsession. Cara was pretty sure Julia had watched more eighties movies than even Cara's mother, and her mother *loved* eighties movies. She'd started with the classics: *Breakfast Club*, *Pretty in Pink*, and *Risky Business*. The last one launched her into a few nights of Tom Cruise's early work, which of course led her to *The Outsiders*, and she'd been Brat Packing it ever since.

"Don't judge. Rob Lowe was some serious eye candy back then."

Another thing to know about a conversation with Julia

Moretti, there were always lots of tangents. "And that's relevant how?"

"It's not," she conceded before circling back. "Time to take control of your life, Cara. All of that feminist jargon means nothing if you're too afraid to ask for what you want."

She had a point. "Fine, I'll do it. Happy?"

"Yes. Just don't do anything I wouldn't do."

"That doesn't leave much." Cara looked at the clock on her laptop. "Shit, it's getting late. If I'm really gonna do this, I better go."

"Wait!" Julia said. "I haven't even told you why I called." Twenty minutes on the phone and she hadn't mentioned why she called? After three years of friendship, Cara wasn't sure how that managed to surprise her.

"Jeremy's got an opening on his desk."

"Get out!" Jeremy Stone was an agent at CTA. He was nearly as powerful as Samantha but with half the attitude. More importantly, he had a reputation for helping his assistants move out of his office and into their own, which was why Cara wasn't at all surprised to learn that the guy who had worked for him the past two years had taken a job as a staff writer on a new Netflix show.

"Has he started interviewing?" Cara asked.

"No. In fact, no one even knows yet. Jonathan isn't giving his official notice to the agency until sometime after the board meeting at the end of next month, which means—"

"I can talk to Jeremy on Tuesday." Made sense. As assistants to the two top producers, Julia and Jonathan would be tasked with making the arrangements for that quarterly meeting. Jonathan would definitely want to keep a low profile until after it was over, which meant Cara would have time to speak to Jeremy before he was flooded with applications and requests. For the first time, Cara was actually happy her trip to Ireland was so short. Working for Jeremy Stone would be a huge step in the right direction. Not only would it be as a first assistant—meaning tasks beyond fetching coffee, making copies, and pampering pets—but it actually might lead to something.

As exciting as this news was, there was nothing she could do about it until she was back in LA. For now, she was in Dublin with the matter of a cute guy, a proper pint, and some sort of Leap Day celebration that would hopefully involve the rest of that interrupted kiss.

Which was why, three minutes later, Cara was off the phone and in the shower. She might not have known how the night would play out—or which top to pair with her favorite jeans—but one thing was certain: there was no way in hell Cara was leaving Dublin without seeing Finn Maguire one last time.

# CHAPTER 7

CARA ARRIVED AT THE BAR at eight thirty, and despite the fact that she'd never been there before, the place was somehow exactly how she'd imagined it would be. The lighting was low, the floors were sticky, and the walls were covered with posters from events held at the venue over the years.

There was a fairly large stage to the left—where from the looks of it, a band was about to play—while to the right, a bar stretched from one end of the building to the other. It was there that she found Finn, leaning casually against the expanse of polished oak while chatting with a bartender who had just handed him a bottle of beer. His confident stance was captivating without being cocky, and Cara found herself drinking in every detail, from the scuffs on his well-worn black leather boots, to the frayed pocket on his very fine denim-clad backside, to the black, long-sleeve Henley that was just tight enough to reveal the muscles in his arms. While simple enough, the overall look would have given him a decidedly rougher edge if it weren't for the warmth of his nearly ever-present smile.

Finn Maguire had a smile unlike any Cara had ever seen before—sincere and inviting, mischievous and playful—and it never failed to draw her in. It was no surprise then that, before she even realized what was happening, she was moving toward him.

He looked up as she approached, and holy hell if the wattage on that smile didn't double. "You came," he said. Was he really that surprised?

Once again, Finn greeted her by pressing a kiss to her cheek. She should have expected it, seeing as how he'd greeted her that same way earlier in the day. But that knowledge, combined with the fact that the custom didn't mean the same in Europe as it would have, say, in a bar in LA, didn't stop a warmth from spreading across her face. On instinct, she looked down and away. When she did, she noticed a large group had not only formed in front of the stage but that the place had nearly filled to capacity. "Did everyone in town decide to show up all at once?"

Finn laughed. "The regulars," he said. "They know we always start a half hour late."

Cara nodded in agreement—as though she had any clue about the regulars or the schedule of their favorite band—but then the pronoun he'd used registered. "Wait," she said. "We? You're a professional musician?"

Finn laughed. "Don't know if I'd call it *professional*." He nodded toward the bartender. "Billy there pays us mostly in free ale."

"Guess that's not such a bad deal."

"Until you end up wrecked and have to crash in one of the hotel rooms upstairs."

Cara nodded. "So in the end, the ale isn't always free."

"Not at all," Finn said in the way he had of making a sentence sound like one long word. *Notattall.* "But these days, we only play special events. No time."

"And today's a special event?" It was a random Sunday in February. What was so special about that?

"Aye." He gave a tight nod. "Leap Day."

Cara's brows drew together. "And that's special?"

"Remains to be seen," Finn said with a mischievous wink. "Either way, it's serendipitous."

"How so?"

Finn lifted the bottle to his lips, then smiled over the rim. "A gig usually helps when I'm trying to impress a pretty lass."

The warmth on her cheeks had no doubt progressed from pink to red. "Plus, it completes the Finn Maguire trifecta."

He cocked his head to one side. "Trifecta?"

"Well, I've seen you drive and give tours. Guess all that was left was to see you play."

His eyes darkened, and his voice dropped. "That's not all that's left."

Forget turning red. If he kept looking at her like that, she might actually burst into flames.

Finn leaned forward to place his empty bottle on the bar behind her, bringing his lips mere inches from hers. He lingered for a split second longer than necessary, enveloping her in the light, woodsy scent of his cologne and a hint of lager. It was an intoxicating mix, and although she hadn't had so much as a taste of alcohol, Cara felt an unmistakable buzz.

A drumbeat echoed through the hall, and the crowd cheered, but it was nothing compared to the pounding of Cara's heart.

"That's my cue," Finn said. "Wait for me?"

As if there were any place in the world she would rather be.

"Billy," he said to the man behind the bar. "Whatever she wants, on my tab."

Cara watched as Finn disappeared into the thick crowd, then turned her attention to the bartender. He was stout with a round face and a welcoming smile.

"What's the craic?" he asked as he wiped his hands on a towel, then slung it over his shoulder.

"Craic?"

His brows shot up. "An American?"

"Let me guess," she said. "My bricíní made you think I was a local?"

The man's smile grew even wider. "Ah, someone's done her research." He winked. "Or met a charmer. My money's on our musician friend, yeah? Would explain why you're a little off the beaten path. Don't get many tourists in here."

Cara stole a glance at the stage where Finn was chatting with the band's drummer.

"Welcome to the Hole," the man said. "What's your whiskey?"

Whoa, way to get right to the hard stuff. "Not sure I have one," Cara said on a laugh.

"How 'bout a Teeling, then?"

"Don't know if I can handle that," she said. "I went on their tour and nearly drowned."

"Drowned? Swam in the vats, did ya?"

"No, but apparently I can't breathe and drink at the same time."

The bartender chuckled. "Ah, failed the tasting. Sip it the old-fashioned way, and you'll be fine." He reached for an amber bottle. "I'll mix it so you'll hardly know it's there." With that, he got to work pouring and shaking, which gave Cara the chance to let her inner groupie out to play. She watched in fascination as Finn lifted the guitar strap over his head and, a few seconds later, played the opening bars of what was clearly a crowd favorite.

"Here ya go," the bartender shouted over the music. He set a squat glass of punch on the bar, and despite her earlier whiskey mishap, Cara had to admit it was quite delicious. So much so that, as the night wore on, she didn't even mind that the drinks were gradually becoming more whiskey than punch. By the third one, she was fighting the urge to sing along with the band, and after glass number who-the-hell-knows-anymore, she actually found herself dancing and not even caring that she didn't have a partner.

When the second set ended, a woman approached the stage and whispered something in Finn's ear. Whatever it was must have been good news judging by the wide smile that spread across his face. As the woman walked away, Finn turned to the other members of the band, and a moment later, the keyboard player began a few synthesized notes. The rest of the band joined in to play a song Cara recognized but couldn't quite place. Snow Patrol maybe? She wasn't sure, but judging by the cheers that erupted in front of the stage, plenty of people knew exactly what song it was.

Cara turned to find her new friend Billy the bartender clapping as well. "Why's everyone so excited?"

"Someone's about to get engaged," he said as the crowd fanned out to form a circle in front of the stage.

Finn strummed his guitar as he sang the refrain of the song Cara now recognized as "Just Say Yes." The woman who had requested the song led her boyfriend to the middle of the dance floor and dropped to one knee, beaming up at him as she pulled a ring out of the front pocket of her jeans. Cara couldn't hear her pop the actual question, but she assumed the answer was yes because not two minutes later, the happy couple was sharing a passionate kiss as the crowd around them went wild. And while she assumed they would have cheered even if the roles had been reversed, there was definitely an extra shot of excitement in the air.

"Hasn't anyone ever seen a woman propose before?" Cara asked. She'd once read an article that said 95 percent of proposals were made by men. But still, it couldn't be *that* rare.

"Not like this," Billy said. "Only happens once every four years."

Cara frowned. "Why only every four years?"

"Leap Day," he said, finally clueing Cara in on why she kept hearing so much fuss over February twenty-ninth. "Been a tradition in Ireland for over a thousand years."

"Of women proposing to men?"

Billy leaned closer, planting his elbows on the bar. "Legend has it that this all started when St. Brigid complained to St. Patrick about how women had to wait around for men to propose. Supposedly, St. Patrick decreed February twenty-ninth as the day it was acceptable for a woman to pop the question. And if the man said no, he had to pay a fine."

"To her?"

Billy shrugged. "Don't know. But according to the stories told by just about everyone's mam, there was a time when turning down the proposal meant a gentleman had to buy a lass twelve pairs of gloves."

"Why gloves?"

Billy chuckled. "To hide the fact that she didn't have a ring, of course."

"Of course." Cara rolled her eyes. "Mighty generous of old Paddy to say it was okay, but only on a day that came around once every four years."

Billy straightened. "If you ask me, women should feel free to propose any day of the year."

"That's very progressive of you."

"He's only saying that because he's hoping I'll pop the question so he doesn't have to come up with some grand plan," a woman behind the bar said. "It's a cop-out, that's what it is."

"Not true," Billy said, placing his hand over his heart. "Is it so hard to believe a man wants to be wooed?"

The waitress's head fell back on a laugh. "Are you drunk?"

"Drunk on love," Billy said.

Even Cara struggled to keep a straight face over that one.

"Wind your neck in, old man," the woman said. But Billy was undeterred.

"Just say the words, and I'm all yours. Even had Liam there ordained." Billy nodded to the busboy. "I'm ready to say 'I do' on a moment's notice."

"Feck off." The actual words might have been an insult, but

the waitress was smiling as she loaded three pints onto a tray. "If you think I'd be married to you in this bar, by a minister of the internet no less, then I know you've been nipping that whiskey while you pour." With that, she hoisted the tray above the crowd and was gone.

"Seventy-nine percent of women say they're not brave enough to propose," the busboy offered, leaving Cara to wonder if he'd read the same article she had. "And sixty-five percent of men said they would turn them down if they did."

"She'll come around." Billy laughed. "And when she does, I'll say yes *and* buy her gloves. If that ain't true love, I don't know what is."

"You two aren't trying to make a move on my girl, are ya?" Finn said. He was standing beside her, radiating an energy Cara swore she could feel. Then again, the tingling sensation rushing over her skin might have had something to do with the way he'd just referred to her as *his* girl.

"That was amazing," she said.

"Thanks." Finn reached for the beer Billy had set on the bar. "Not our best effort, but the guitar player was a bit nervous."

Cara giggled. And not in a subtle way either. No, the sound that came out of her mouth was a full-on schoolgirl giggle. "Is that so?"

"Aye. Tryin' to impress a lass, from what I heard." He took a long pull of his beer, never once taking his eyes off hers.

"Well, I can't speak for the woman he was trying to impress," she said, playing along with his game. "But I thought the guitar player was pretty great."

"What was Billy bending yer ear about?"

"He was telling me about Leap Day."

"Always a crowd-pleaser. To be honest, I'm surprised there's only been one tonight. Most pubs get at least half a dozen."

While Cara was all in favor of women taking their romantic destiny into their own hands, it struck her that those kinds of statistics meant there were a lot of women who had grown tired of waiting for a man to decide they wanted something long term.

*Long term...*

"Can I ask you a question?"

Finn smiled. "You just did."

She narrowed her eyes at him. "You're a cheeky one, Finn Maguire."

"You love it though."

Not yet, but she was beginning to think she could.

"Well, then can I ask you one—I mean two"—she quickly added, not wanting to fall for the same joke twice—"more?"

Finn tipped his bottle toward her in salute. "Nice catch."

"I'm a quick study." Not really, at least not when it came to men. Those lessons she seemed destined to learn again and again.

"Go on, then," he prompted.

If she hadn't had three—or was it five?—glasses of Billy's punch, she never would have asked, but since that wasn't the case...

"Do you think I'm the kind of girl a man would marry?"

The smile slipped from Finn's face. "Why in the world would you doubt that?"

"My ex told me I wasn't long-term potential." Whiskey-fueled or not, once the words were out of her mouth, Cara couldn't help but feel a little stupid for blurting out such an embarrassing detail. Not that there was anything she could do about it. And why stress over it anyway? She only had a few hours left with Finn. If he was going to be turned off by her penchant for oversharing, there wasn't any real damage done. *Yeah, keep telling yourself that, Kennedy.* Fortunately for her, Finn was unfazed.

"Your ex is a feckin eejit."

Cara didn't know what an *eejit* was, but judging by the sour expression that crossed Finn's face when he said the word, it probably suited Kyle to a T.

"You need to put him out of your mind and enjoy yourself," he said. "Like my mam always says, 'Better to enjoy the moment than think it to death.'"

Cara couldn't help but smile, not only at what he said but the way he said it. She loved the way *"think"* sounded like *"tink"* and how his voice went up at the end of a sentence, making nearly everything he said sound more like a question than a statement.

"Your mam sounds like a wise woman."

"Oh, she's got a few that would make you laugh your tits off," he said. "But on this one, she's spot-on. None of us knows what lies ahead. Seems to me, 'so far, so good' is all you really need to worry about."

Cara nodded, then drained the last of her whiskey punch. Judging by the color, that one had been a *lot* more whiskey than punch, although she'd have never known it by the taste.

Finn reached into his pocket for his guitar pick, shoving his jeans a little lower in the process and revealing a smattering of dark hair just above the waistband of his blue... *Hmm, boxers? Or maybe briefs?*

"We've got one more set to play," Finn said, yanking Cara away from the Calvin Klein fashion show that had started playing on a loop in her head. "Then I'm all yours." He winked. "If you'll have me?"

*If she'd have him?* Holy moly, she'd have him right there on the bar if she could. Finn Maguire was a walking, talking aphrodisiac as it was. After two hours of watching him sing and play guitar, she was ready to damn near combust as it was and now...*if she'd have him?* The words held so much unspoken promise that when she opened her mouth to speak, Cara was sure her voice would reveal the way her breath had caught in her throat. "I'll be right here."

Cara watched as he disappeared into the crowd before bounding back onto the stage. In the corner of her mind, a tiny part of her rational brain wondered if this was his go-to foreplay for all the women he met. Would be a smart move, seeing as how it was working like a charm. But Cara's rational brain wasn't in control at the moment. She was a live wire of hormones and whiskey.

"This one's on the house," Billy said, setting another glass on the bar.

Cara giggled. It was becoming a trend. "Like a punch card?" she asked. "Buy five, get the sixth one free?"

Billy chuckled. "Nah, just that I couldn't help but overhear what you were saying there. Whoever the bloke was that told you that you weren't long-term potential is a gobby shite."

"You've got a way with words, Billy Donnelly." The waitress

was back. "But that couple there"—she set her now empty tray on the bar and nodded to a man and woman seated at the far end—"need you to be pouring instead of yapping."

She waited until the bartender was out of earshot, then turned her attention back to Cara. "Billy was bang on. That one wasn't the guy for you." Her gaze shifted back to him. "But he's out there. Every pot has a lid."

"And Billy's yours?"

The waitress smiled. "For six years now."

"Then why aren't you two married?" Cara asked without thinking. "Sorry, that was way too personal a question for a total stranger to ask." She winced. "Can I blame the whiskey?"

The waitress wiped her hand on the dark-green apron she wore tied around her waist, then stuck it out. "Eileen."

"I'm Cara," she replied as they shook hands.

"There, now we're not strangers." Eileen flashed her a smile that wasn't the least bit fake. "And to answer your question, Billy and I like to take the piss out of each other, but the fact is, he'd propose if he thought that's what I wanted."

"You don't?"

Eileen laughed. "Naw, I just like giving him a hard time. Neither of us cares if we ever get married." She glanced down the bar at her boyfriend. "We love each other and that's enough."

Cara nodded.

"But if I *did* want to get married, Leap Day or not, I'd ask that man in a heartbeat."

"Really?"

"Sure as hell would. I'm not about to stand around waiting

for a man to decide my fate." Eileen set two shot glasses on the bar, then reached for a bottle of Jameson and sloshed the amber liquid back and forth across the glasses until they were full. When she was finished, she slid one in front of Cara and raised the other in the air. "To finding what you want and having the balls to ask for it."

Cara lifted her glass. As she did, her gaze instinctively shifted to the stage where Finn was strumming his guitar. "To asking for what you want," she said before downing the shot. She knew straight whiskey should have burned on the way down, but Cara swallowed it without so much as a wince. Maybe that was what people meant when they said whiskey was an acquired taste. That or she'd had enough that she didn't notice the burn anymore. Either way, there was enough liquid courage coursing through Cara's veins to not only ask for what she wanted but to follow through with it as well.

A hiccup bubbled up from inside her, and she smiled.

"You okay?" Eileen asked.

Cara was more than okay. She was great. She was in Ireland, thousands of miles from her real life. She could be any version of herself she wanted to be, even the one who lived deep down inside her. "Never better," she said. Then she placed the shot glass on the bar and made her way toward the stage. For once in her life, Cara Kennedy was going after exactly what she wanted.

# CHAPTER 8

A KNOCK ON THE BATHROOM door pulled Cara out of her daydream and back into her nightmare.

She sat up and slumped against the wood door she didn't remember closing. Thank god for small victories, she thought, although there was little doubt the tile floor had left a mosaic imprint on her cheek.

"You okay?" Finn asked from the other side.

Cara wanted to reply, but when she opened her mouth, saliva pooled in the back of her throat. So much for the short rest calming her whiskey-logged stomach.

"Can I come in?"

"No!" she managed to not only say but somehow shout. Then after a few seconds, she added a quiet, "I'm naked."

"We already established that."

"That was before."

"Before what?"

*Before I realized you were still dressed.*

*Before I saw myself in the mirror.*

*Before I knew I was your wife.*

In a perfect world, she would have fallen asleep on the floor, only to wake up in a few hours to find she was both hangover and husband free. But the world wasn't perfect, and this wasn't merely a bad dream. It was her shit show of a life, and she needed to deal with it. First, she needed to get dressed. "Can you bring me my clothes?"

There were footsteps in the hallway and, a moment later, a tap at the door. "Here you go."

Cara sat up and reached for the knob. "Thanks," she said, opening the door just enough for Finn to pass the items to her while she stayed safely hidden from view.

Once she was dressed in the jeans and the black blouse she'd worn the night before—both of which now smelled more like a bar than the *actual* bar had—Cara joined Finn in his room. He was sitting on the edge of the bed. The jeans he'd slept in were now paired with a tattered Lumineers T-shirt, and his hair was standing up as though he'd stuck his finger in an electric socket, but damn if he didn't look good.

"Whiskey should come with a warning label," she said as she shuffled past him.

"I usually avoid the stuff but—"

"Wait." Cara turned toward him so quickly, she nearly fell down. "You were only drinking beer." At least as far as she could recall.

"During the sets, yeah. But you insisted I catch up to you."

Fuzzy images played through her mind. Her chanting for Finn to do shots. Billy laughing. Eileen flashing her a knowing grin.

Cara slumped into the chair next to the bed. "The last thing I remember…" She tried her best to recall the night but was only able to grasp small threads. "I was talking to Eileen, you were about to finish your last set, and…" A thought broke through the fog. "I was going to ask you to dance with me."

"You did. But first there was a smoking-hot kiss."

*That* she did remember, in surprising detail considering the fact that her mind drew a complete blank after that.

"Then there was the matter of catching up. Something about a punch card—at least I think that's what you said. All I know is you had five shots lined up on the bar and told Billy to give me a sixth one for free. You had a few more as well."

"And *then* I asked you to dance?"

He nodded slowly. Cara wasn't sure if the pace was because of the way his own head felt at the moment or if he was waiting for her memories to return. When she said nothing, he quietly added, "That's not all you asked."

Cara closed her eyes and drew a deep breath, and after a few seconds, more images flashed through her mind. Unlike her memories from earlier in the night, these played like clips from one of those old silent movies—grainy and at the wrong speed.

Dragging Finn to the dance floor.

Laughing, dancing, grinding.

Kissing. Lots and lots of kissing.

"I remember telling you not to overthink…" Cara frowned as the thought evaporated. "…something." Again, she tried to think back.

Her hands under his shirt. His lips on her neck.

A low groan in her ear. A hand on her ass.

Wanting him. Now. Always.

Pots and pans. A smiling cook. *What?*

Cara opened her eyes. "Was I in the pub's kitchen?"

"Aye."

"Why in the world—"

Finn held up his hand and wiggled his fingers. Oh, right. The tinfoil rings. But why...

The music stopping. A circle forming.

Dropping to one knee.

*Oh god...*

"I proposed?"

"You did."

"What was I thinking?"

"That being in Ireland on Leap Day was a sign."

"What were *you* thinking?"

"Clearly, I wasn't."

"Clearly."

"Those six shots hit me kinda fast, and you looked so damn cute looking up at me. I don't know why really, but I couldn't say no."

Great, the one time a guy found her irresistible. Cara picked at a mysterious stain on the thigh of her jeans. "Couldn't you have just bought me twelve pairs of gloves?"

"What?"

"Never mind." She shook her head. "Who did the...I'm not Catholic...was there a priest in the pub?"

As soon as she asked the question, she remembered the in-house internet minister.

"The busboy," they said in unison.

"Look," Cara said. "It's not that I haven't had loads of fun with you, but obviously my proposal was fueled by a lot of whiskey. Cute or not, why in the world would you agree to marry a woman you barely knew? And, I mean, it's not like that was gonna change with me leaving town the next day."

The next day.

Today.

Shit.

Cara sprung to her feet, her eyes darting around the room as she turned left, then right. Why didn't people have clocks anymore?

Finn crossed the room, placed one hand on each of her shoulders to settle her, then bent his head so he could look her in the eyes. "Don't panic, luv. This can all be fixed."

"It can?"

He nodded. "We'll just pop over to the pub and tell Liam to tear up the paperwork. As long as he doesn't file it with the county, then it will be like it never even happened."

Relief flooded her body, and she relaxed like a balloon that had been untied. But she'd no sooner let go of one anxiety when another gripped her chest.

"What time is it?"

"About ten."

Her words came out so quickly, they sounded like one long sentence. "My flight is at three which means I need to be there by noon which means I should be packing right now or at least be in the shower."

"Breathe." Finn said. Then with a smile, he added, "Don't want my wife passing out."

He had a point, although to be fair, referring to her as his wife wasn't helping matters. Still, Cara took a deep breath.

"I'll run down to the pub, and you go back to the hotel. Once I've got it all sorted, I'll pop 'round to say goodbye."

Under normal circumstances, the thought of saying goodbye to a vacation fling would have sounded bittersweet, but missing Finn Maguire would have to wait until she was home. Right now, all she could think about was how happy she was going to be when he turned up at her hotel holding a torn-up marriage certificate in his hands.

But an hour later, when she opened the door, Cara didn't find him holding a ripped-up paper or anything else for that matter. And after seeing the look on his face, she sure as hell wasn't happy.

"What happened?" she asked. The pit of her stomach had already registered the outcome, but her brain still wanted to know.

"I was too late."

"Too late?"

Finn nodded. "He'd already taken the papers to the courthouse."

It wasn't even eleven a.m. How the hell had she somehow managed to not only get married but by an internet minister/busboy who was an early riser?

Cara felt as though she might actually pass out. "I need to sit down," she said, moving toward the padded bench at the foot of the bed.

Finn stepped into the room and closed the door behind him. "We can have the marriage voided." He sat down next to her and placed his hand over hers in a move she knew was meant to soothe her, but the sight of his homemade wedding band killed any hope of that.

*Why was he still wearing it?*

"As soon as the county finishes the processes of declaring the marriage legal," he said, "we can petition the courts for an annulment."

There were no two ways about it. This was a disaster. "How long will that take?"

"Not long. I'm sure we can have the whole thing wrapped up in a matter of weeks."

"*Weeks?*" she squeaked.

Finn nodded. "Four or five at most."

"And in that time, we'll just be...married?"

"On the bright side, now you'll have a chance to visit the west coast, see where your ancestors lived."

This was *not* happening.

"I'll take you there myself," he continued, clearly oblivious to her internal meltdown. "Been ages since I went to—"

"I can't just stay here for a month."

"You won't have to worry about a hotel. You can stay with me." He flashed her a grin. "You are my wife after all."

Was he actually making a joke?

"It's not just hotel bills, Finn. I have to work."

"You've got your laptop," he said, nodding to the case resting atop her suitcase. "You can work on your next screenplay from here."

"It's not that simple," she said. "I've got a big meeting on Tuesday that could be a game changer for my whole career." What she should have said was, while that part was true, she hadn't been entirely honest with him and that she was only a screenwriter under cover of night and that by day she was a lowly assistant who would never accrue enough vacation time to take a month-long holiday. But that conversation required more time than she had at the moment, because she had to be at the airport in—she glanced at the digital clock on the nightstand—just under an hour.

"Come with me," she blurted out.

Finn's eyes grew wide. "What?"

Cara froze. Did she really just ask Finn to come home with her? Part of her knew it sounded like a ridiculous idea, but another part knew it made perfect sense. He was right about one thing. If she stayed, it might only take a few weeks to settle the matter. But if she left, it could be months—hell, maybe as long as a year—before she was able to negotiate an annulment with a relative stranger across not only the Atlantic but the span of the United States.

"Come with me to LA, and we can have the marriage annulled there."

"Quit acting the maggot."

"What?"

"That's crazy talk."

"How is it any crazier than me staying here?"

She had a point, and if the frown on Finn's face was any indication, he knew it too.

"You're right about it being easier if we're in the same country," she said. "Can you imagine the red tape if we try to have lawyers from two different countries handle this?" Not to mention the bills. "All I'm suggesting is we do it in my country instead of yours."

Finn didn't say any word, but Cara could tell he was considering it.

"Can you take time off from the jail?" Words she never imagined asking anyone, let alone her husband. *Husband!*

"That wouldn't be a problem but—"

"Great. Look at it as a holiday. You said you've never been to LA, so now's your chance. There's loads to do, so you won't be bored while I'm at work and..." Cara stopped herself midsentence. "We can talk about all this later. Right now, you need to go home and get your passport and meet me at the airport in forty-five minutes."

"Married only a few hours and already the little woman is bossing me around." He was shaking his head, but his eyes were smiling.

"Cute," she deadpanned. "Now go." There was no time to joke or even think. There'd be plenty of time to obsess on her greatest lapse in judgment on the eleven-hour flight to LA. Next to her husband. Her very sexy Irish husband. Who, for the immediate future, was going to be living with her in her very tiny apartment.

Yep. She was screwed.

# CHAPTER 9

CARA HAD BEEN WORRIED SHE wouldn't have enough room on her credit card to afford a last-minute ticket to LA, and even though she was fairly sure Finn would at least offer to split the cost with her, the truth of the matter was, she didn't know if he could afford it either. The guy worked two jobs, and if his apartment and car were any indication, he lived a pretty simple life. At least as far as she could tell. For all she knew, Finn could have been a billionaire's son. A former bad boy now living a more low-key, trust fund existence in order to avoid the tabloid press while taking part-time jobs to break up the monotony of spending his father's money. The thought nearly had her laughing out loud in the ticket line. Stuff like that only happened in a movie, which, once she'd thought of it, didn't seem like such a bad idea. Normally, a plot bunny like that would have gone straight to the file she kept in her phone's notes app, but there'd been no time for that. Cara had bigger issues than coming up with her next screenplay idea, and at the top of that list was getting her husband on her flight.

Turned out that purchasing the ticket was the easy part. Finn insisted on covering the full fare and, more than that, didn't even flinch when he handed over his credit card. Convincing the airline that Oscar was Cara's therapy dog was a bit trickier. In the end, Oscar's affection for her combined with her slight panic attack—that she didn't even have to fake thanks to the day she was having—was enough to convince the desk agent that there had been some mistake in the paperwork and that the needy pup was, in fact, *her* support animal. Finn had thanked her profusely, although to be fair, he hadn't left her much choice. He'd shown up with only minutes to spare, with his rucksack and dog in tow. All was well that ended well though—or so she thought—because the real fun began after they were on the plane.

Even though she'd only made the trip once before, Cara could say with all certainty that transatlantic flights were a lot more enjoyable when you were *going* on vacation than when you were flying home. Then again, she'd been quite tipsy for the flight to Ireland, which was a lot more fun than the hangover she was sporting on the return. To put it simply: it was hell. Turbulence had her reaching for the airsickness bag, and headwinds had the flight running an hour longer than scheduled. And all this took place while she was seated next to the man she'd married. *Married!* Not that either of them broached that subject. In fact, they hardly talked at all. Cara couldn't speak for Finn, but their surprisingly comfortable silence was just fine with her. There was no way she could begin to unravel the mess she'd made until she'd had a good night's sleep and several doses of Tylenol.

It was nearly eight o'clock by the time they got to Malibu. Penelope's house wasn't the flashiest home on Colony Beach, but it was definitely Cara's favorite. Unlike the glass box houses with infinity pools and landscaping that looked as though it had been grown in outer space, Penelope's home featured warm stucco walls and a clay tile roof that gave it a decidedly Tuscan feel. Cara had seen photographs from some of the parties Penelope had thrown back in the eighties, and from what she could tell, the house had been quite the show place back in the day.

"This way." Cara led Finn through a gate on the side of the house and down a path that at one time had been perfectly manicured but was now overgrown to the point that a machete would have come in handy, especially when dragging a suitcase. The main floor of the house was dark, but above them Cara could see the lights on the second floor were still on.

"Looks like Penelope is still awake," she said as they reached the rear of the house. The pool lights were still on as well, casting the oceanfront deck in a soft, blue glow.

"Penelope?"

"The woman who owns the house."

Finn frowned. "This isn't your house?"

"No, I live out here," Cara said, nodding to the small bunga-low on the other side of the pool. The fact that Cara didn't actually rent a house in Malibu, let alone own one, was one of the many things about her life she hadn't been completely honest about. To be fair, she hadn't actually lied, per se. More like she'd left out a few key details. She'd have to lay it all out for Finn, but at the moment, she was so tired, she could barely stand up. Having a conversation with her new husband about the cold, hard facts of her life ranked about as high as a trip to the dentist, and Cara hated going to the dentist. All those tools and the gritty toothpaste. No thanks. And why did all of them ask you a question the minute they stuck their hand in your mouth? Was that something they learned in dental school?

"Wow," Finn said, interrupting Cara's wandering thoughts. She turned to find him staring out across the water. It was dark outside, but the moon was full, reflecting off the waves as their whitecaps crashed into the sand just below the deck.

"Yeah, that view never grows old." And it was true. Cara had lived in Penelope's pool house for nearly two years, and yet every morning when she walked outside, she wanted to pinch herself. Her personal life and career might have needed help, but thanks to Penelope Parker, Cara was killing it when it came to prime real estate.

She drew a deep breath of the salty air. No matter what was going on in Cara's life, the smell of the ocean never failed to calm her. It was her favorite aromatherapy, and it was right outside her door.

Finn looked at her. "Beautiful."

Cara assumed he was still referring to the view, but that didn't keep her heart from racing. Then again, that might have been due to the fact that she was about to show her new husband and his dog their temporary home.

She unlocked the door and pushed it open. For a moment, the two of them stood staring at the doorway, as though each was waiting for the other to make the first move.

It was Finn who finally spoke. "I feel like I should carry you over the threshold," he said on a laugh.

"Maybe we could skip that tradition," she said.

"After you, then."

Cara stepped into the one-room bungalow and flipped on the lights. It was something she'd done hundreds of times, but this time was different. This time, she was seeing her home through the eyes of a relative stranger who was now, well, a relative.

"This is weird, isn't it? I mean, of course it's weird. But I want you to feel welcome. It's just a small space and—"

"It's grand, Cara," Finn said. "I've never seen the Pacific Ocean, and yet here I am, practically living on the beach." He smiled, then quickly added, "at least for a week or so."

Cara didn't know how long it took to sort out an annulment, but something told her it would take a lot longer than a week.

Finn set his bag down, then walked farther into the room. Cara watched as he took in his surroundings, which didn't take long. A small kitchen lined one wall, while a bed sat against another. That was really it aside from a desk, a table for two, and a couch. He didn't say anything, but the expression on his face told her he liked what he saw. Not that it should have surprised her. Yes, her place was small, but it was also pretty terrific. Penelope had decorated the pool house in the early sixties. And while for many years it would have been considered "dated," mid-century modern had made a huge comeback of late, which meant Cara had a vintage "pad" that was the envy of all her friends. All she'd had to do was buy the bed.

*The bed.*

The bed that would comfortably sleep two, if the two in question happened to be sleeping together. But were they? They certainly had the night before—not that she remembered—but that night had been fueled by enough alcohol to result in spontaneous nuptials. The fact that they'd fallen into bed together shouldn't have been too surprising. But that was then, and this was now, and both of them were sober and...*gah*! Why did everything have to be so damn complicated?

"Is that Penelope?" Finn asked, pulling Cara from what had to have been her hundredth spiral of the day. He was standing in front of one of the black-and-white photos that hung along the wall.

"Mm-hmm." Cara moved so she was standing beside him. The photograph Finn was studying featured Penelope wearing a two-piece bathing suit and some sort of groovy hat that was basically a swim cap covered with feathers. She was holding a glass of champagne in one hand and a small dog in the other and had not one or two but three men offering to refill her glass. "Apparently she had some pretty epic parties here back in the day."

Finn narrowed his eyes. "Is that Warren Beatty?"

"Yep. Penelope's photos are like a who's who of Hollywood," she said as he moved from one framed photo to the next.

"How do you two know each other?"

"She and my grandmother grew up together. When I moved out here, she sort of adopted me as the granddaughter she never had," Cara said, leaving off the part about her also being one of CTA's oldest clients, as that would require Cara to come clean about her actual day job. There was no sense hitting him with all the info at once. Although to be fair, he was taking the whole

"I live in a pool house" thing fairly well. Still, it was late, and both of them needed sleep a lot more than they needed additional revelations.

"I think she gets lonely out here sometimes and likes the idea of having someone else around," she added with a shrug. "Speaking of which, I should run up to the main house and let her know I'm back and that I have a...friend staying with me. Make yourself at home. I won't be too long."

Cara found Penelope watching television in a small room off the kitchen. The woman had nearly four thousand square feet of prime, oceanfront real estate, and yet her favorite place to hang out was a wood-paneled room that looked like any middle-class home from the sixties. Go figure.

"Hey there, Pippa," Cara said as she tapped on the doorframe. When she'd first met Penelope, she'd called her Ms. Parker, same as she did any of her parents'—let alone grandparents'—friends. But after she moved into the pool house, her benefactress had insisted she call her Penelope. Maybe it was Cara's Midwestern upbringing, but calling a woman of that age by her first name seemed disrespectful. Then again, not wanting to feel, as she put it, "as old as the MGM lion" was probably one of the reasons Penelope preferred less formality. They'd settled on Pippa, which according to a story Penelope had shared one night after far too much wine, was a nickname Paul Newman had bestowed on her back in the day.

Penelope turned around, and a wide smile spread across her face. "Cara, dear, you're home."

Her words, combined with the warmth in her eyes, released

the knot that had formed between Cara's shoulders, and she exhaled a deep breath.

"Come, sit," Penelope said, patting the sofa cushion. Cara joined her, taking in her outfit as she did. Penelope was the epitome of style, as long as that style was from *The Golden Girls* wardrobe department. With her satin caftans and sparkling accessories, she often reminded Cara of Dorothy. Her personality, however, was all Blanche.

"How was Ireland?" she asked. "Did you bring back any fun souvenirs?"

"I bought a watercolor by a local artist," Cara said. "And I have something for you as well."

Penelope clapped her hands. "Oh, I love presents." Cara couldn't help but smile. Penelope's childlike enthusiasm was one of the many characteristics she found so endearing. Hopefully her understanding would fall into the same category.

"So," Cara began with a wince, "I may have brought back an Irishman as well."

"May have?" Penelope raised a perfectly sculpted, pencil-thin brow. "Is there a chance you left him at baggage claim?"

"No," Cara laughed. "I definitely brought him home. And his dog."

"Is it too much to hope that's the souvenir you brought me?"

"The dog?" Cara asked, although she suspected she already knew the answer.

"Wouldn't be my first choice, but I'm assuming the young man is already spoken for."

Cara felt her cheeks flush. Penelope had no idea just how

"spoken for" Finn was. At least until the lawyers worked their magic.

"Hmm." Penelope studied Cara's face. "You like this boy." It wasn't a question.

"I do," Cara said. "I mean, I think I do. I hardly know him." *But I married him* was what she was thinking, although she left that part out, at least for now. She knew Penelope would never judge her. In fact, she was probably the one woman Cara could trust to not only understand her predicament but offer the advice she was so desperately going to need. But she needed a few hours of sleep before she could have that conversation with anyone, even Penelope. "I hope you don't mind. I promise he won't be here long."

"Mind? Of course not. It's been ages since I had a young man around the house." Cara shouldn't have been surprised that Penelope wasn't at all fazed by the fact that she'd brought a guy home from Ireland. Then again, Penelope had not only invited a relative stranger to live in her pool house, but it was rumored that for about a year, she'd been working undercover for the CIA. And that was nothing compared to the stories Penelope herself had told her! Cara didn't know if they were all true, but even if only a fraction of them were, then Cara's misadventures didn't hold a candle to Penelope's. "Tell him to feel free to use the pool. No swim trunks required," she added with a wink.

Cara laughed, although to be fair, the thought of Finn swimming buck naked in Penelope's pool was definitely something she'd revisit once she wasn't on the verge of lapsing into a coma. "I can tell you more tomorrow—I'll bring your souvenir by then too—but for now..." Her words trailed off as she yawned.

"Get some sleep. We can gossip about Irish boys tomorrow. Oh, and remind me to tell you about the time I filmed a movie in Dublin with Robert Redford."

"Will do." Cara leaned over and gave Penelope a kiss on her cheek. "Night, Pippa."

As she made her way back to the pool house, the reality of the situation, or maybe just the bone-crushing fatigue, hit her like a ton of bricks. But as anxious as she was to get off her feet, she still hesitated before opening the door. Her husband was waiting inside. *Her husband.*

She was married to Finn Maguire, and for the next few weeks, he would be living with her in her tiny, one-room bungalow.

One room.

One bed.

Sweet Jesus. As if the day hadn't been stressful enough, now she had to deal with the question of sleeping arrangements. No sense putting off the inevitable, she thought. But when she opened the door, Cara realized the decision as to where Finn would sleep had already been made. He was sprawled—fully clothed in his jeans and a vintage Doors T-shirt—on the sofa with one arm thrown over his head and one leg casually bent at the knee. Finn was a large presence in her home but an even larger one on her couch. To put it bluntly, he barely fit, which left poor Oscar to fend for himself on the floor.

Cara grabbed one of the blankets off her bed and arranged it over Finn's body. As she did, he stirred, and for a moment, she thought she might have woken him, but his eyes remained closed as he shifted onto his side.

She watched him for the span of three or four breaths, then turned, giving Oscar a pat on the head as she passed him on the way to the bathroom. That wasn't so bad. Easy peasy actually. No awkward conversation, no confusing emotions. Just two people sharing separate accommodations that happened to be under the same roof. No biggie. But as she was about to close the bathroom door, every fiber in her being went from calm to full alert as she heard Finn's voice, thick with sleep as he said words she didn't quite understand but somehow still loved. "Night, ann-am Cara."

# CHAPTER 10

CARA PULLED THE BLANKET TIGHTER around her shoulders. Having coffee on Penelope's deck was one of her favorite ways to start the day. But that required a luxury of time she usually only had on the weekend, and even then, it was never early enough to watch the first glow of sunlight hit the waves. Not today though. Thanks to jet lag, Cara found herself up long before the sun. Of course, her inability to sleep might have also had something to do with the colossal mess she'd made of her life. Or the fact that the result of that mess was currently asleep on her couch. Or maybe it was the idea of interviewing for a position that had the potential to finally break her out of her career rut. In all likelihood, it was a combination of all those things that had Cara sitting outside at an hour when no sane human would be awake.

Which was why it scared the crap out of her when she heard someone coming down the path.

She turned to find Julia crossing the pool deck, confirming her earlier thought that no sane person would be awake at that hour.

"What are you doing up so early?" Cara narrowed her eyes at

her friend. She was a bit overdressed for work—wearing a pair of dark jeans with a black halter-style top that tied in a bow behind her neck—and had her hair swept up, showcasing a pair of silver hoop earrings. All in all, she seemed ready for a night out instead of a day at the grind, and while her clothes didn't look wrinkled, that didn't mean they hadn't spent the night in a pile on some dude's bedroom floor. "Or are you just heading home from the night?"

"Hey, I resemble that remark," Julia teased, intentionally swapping *resent* for *resemble*.

Cara laughed. "Between the hour and the outfit, you can't really blame me."

"The outfit is so it won't seem odd to Samantha when you're a bit overdressed today—you know, for the interview. This way, I can tell her we're going out after work."

Cara hadn't even thought about what she'd wear to meet with Jeremy, but Julia was right, she definitely needed to up her game. "Smart thinking."

"And as for the hour..." Julia set a cardboard drink carrier on the table beside Cara's chaise. "Figured you were missing these bad boys," she said, nodding to the two blended iced mochas. "Plus, I thought I'd have to drag you out of bed to get you to work on time...jet lag and all that."

"Works the other way this direction," Cara said. Although to be fair, she was in Ireland for such a short amount of time, she wasn't sure if she had adjusted to their time zone enough to even *have* jet lag. "Been out here since before the sun came up."

Julia had been about to plop into the other lounge chair, but

Cara's words stopped in her tracks. Jet lag or not, she knew Cara never watched the sun rise. Not unless she was still awake from the night before.

After taking a beat to study her, Julia stretched out on the lounger and reached for one of the whipped-cream laden drinks. "What's up, buttercup?"

Cara exhaled a heavy breath. "Honestly, Jules, I don't even know where to start."

"The beginning is usually a good place," Julia said with a smile that was half lighthearted teasing and half genuine concern. Cara was about to unload when a shiver racked her friend's small frame. "But first let me grab one of your sweatshirts. It's a lot colder here than it was in the canyon." She laughed through chattering teeth. "Don't know what I was thinking bringing frozen drinks."

Julia was halfway to the door when Cara's brain caught up. "Wait," she said. "Don't go in."

"Oh shit, is that dog here?" Julia asked. Samantha's poodle didn't get along with anyone, but for some reason, she really hated Julia. "Tell me she didn't ask you to dog-sit on your first night back in town."

"No, it's…"

A light bulb went off in Julia's oversexed mind. "Cara Maureen Kennedy, do you have a man in there?"

"Yes, but—" Cara began, but Julia's feet and mouth were already in motion.

"Ho-ly shit," she said as she plopped back into the chaise. "Was he on your flight?"

"Yes, but—"

"Oh my god, did you have sex on the plane?"

"No, but—" Cara reached over and grabbed her friend by the arm. "Julia, stop. Let me explain."

Julia's shoulders sagged, but her smile remained firmly in place. "Sorry," she said. "Tell me everything."

Cara took a deep breath. She really had no idea where to begin. The full story was probably going to knock Julia right out of her chair, which was why Cara decided to start small.

"It's Finn."

A crease formed between Julia's brows. "Finn?"

Cara nodded, then watched as reality dawned.

"The hot guy from the jail?"

Another nod.

Julia whistled through her teeth. "Damn, girl. That's one helluva souvenir. I mean, most people only come back from Ireland with a suitcase full of wool sweaters and pint glasses. Not that I'm criticizing—I think a roll with Mr. Sexy Brogue is a good idea no matter what continent—but wouldn't it have been easier to close the deal before the trip ended?"

"I couldn't leave him there."

"Oh god, please tell me you haven't fallen for this guy. You barely know him."

Cara took a deep breath. It was the moment of truth. "I married him," she said, then braced herself for her friend's reaction.

At first, Julia's eyes grew wide, but then her gaze shot to where Cara's left hand held her drink and, after finding her ring finger bare, she laughed. "Good one. You almost had me there." She took a pull from her paper straw, then smiled and shook her head.

"You're the last person in the world who would ever do something that impulsive, but even if you did, I know you'd want a ring on that finger."

"I'm not joking."

Julia's smile slipped from her face. "You really married him?"

"Yes."

Julia had gone completely still.

One.

Two.

Three.

"Have you lost your damn mind?" she practically shrieked.

Cara shushed her. "Keep it down. I don't want to wake Penelope."

Julia lowered her voice. "What the hell, Car? I told you to speed things up a *bit*, not to warp speed. You were supposed to find a fling, not a husband."

Cara cringed. "Can I say the whiskey made me do it?"

"Well, duh, I figured that much. But the whiskey ain't gonna help you now."

Her friend was right. Being drunk might have been her excuse, but it still didn't change the facts.

"Start from the top," Julia said. "And I swear to God, if you leave out so much as one single detail, I'm going to beat you to death with this soggy straw."

Cara recounted the details she could remember—along with a few Finn had filled in—about that fateful night in the pub. When she was finished, Julia circled back to her original thought.

"So where's your ring?" she asked. Cara had no idea why the

idea of her bare finger bothered Julia so much when clearly there
were bigger fish to fry.

"My ring was made of tinfoil." Either way, it wasn't like
she was going to walk around the office wearing it. Although, if
pressed, she would have admitted that she hadn't exactly thrown
it away either.

"Didn't you need it to get him into the country?"

Cara shook her head. "No. We thought it would be easier
if Finn just went through customs as a tourist. It's fairly simple
for Irish folks to visit the US, and it's not like we had any of the
paperwork or even our license. There would have been so many
questions we couldn't answer. And then there was the whole thing
with the dog..."

Julia's brows shot up. "The *dog*?"

"Yeah, he brought his dog. It's a long story."

A few long beats of silence passed before either of them spoke.

"I miss the purple straws," Julia finally said as she stabbed the
clump of whipped cream at the bottom of her cup. There was a
time when the frozen concoctions they both loved were synonymous with bright-purple straws. It had been ages since they'd been
replaced by paper ones, which meant Julia was making small talk
while she considered the situation.

"Plastic straws are bad for the environment," Cara said, giving
her friend the time she needed to digest the information.

"At least they didn't dissolve as you drink." Julia took a final
sip through her limp straw, then stared out across the waves. The
sun had nearly fully risen, casting the water in a yellow and amber
glow. "What are you going to do?"

"I was hoping you might have some ideas."

Julia laughed. "Well, I'd start by finding a lawyer as soon as possible." Her gaze shifted over Cara's shoulder, and her jaw dropped. "Then again, maybe there's no rush."

Cara turned to find the subject of her friend's less-than-subtle gawking standing in front of the French doors wearing nothing but a pair of low-rise jeans and the crooked smile that never failed to make her stomach flutter.

Finn opened the door, and Oscar came bounding out onto the pool deck and into Cara's lap.

"Good morning to you too," Cara said between slobbering kisses.

"Sorry, luv," Finn said. "I didn't want to interrupt, but he was desperate to get out."

Julia's dark brows shot up. "*Luv?*" she mouthed in Cara's direction before turning her attention to Finn. "I'm Julia, the best friend."

Finn stuck out his hand. As he did, a ray of the early morning sun reflected off the foil band on the ring finger of his left hand. *He was still wearing his ring?* Had he had it on this whole time? Cara tried to think back to the flight but drew a blank.

"I'm Finn, the..." He stopped midsentence, and his eyes darted to Cara's.

"...husband," Julia said, finishing his sentence. "Which makes you family, and we don't shake hands with family."

Cara rolled her eyes as her best friend greeted her new husband with a hug that bordered on molestation.

"Uh, nice to meet you," Finn said, smiling at Cara over Julia's shoulder.

"Julia was just leaving."

"I was?"

Cara shot her a pointed stare.

"Right, I was." Julia looked back and forth between the two newlyweds, then laughed. "Three's a crowd on a honeymoon." With that she turned to leave but not before mouthing two more words in Cara's direction—*holy shit*, if she wasn't mistaken. There might have been a chance the exchange went unnoticed by Finn, until Julia fanned herself in an exaggerated gesture that even a passing beachcomber would have found hard to miss.

They stood in silence for a few moments as the word *honeymoon* floated around on the ocean breeze.

"She seems lovely," Finn finally said. He shoved his hands into the front pockets of his jeans, pushing them even lower on his hips in the process. But it wasn't a blue Calvin Klein waistband she saw this time. Not a red or green one either. Just...skin. Sweet Jesus, was the boy commando?

"So what's next?" he asked.

"Next," Cara said, forcing her eyes back to Finn's face. "I need to go to work."

"That's right. It's a big day for you."

"Hopefully." When it came to Samantha, anything was possible.

"I'm sure it will be smashing, and when you get home, we can—"

"Talk about the annulment?"

The corner of Finn's mouth turned up in a smile Cara was starting to associate with trouble of the best and worst kind. "I was going to say we could celebrate your success."

*That works too*, she thought. "I'm going to…" She gestured toward the house. The pool house wasn't designed to be an apartment. It was more of a guest bedroom than anything, which meant close quarters. In other words, it wasn't ideal for showering and getting ready for work. Not unless she wanted to do it with a hot guy she happened to be married to but had never seen naked watching her every move from the couch.

It took a moment for Finn to connect the dots. "Oh, yes, yeah, sure," Finn said. Utilizing three words to convey the same message was one of Cara's trademark moves. Finn, on the other hand, never suffered from that affliction. Was he thinking of the close proximity as well? Or better yet, had Julia's comment conjured a few ideas? Cara tucked that little nugget away for the time being. The sun was up, which meant Samantha was too. There was no time for honeymoon thoughts. At least for now.

# CHAPTER 11

NO ONE COULD WELCOME A person back from vacation quite like Samantha Sherwood. There was no "how was your trip?" or "bring back any cool souvenirs?" small talk. And there was certainly no request to see her photos. All Samantha cared about was the day's calendar, which, as always, was jam-packed.

"Both of you, my office in five," she said as she breezed through the small reception area that held the desks Cara and Julia called home for ten to twelve hours a day.

When four minutes had passed, they grabbed their tablets and made their way into Samantha's office. To say it was minimalist was putting it mildly. White walls, white sofa, and white carpet were framed by floor-to-ceiling windows that met in the corner of the building's largest office. The only color in the room was provided by the view outside the windows and the large, framed photos of Samantha and her clients at various industry events that hung on the two interior walls.

"Take me through the day." Samantha was always dressed in either black or white, and today was no exception. Julia had a theory that her color choice either dictated the mood or predicted how the day was going to go, but she was still trying to figure out which came first, the chicken or the egg. In Cara's opinion, it was both, one feeding the other. Samantha chose black when she was in kick-ass mode and white when she was feeling more relaxed. At least her version of it. Today Samantha was wearing black—a power suit with a fitted jacket—which meant they were in for a bumpy, high-speed ride, something Cara braced for as she and Julia settled into the white leather chairs on the opposite side of their boss's glass-and-chrome desk.

Julia ticked through the details of Samantha's calendar while Cara took notes as her boss made comments. If there was one thing she'd learned early on, it was that Samantha never gave specific instructions after the morning rundown. More that she would react to calendar events and meetings in a way that just assumed her needs and desires would be met.

"That will be all," she told Julia when she was finished. "Oh, and, Cara, I need you to get more of that shampoo Coco loves." *There goes half the day*, Cara thought. Coco's "groomer to the stars" was all the way in Venice. By the time she made it to Abbot Kinney and back, half the day would be gone. Cara would have loved to have asked Samantha how she knew her pampered poodle preferred one shampoo over another, but instead all she asked was how many bottles she should pick up.

"Just one is fine," Samantha said.

Cara made a mental note to grab two bottles even if she had to pay for the second one with her own money. That way, if she was sent back in a week, she could spend the time writing at the Coffee Bean instead of sitting in traffic.

"Great outfit, by the way," Julia said as soon as she and Cara were alone.

Cara glanced down at the dark jeans she'd paired with an ivory silk top and taupe open-toe suede wedge booties. She'd finished the look with the brushed-gold Kendra Scott necklace and earrings her mom had given her for her birthday. It was professional enough for an interview for a potential job but could totally go along with Julia's cover story of going out after work. Speaking of...

"When do you think I should try to see Jeremy?"

"I already booked you ten minutes with him on your lunch break," Julia said.

While Cara appreciated Julia taking the initiative to set up the meeting, there was one small problem. "I don't get a lunch break," she said. Well, technically she did. The law required it. But when you worked for Samantha Sherwood, your lunch was whatever you could sneak at your desk, and even that was mostly broken up in five-minute intervals throughout the afternoon. None of this would have been new information to Julia, seeing as how she'd worked for Samantha even longer than Cara had, which was why she didn't bother saying any of her thoughts out loud.

"Today you do," Julia said, but even as she said the words, a smile formed on her lips. "Okay, fine, if she asks, I will tell her you had to run to CVS for tampons."

"That's the best you could come up with?"

"It had to be something I had lying around the house, so yes." Julia slid open the bottom drawer of her desk and pulled out a reusable grocery bag that contained an unopened box of tampons. "But at least now you won't come back empty-handed."

Right, she just had to take a box of tampons with her to her interview. Not that Jonathan would have been phased by Cara arriving with feminine hygiene products in tow or really anything else, for that matter. He'd been out drinking with Cara and Julia enough to be considered one of the girls, and after witnessing the night Julia confused an actual LAPD officer with a stripper, nothing would surprise him.

As expected, Jeremy's current assistant was quick on the uptake. "Told her you had a feminine emergency?" he asked, nodding to the bag Cara held in her hands as she approached his desk at exactly noon. He was impeccably dressed, as always, in a slim-leg suit that made him look more like the high-powered agent than his assistant.

"Only way I could actually take a lunch break," she said.

"That's one thing you won't have to worry about if you end up on this desk. Jeremy believes a fed assistant is a productive assistant." Jonathan's brows shot up. "And the best part? If he has me ordering in for him—coffee, lunch, or dinner—he always tells me to put something for myself on his tab."

Now that would be one hell of a perk. Even with the free rent, living in Los Angeles on an assistant's salary left Cara in a constant state of budget juggling. If she got the occasional coffee—not to mention meal—paid for by the company, it would definitely improve her weekend situation.

"At the rate you're going, you'll be buying lunch for him soon," Cara said.

Jonathan laughed. "Hardly." He was being modest, but Cara had complete faith that her friend was on a fast track. And why wouldn't he be? He had the talent and the personality to go far in this town.

"He's on a call," Jonathan said. "But it shouldn't be much longer."

"Good," Cara said, then, on a laugh, added, "I figure it's about an eight-minute walk to CVS, so..." She glanced at her phone. "I have about sixteen minutes plus check-out time."

"Say the line was long."

Cara nodded. "Nice suit, by the way."

"Thank you." Jonathan sat a little taller in his chair. "I decided to splurge a little." He leaned forward and lowered his voice. "After I found out about the thing that shall not be discussed yet."

Cara smiled. "My lips are sealed." Aside from Julia, Jonathan was her closest friend at CTA. She was going to miss his tension-busting humor, but she couldn't have been happier for him. Landing a staff writer job on a Netflix show was something they had both dreamed of for years now. Seeing it actually happen to her friend gave Cara hope that someday it would happen for her as well, and working for Jeremy would definitely be a step in that direction.

An alert flashed across Jonathan's computer screen. "Jeremy is ready for you," he said, relieving her of the bag of tampons. "Go on in."

Cara pushed through the glass door into what was the second-largest office at CTA. Like Samantha's, Jeremy's office occupied one of the corners of the building. His office had the same floor-to-ceiling windows overlooking Wilshire Boulevard, but unlike her current boss's, Jeremy's office was far more reflective of the man who occupied it. His furniture was still modern with clean lines but with a palette of green and taupe, and his walls didn't contain photographs of him with his client roster but rather shots of him with his partner and their two children.

"Thank you for agreeing to meet with me, Mr. Stone."

He stood, then crossed the room to shake her hand. "Please, call me Jeremy." He waved to the chairs directly across from his desk. "Have a seat."

They moved to their respective sides of the teak desk. Jeremy waited until Cara was settled, then got right to the point. "I take it you heard the news about Jonathan?"

His directness wasn't a surprise. Didn't take a rocket scientist to figure out why an assistant within the agency would ask for a meeting. But still, the news of Jonathan's departure wasn't yet public knowledge. "Yes," Cara said. "But don't worry. I won't say a word to anyone until he gives his official notice." Her motivation wasn't merely because Jonathan was her friend. That alone would have been enough, but in this case, keeping the job vacancy quiet was in Cara's best interest as well. No sense giving the competition a heads-up.

Jeremy leaned back in his chair. "I started in the mail room here," he said, his words and the fact that his smile reached his dark-brown eyes putting Cara instantly at ease. "I haven't been in this office so long that I forgot how the assistant network works." He laughed, and the sound was warm and rich and genuine. "Hell, I think sometimes that was the only thing that got me through the fifteen-hour days."

"It's nice to have somebody who understands what you're going through," Cara agreed.

Jeremy nodded. "And who's got your back." He reached for a blue folder that sat in the middle of his desk and opened it. "Julia took the liberty of sending over your résumé." He lifted the piece of paper, but the markings scribbled in the margins made it obvious he'd already read it. "Your credentials are impressive, and something tells me you didn't get that creative writing degree so you could shuffle papers around for somebody else."

"No, Mr.—" Cara caught herself. "No, Jeremy, I didn't. My passion is screenwriting," she said, deciding to be honest and upfront right from the start. "But I know I have to pay my dues, and I'm more than willing to put in the work. Whatever it takes."

"Seems like you've been doing that already." He put her résumé back in the folder, then looked her right in the eye. "I'm going to level with you, Cara. Yes, I will ask you to get coffee for me—I'm afraid that comes with the territory—but I'll always tell you to add one on the order for yourself. Yes, there will be a lot of paperwork—again, that's sort of what we do. But I will absolutely never ask you to run personal errands." He closed the folder and leaned forward so his elbows rested squarely on the desk. "And no, I don't have a dog."

Cara met his grin with one of her own. "Good to know."

"I will also never lose sight of the fact that this isn't your endgame. I pride myself on helping my assistants move into their chosen path. No one has stayed on my desk longer than two years, and I don't plan to break that streak now."

Cara felt like she'd died and gone to heaven. But while his

words were thrilling, they were also a bit confusing. It was if as if she were the one interviewing him and not the other way around. "So does that mean you're considering me for the position?"

He gave a tight nod. "I've watched you for the past two years, Cara. I know the hours you've put in, the dedication you've shown, and I know the conditions under which you've done it."

Cara didn't know what to say. It was all true. She just hadn't realized anyone else had noticed.

"As far as I'm concerned, the job is yours," Jeremy said, standing and once again extending his hand. "My schedule is insane over the next four weeks, and Jonathan doesn't start at Netflix until later next month, so I've asked him to hold off on giving notice. Once he does, I'll speak to Samantha, and then we can run the paperwork through HR."

They shook hands, sealing a deal that would hopefully restart a career that had definitely stalled. As she walked back to her office, Cara realized that, as excited as she was to drag Julia to the ladies' room so she could share the good news, there was someone else she wanted to tell as well. There was only one problem. Before she could tell Finn about her new position, she'd have to come clean about the job she already had, which was a far cry from how she'd portrayed her life in LA. Her stomach twitched as she imagined how her new husband would feel about her embellishment, but then she paused midstride and gave her head a hard shake. What was wrong with her? She might have been married to Finn, but he wasn't her husband. Not in the true sense of the word. Still, that didn't stop her from checking her phone to see how many hours were left before she would be back at the beach house with the man who, real husband or not, seemed to occupy her thoughts far more than she'd have cared to admit.

And who, as of this morning at least, still wore her tinfoil ring.

..................................................

When Cara arrived at the beach house, she was greeted first by Oscar, who bounded through the door the minute she opened it, nearly knocking her to the ground in his excitement, and then by Finn.

"Hey," he said from behind the small kitchen island. Plates sat in front of both the barstools, along with a single votive candle, and from the smell of it, something amazing was cooking in the oven.

"You made dinner?" And quite an impressive salad from the looks of the assorted greens he was tossing in an olive wood bowl. *She had one of those?*

"Indeed."

"How in the world..." Her fridge had been practically empty considering she'd been gone the past few days. Not that it was ever really that well stocked. For the most part, she lived off grocery store salad bars and Grubhub deliveries.

"I walked up to the market." He paused with the salad tongs in midair, and a small crease formed between his brows. "Can't recall the name, but it was your version of Tesco."

"Ralph's?"

"That's it."

"You really didn't need to..."

"Least I could do to thank you for your hospitality." He

flashed her a smile as he set the salad bowl between the two plates. "Plus, I was confident you'd have news worth celebrating."

"I...this is..." Cara found herself at a loss for words. No one aside from Cara's mom had ever made her dinner. And when it came to the men in her life, she was lucky if they made her a cup of coffee.

"Don't get too excited. It's only a cottage pie."

"I thought it was called shepherd's pie?" *For the love of god, Cara, just say thank you.*

"Not when it's made with ground beef. Seems the fine folks of Malibu don't have much call for ground lamb." Finn opened the oven to reveal a casserole—where did he get a casserole dish?— topped with perfectly browned mashed potatoes. "Had to borrow a few kitchen items from Penelope," he said, explaining how he managed to cook in a kitchen that, aside from a coffeepot and toaster, was only stocked with two pots, a cookie sheet, and a frying pan. "She's lovely, by the way. Told me some of the most fascinating tales."

Cara laughed. "I bet she did."

"Have a seat," Finn said.

Cara slid onto one of the barstools, and Finn joined her on the other. After serving them each a healthy portion of salad and pie, he cracked open a can of Guinness and took a sip. "Christ on a bike," he said, wincing as he studied the can that he still held in his hand. "This is what you Americans think a Guinness tastes like?"

"We can't all get it right from the source," Cara teased. She popped the top on her own can and, after taking a sip, had to agree. After only three days in Dublin, even she could taste the difference.

"Might need to sample some of the local brews," Finn said.

"When in Rome..."

"Aye."

"This is delicious by the way," she said after her first bite.

Finn smiled. "How did the meeting go?"

Were they really eating dinner by candlelight like some sort of normal married couple?

"Cara?"

"Um, oh yeah, it went really well. At least I think it did."

"You told me it was a big opportunity, but you didn't say what."

Time to come clean. Cara wiped her mouth with her napkin and placed it on the counter beside her plate. "Finn, I need to talk to you about something."

An emotion she couldn't quite place flashed across his eyes— concern or maybe even panic. Either way, it wasn't good.

# CHAPTER 12

CARA DREW A DEEP BREATH. *Here goes nothing.*

"There are a few details about my life in LA that I may have stretched a bit." That was more than an understatement, but it felt like a safe place to start.

The tension in Finn's shoulders eased. "I don't care that you live in a pool house, luv. You've seen my flat, and while it's a tad larger, it doesn't have a view like this one." He laughed. "And it's sure as hell not this tidy."

"It's more than just where I live. I wasn't exactly honest with you about my job either."

He cocked his head to one side. "So you aren't a writer?"

"No, I am—it's what I went to school for—and I mean, I do write screenplays. Well, I've written one a few times now, or rather, I keep rewriting it." *Oh boy.* Even she knew she was rambling. She paused to collect herself, and when she had, she slumped against the back of the barstool. "It's something I do in my free time, and I definitely don't get paid for it."

"Yet," he said.

"Yet?" That was all he had to say after his wife told him she'd basically lied about every detail of her California existence. Not that she was really his wife, but still.

"You haven't been paid *yet*." He flashed her one of his familiar grins. "But you will. Give it time."

Cara smiled at his optimism. That was how it was with people who weren't in the business. Their intentions were always good, but their encouragement wasn't necessarily in line with the reality of Hollywood.

"So you're not mad?"

"Mad? Why would I be mad?"

"Because I led you to believe I was a big deal," she said. "When in reality, all of my time in LA has been spent working at CTA."

Finn's brows shot up. "That *is* a big deal, Cara. Even I've heard of CTA, and I'm just a bloke from Dublin."

"Don't be too impressed," she said on a laugh. "I'm an assistant, second desk at that. And while I might work for the biggest name in the building, my duties typically range from fetching coffee to taking her dog to the groomer, which is a far cry from working as a writer."

"It's fine, luv, really." Finn placed his hand over hers. She knew it was meant to be a reassuring gesture, but in reality, feeling his skin against hers—even in such a seemingly innocent way—set off an entirely different reaction. It was as though a current passed from his hand to hers before settling somewhere deep inside her. "Besides, it's not like I married you because of your career." He winked. "I just needed a mother for Oscar."

At the sound of his name, the dog lifted his head from where he'd been sleeping on the couch and gave a small bark.

"See, he agrees."

"Glad he approves," Cara said as they shared a laugh. She slipped her hand out from under Finn's and reached for her water. Partly because she was thirsty and partly because, with the way her heart was racing, if she didn't stop holding hands with Finn, she was liable to climb right into his lap.

"As for the writing," Finn said. "It will come." His smile remained the same, but his tone had grown more serious. "Just have to keep putting in the work." For some reason, his words seemed to carry more weight this time, and Cara found herself wanting to share the events of the day.

"I might have taken a step in the right direction today."

"Yeah?"

"A new position opened up at the agency. I'd be working for a less senior agent but as his only assistant, and more importantly, he's someone who realizes people like me only take jobs like that as a means to an end."

"A foot in the door."

"Precisely."

"I take it your current boss doesn't see it that way?"

"Oh, I'm sure she knows. She just doesn't care. The only 'in' I've had on Samantha's desk is proximity to A-list celebrities, and while meeting the Avengers was definitely a perk, it's not the reason I'm in that building. The most Samantha has ever done for me personally was to give me that Prada bag last Christmas," she said, nodding to the tote bag she'd left by the door. "But even that was a regift from a client. Jeremy, on the other hand, has a reputation for helping his assistants move off his desk and into their careers. The guy who has the job now—my friend Jonathan—was just hired as a staff writer for a show starting production next month."

"When will you find out if you got the job?"

"Jeremy said the interview was just a formality." Cara shrugged. "I don't want to jinx it because nothing is official yet, but it feels like a lock."

"Well done, you." He tipped his beer can in her direction. "Sounds like it was a great day."

"It was," she admitted. "Busy one too. I didn't have a chance to look into divorce lawyers, but I will make some calls tomorrow."

The word *divorce* hung in the air like a dark cloud over their lovely dinner. Time to redirect the conversation.

"Oh, that reminds me…" Cara walked over to her bag and reached inside. "Here," she said, handing Finn the pay-as-you-go phone she'd picked up on her way home from work. "I already programmed my number into it." She hadn't really given it much thought at the time, but as she said the words to Finn, Cara realized just how ridiculous it was that her husband didn't even know her phone number. And that was just the tip of the iceberg. Finn knew next to nothing about Cara, and she knew even less about him. Her stomach turned. Over the last thirty-six hours, she'd moved through life like it was one giant to-do list. But now, in the quiet of her bungalow, the reality of their situation sunk in. She was not only married to a stranger; she'd brought him home to live with her. Still, as crazy as that sounded, there was no denying the fact that she was finding herself more drawn to him by the hour.

What. A. Mess.

"You okay?" Finn asked.

"Yeah." She had planned to leave it at that, but as she sat back down, she added, "It's just...we don't really know all that much about each other, do we?" It was the understatement of the century. Cara didn't even know the most basic facts about Finn.

He chuckled. "Enough to want to get married." Cara knew his words were meant to break the tension that was suddenly vibrating through her body, but she was far too amped for his charm to put her at ease. At least not this time.

"I'm serious," she said. "I was going to buy some food on my way home, but then I realized I don't even know what you like for breakfast. Do you even eat breakfast? Do you drink coffee, or do you prefer tea? I mean, I wouldn't even know what kind of snacks to buy. Do you like salty or sweet? Ice cream or frozen yogurt? Boxers or briefs?" Cara had no idea why that last one popped out, but it didn't matter. She was on a roll. "And it's not just the little stuff. I don't know any of the big stuff either, like how many siblings you have or what you studied in school or—"

Finn placed his hand on her shoulder. "For breakfast, some toast is fine. Oatmeal if I have time. Salty is good if you're having a pint, but I fancy sweets as well. Ice cream every day and twice on Sunday." His fingers worked the knot that had formed between her shoulder and her neck, and all at once, the tension that had coiled deep in her belly began to ease. "I didn't go to uni, but if I had, I would have studied landscape design as I've always enjoyed working outdoors. I have two sisters, who would both tell you my mum spoilt me rotten. As for pants..." The corner of his mouth quirked up in that half smile that slayed her every darn time. "Boxer briefs."

"I'm sorry. I think it all just hit me...I mean, this is really weird."

"It is," he agreed, the two words rolling off his tongue as one. *Ittis.* "But sometimes life hands you adventures you weren't expecting, and those can be grand."

Cara's emotions were strung so tight that she'd been walking that fine line between laughter and tears. But Finn's words tipped the scales in the right direction. "Is that something your mam says?"

"No, that's all mine," he said on a laugh. "Your turn."

"My turn?"

"To answer the questions."

"Oh, okay." Cara thought back to the list she'd fired off during her meltdown. "Breakfast is usually a latte from Starbucks, an omelet if I'm feeling fancy, but I only have time for those on the weekends. I'm an equal opportunity snacker but would walk through fire for chocolate. And you're right, definitely ice cream," she said with a smile. "I grew up in Chicago, studied creative writing at Iowa, and I have one younger brother, who is most definitely spoiled."

"What kind of music do you like?"

Now that was a question that didn't require any words at all. Cara picked up her phone and opened the Spotify app. "My musical tastes are varied, but lately I've been obsessed with the eighties," she said. "Probably because of Julia's John Hughes binge." She pulled up her most recent list and "Please, Please, Please, Let Me Get What I Want" began to play.

"Bloody hell. I love this song."

"You know the *Pretty in Pink* soundtrack?"

"No, but I know the Smiths." He slid off the kitchen stool and took Cara by the hand.

"What are you doing?"

He flashed her a cheeky grin as he placed his other hand on the small of her back and pulled her close. "Dancing with my wife."

"Like a first dance?" Cara narrowed her eyes, but her tone was teasing. "Is this because I didn't let you carry me over the threshold?"

"First," Finn said, matching her vibe, "if I'd wanted to carry you over the threshold, there'd have been no *letting* required."

"What, you'd have thrown me over your shoulder like a caveman?"

"Something like that." He laughed as they swayed to the music. "But we were both knackered. I figured we'd had enough excitement for one day."

Excitement? Meaning the carrying wouldn't have ended at the threshold? Would he have carried her to the bed? Would they have consummated a marriage that never should have happened in the first place? The guy had spent their wedding night sleeping in his jeans, and he hadn't even so much as kissed her since they'd gotten to LA, something they'd done a few times in Dublin. But that was before they'd woken up married. Cara had started to think maybe the spark had been snuffed out, at least for Finn. But now...

Images flooded her mind, but she pushed them aside. No sense getting ahead of herself. Not without more information. "And second?" she prompted.

"Second, we already had our first dance."

"We did?" One more thing added to the list of memories lost to whiskey.

Finn nodded.

Cara wasn't sure she wanted to know the answer to her next question, but she asked it anyways. "What song?"

"Still Haven't Found What I'm Looking For."

Her mouth dropped open. "You can't be serious." Then again, given the way things had gone, it really shouldn't have surprised her that their bridal dance was to a song about restless spirits.

"It wasn't my choice, luv. You insisted it had to be an Irish band, but you wanted it to be one you'd heard of so…"

She nodded. "U2."

"It was the only song of theirs on the juke," Finn explained. "We can call this one a do-over, if you'd like."

"A do-over?" Cara laughed. "That's about as ridiculous as dancing in the kitchen on a Tuesday night."

Now Finn was the one to laugh. "Dancing isn't specific to a certain night."

"It feels like a weekend activity."

"There's fifty-two weekends in year. Multiply that by how many years we have on this earth, and that's not nearly enough. If you want to live life to the fullest, you're gonna have to dance on some Tuesday nights."

His words were like an incendiary device straight to her lady parts. "Now that had to have been a bit of Mam philosophy," she said in an attempt to keep her brain on track even if her body wasn't.

"Nope. But it sounds like something she would say." Finn

spun them in a tight circle. When they came to a stop, Cara felt a bit light-headed, although she was pretty sure it had nothing to do with the spinning and everything to do with how tightly Finn held her against his body.

"Back to the questions," he said, seemingly unaffected by their proximity. Then again, maybe she wasn't the only one trying to distract themself.

"Shoot."

"Beach or mountains?"

"Well, I live at the beach," she teased.

"True, but if you had a choice?"

"Still beach. But I'm not averse to mountains."

"Netflix or a club?"

"You sound like a dating app."

He laughed. "Fair point. And those things are bloody awful."

"Agreed. But to answer your question, Netflix every day and twice on Sunday," she said, echoing one of his earlier replies. "I'm not a huge fan of clubs. Pubs are nice, but apparently I can get in a whole lot of trouble there."

"True. But sometimes it's trouble of the best kind."

Surely, he wasn't talking about her proposal?

"Do you ever wonder how our parents' generation managed to date without apps?" Her question was an attempt to quickly divert the spotlight from their night at the Hole in the Wall, but it was still a legitimate one. "I mean, as bad as they are, at least they provide more options. And what about our grandparents' generation? They had even less opportunity to expand their circle. It's amazing anyone met their soul mate before Bumble."

Finn stopped swaying as the song came to an end. A beat passed while his eyes roamed over her face, taking in every detail as though seeing her for the first time. "I think fate has a lot more to do with meeting the right person at the right time than a little yellow app."

"You do?" she asked. Her voice was quiet and shaky and sounded nothing like her.

He nodded. "It wasn't an app that put you in the back seat of my car."

*The back seat of my car...*

His charged words, the dark look in his eyes, the way his tongue darted out to wet his lips...Finn was about to kiss her. Too bad Cara realized it a second too late.

"Well, technically it was," she said. "The Uber app, but still." The breathy tone of her voice was gone, probably due to the fact that she'd just stuck her foot in her mouth. She was right, of course, but really, when a hot guy was about to kiss you wasn't exactly the best time to prove a point.

But Finn was undeterred, even by her awkwardly timed observation. He leaned forward, covering her mouth with his while his hand flattened against the small of her back, pulling her against him as a low groan vibrated in his chest.

This was it. The moment Cara had been waiting for. She'd wanted to kiss Finn, *really* kiss him, since their lips had barely touched in the Kilmainham chapel. Sure, they'd made out that fateful night at the pub—one of the few memories that had come back to her the next morning when she woke up married—but that was all it was, a memory, and a fuzzy one at that. Like watching someone else kiss the leading man in a movie, which wasn't a totally unfair comparison, considering Cara might as well have been someone else that night. She'd been in a different country then—determined to live like another woman as well—and not only that, she'd been drunk enough to ask a virtual stranger to marry her.

This was different.

She was back in LA, in her home, totally sober, in the middle of a week in her very real life. More than that, Finn wasn't just a hot Irish brogue with the potential of a passionate vacation fling. He was her husband. A husband she planned to divorce. Kissing him there, under those circumstances, it all felt much more… consequential.

Cara stepped back. "It's late," she said. "We better get some sleep." She'd wanted to sound breezy and nonchalant, but her racing pulse and quick breaths made that impossible to pull off.

"Right, then," Finn said. His ever-present smile was on his face, but in his eyes, she saw confusion.

"You can use the bathroom first if you want," she offered. "And I'll clean up from dinner. Only fair since you cooked."

"Are you sure? I don't mind helping."

"Absolutely. More time efficient as well." More time efficient? Since when did that matter? *Since you freaked out kissing the man you accidentally married.*

She waited until Finn had closed the bathroom door behind him, then began loading everything into the dishwasher—prerinse be damned. If she had everything done by the time he finished, she could slip into the bathroom before an awkward "where should

I sleep" conversation could take place. It was a topic that hadn't come up the night before, seeing as how Finn was passed out on the couch by the time she came back from talking to Penelope. But now...should she just assume he wanted to sleep on the couch again? Or did he want to sleep in the bed with her? Did *she* want that? If only there were some sort of guidebook for navigating the world of cohabitation with a husband you barely know and don't even remember marrying. Sure, the market for idiots who found themselves in that situation was undoubtedly small, but still, it would have been helpful.

"All yours," Finn said as he stepped out of the bathroom.

Cara was already waiting with her pajamas in hand. "Thanks." Once inside, she scrubbed her face, brushed her teeth, and combed her hair. She knew there was little hope it would stay that way. By morning, her hair would no doubt be sticking up in a hundred different directions like some fuzzy version of Medusa, but if the bedtime brushing upped the odds of her looking presentable to slim from none, then it was worth a shot. Of course, all this had to be done in record time because god forbid she was in there long enough for him to get the idea she was *pooping*. The thought had no sooner crossed her mind than it was followed by two that were even more horrifying: What if she snored? Or worse, what if she farted in her sleep?

Ugh. This hot husband-roommate life was proving to be way more stressful than she first thought. At this rate, actually getting the divorce was going to be the easy part.

At least the sleeping arrangements were settled. By the time Cara came out of the bathroom, Finn was already tucked in on the couch. Well, if you could call sleeping on a sofa with nothing but a toss pillow and her extra blanket as *tucked in*. As her eyes adjusted to the darkened room, she noticed that he wasn't wearing a shirt. Her gaze traveled across the smooth planes of his chest, then lower to his abs, which quite frankly resembled more of an eight pack than a mere six, and finally to the smattering of dark hair that disappeared below the blanket.

Stop.

That.

Now.

She turned toward her bed, trying like hell to keep her mind focused on the ticking of the clock in the kitchen, the crashing of the waves on the beach, or even the soft snores coming from the small rug Oscar had claimed as his own. Anything besides the image of Finn lying half-naked—he *was* only half-naked, wasn't he?—on her couch.

It was no use. Finn Maguire was in her house. On her couch. And he may or may not have been naked, a thought that no amount of distraction was going to keep from the forefront of her mind as she slipped beneath the covers.

She just had to fall asleep. That was all. But as Cara lay in bed, she was acutely aware of every breath Finn took. And while the space they shared felt small, somehow, he still seemed far away.

The wood frame of the sofa creaked as he shifted his weight. Mid-century modern sofas were practically works of art, but for sleeping, there was no two ways about it: they sucked. The cushions were hard, and the angles were sharp.

"Finn?" she whispered.

"Yeah?"

Cara pushed up on her elbows. Thanks to the moonlight shining in through the skylight, she could see him clearly now, stretched out on the sofa with one leg dangling over the side. "That couch is barely comfortable for sitting. I can't imagine trying to sleep on it, and I'm a lot shorter than you are."

"It's fine," he said. Then with a small laugh, he added, "I've slept on worse."

"I'm just saying… If you wanted to sleep on the bed, I wouldn't be opposed to it. I mean, we slept in the same bed at your apartment, and you didn't molest me, so…"

*Crap.* Why did she say that? In Dublin, before the fateful night in the pub, Cara had absolutely wanted to have sex with Finn. Now there she was, inviting him to sleep in her bed because she felt safe in the knowledge that he *wouldn't* have sex with her. Some femme fatale she turned out to be.

"That would be grand," Finn said. He stood, revealing that he was in fact wearing clothes beneath the blanket—a pair of navy-blue boxer briefs, to be exact—and made his way across the tile floor. "Not that I wasn't appreciative of your hospitality."

"No, totally, I get it."

He lifted the covers and settled in beside her in the double bed. They were only inches apart. Close enough for her to feel the warmth of his skin and to smell the faint scent of his soap. It was all she could do to fight the urge to reach out and touch him, to run her fingers down his bare chest before slipping them beneath the blanket.

"Well, good night," she said.

"Good night, ann-am Cara."

*Ann-am Cara...*

They were same words he'd said to her the night before, so softly that she'd wondered if he'd said them in his sleep. There was no such doubt this time, and whispered across the pillow on a gentle breath, his words felt like a caress. She wanted to ask him what they meant, but more than that, she wanted to curl her body around his until they couldn't tell where one of them ended and the other began.

Instead, she turned on her side, facing away from him. When she did, she saw Oscar watching her from his spot on the rug. *Don't judge me*, she silently told the dog. Although he did have a point. Having sex with Finn didn't have to mean anything more in LA than it would have in Dublin. Sure, they knew each other a little better, but that would only make the sex better as well, right? Then again, maybe it would make things *way* more complicated. Oh, who was she kidding? Sex with Finn would definitely make things more complicated. She was crazy to think otherwise—and even crazier to be having this silent debate with a dog. That didn't stop her from thinking about it as she was falling asleep—in far greater detail than she would have cared to admit—which was fine. She just had to come up with a way to keep from actually doing it.

# CHAPTER 13

"THAT'S EXACTLY WHAT YOU SHOULD have done," Julia said the next day. It was a reaction not unlike the one she'd had when Cara had called her from Dublin. Only this time, they weren't on FaceTime talking about a cute Irish guy Cara had chatted with on the way to the hotel. They were in the bathroom at CTA talking about a cute Irish guy Cara had accidentally married. It was a game-changing distinction in Cara's opinion, and although she tried her best to make her point, Julia wasn't buying it.

"It's the one and only perk of this situation," Julia said as she finished washing her hands. "Well, aside from the home-cooked meals."

"That might have been a one-time deal." Cara grabbed one of the neatly folded towels from the wire basket on the counter and handed it to her friend.

"The possibility of sex or the dinner?"

"I don't even know for sure if sex was a possibility last night. As for the dinner, cottage pie might be the only trick he's got up his sleeve."

Julia leaned her hip against the marble countertop. "Something tells me he's got a few more tricks when it comes to—"

Cara covered Julia's mouth with her hand. "Let's keep it PG while we're at work please."

"Fine. But answer me this. Why am I only just now hearing about this at"—Julia glanced at her watch—"six o'clock?"

Cara shrugged. "It's been a busy day."

"Bullshit. It's because you knew I would yell at you for passing up another golden opportunity."

"No." *Yes.*

Julia raised a brow.

"Okay, fine, you're right. But only about the yelling part. I'm not convinced it's a golden opportunity. Might be the kiss of death."

"Death by orgasm maybe," Julia said as she pushed through the bathroom door.

"Now this I've got to hear," Jonathan said. Unlike the previous day, he was dressed a bit more casually, opting for a pair of chinos and a pale-blue sweater—cashmere, best Cara could tell.

Julia stopped short. "What are you doing loitering outside the ladies' room?"

"Just on my way to the break room." He nodded to the empty mug he held in his hand. "But please, don't let me stop you." He leaned one shoulder against the wall.

"I heard they restocked the Nespresso," Cara offered in an attempt to hijack the conversation. "With the good stuff this time. None of that generic crap."

"Oh no, you don't," Jonathan said. "No way you get to leave the word orgasm dangling in the wind. Spill."

Cara shot Julia a pleading look. Jonathan was a good friend, but as far as she was concerned, the fewer people who knew about her marriage to Finn, the better.

"I don't know, Car. You might want to tell him." Julia turned her attention to Jonathan. "You went to law school, right?"

Jonathan narrowed his eyes at her. "Yes. But I never took the bar."

"Still, you can give some basic advice. Make a referral, that sort of thing?"

He laughed. "If you're about to tell me you murdered someone with too much sex, I will *not* help find a lawyer to represent you."

"I'm not the one who needs a lawyer."

It was at that moment that Jonathan realized he was the only one smiling. "Oh shit." His eyes darted to Cara's. "Are you okay? If you're in some kind of trouble, I can—"

"No, I'm not," Cara rushed to assure him. "In trouble, that is. Well, I guess I sort of am, but not in the way you're thinking. At least the way I *think* you're thinking." She took a quick look around to make sure no one else was in earshot. Given the hour, it wasn't likely, but it never hurt to be extra careful, especially when airing dirty laundry. "I may have brought someone back with me from Ireland."

"I see," Jonathan said. "So you need an immigration lawyer." It was a statement, not a question.

"No, I…" *Shit*. Why was this so hard to say?

"She brought back a husband," Julia said.

"Whaaaaat?" It was a good thing Jonathan's mug was empty, because if it hadn't been, the way he pushed away from the wall would have surely spilled the contents all over the ground.

Cara nodded.

A beat passed where the only sound was Jonathan's slow exhale whistling through his teeth. "Okay, no reason to panic," he seemed to tell himself as much as anyone else. "We can figure this out." He glanced down at his mug. "But we are going to need something a lot stronger than tea."

..................................................

Cara eyed her friends over the rim of her wineglass. With the two of them on one side of the dark booth and Cara on the other, it felt more like a job interview, or maybe an intervention, than a brainstorming session on how to fix a life.

They'd barely said a word since they'd arrived at the bar—a dimly lit place that had offered privacy not only via the rows of high-backed booths that lined the walls but from the nineties music that pumped from the digital jukebox. Cara wasn't sure if it was because neither of them knew what to say or if they were each waiting for the other to begin, but either way, the silence was unnerving.

It was Julia who finally spoke. "Did you tell the ball and chain you're gonna be late?"

Cara shot her a look. "*That's* your opener?"

She shrugged. "Thought I'd lighten the mood with a little humor."

Jonathan shook his head. "The only thing that's going to lighten this mood is a little—"

"Do not say whiskey," Cara and Julia said in unison.

Jonathan held his hands up, palms out, and laughed. "Vodka."

On the ride to the bar, Cara had clued Jonathan in on what had transpired in Dublin. She'd stuck to the basic facts, but even those were enough for him to understand why Julia planned to order Cara a T-shirt that said "The Whiskey Made Me Do It."

His phone vibrated against the table.

Cara sat up straighter. "Is that your friend?" she asked. Jonathan had left a message for a law school buddy before he'd even parked his car. If she were lucky, this guy—Mark somebody—would be able to answer all her questions.

Jonathan glanced at the screen. "It is," he said. "I'll take this outside. Be right back."

Cara watched as he strolled out of the bar, his phone already pressed against his ear.

"We'll figure this out," Julia said, echoing the words Jonathan had said at least a half dozen times since they'd dropped the bomb. "You and I might not have a clue, but Jonathan is a genius, and his friend works at a big firm—"

"Meaning I can't afford him."

"*Meaning* he'll tell us what the next step is," she corrected. "Gotta have a little faith. After all, Jonathan was already right about one thing."

"What's that?"

"We need vodka." Julia caught the eye of the waiter and flagged him over. "Can we get a few martinis, please? I'll take mine straight up, two blue cheese olives on the side, and she'll have a lemon drop, sugar on the rim."

The waiter nodded to Jonathan's empty seat. "And your friend?"

"Bring him one of each, and he can choose," Julia said.

Cara gaped at her.

"What?" she asked, feigning innocence. "It's not like one of us won't drink the extra one." She slid out of the booth. "I'm going to hit the little girls' room while you text Finn."

"How do you know I haven't already?" Cara asked. As usual, Julia was right, something Cara both loved and hated at the same time.

"Just do it," Julia said before heading to the rear of the bar.

Cara dug her phone out of her purse. The screen was blank. Nothing from Samantha, which was good, but also nothing from Finn. Not that he should have texted her, but it was almost seven. Wasn't he wondering when she'd be home? Then again, maybe he was enjoying having some time to himself. *Shit.* She was doing it again, overthinking everything just like she always did when she started dating a new guy. Except they weren't dating, were they? No. They were just hanging out while they straightened out this mess, something she was trying to facilitate by getting legal advice. Wait. Should she tell him that? They hadn't talked about the next steps. Shouldn't they have decided what to do together?

*Ugh.* Forget awkward small talk. Cara's real superpower was apparently analyzing a situation to death.

*Keep it simple*, she told herself. And that was exactly what she did, sending Finn a short, matter-of-fact text that said she had a work "thing"—which was true. She *was* with people from work— and wouldn't be home for dinner. He replied almost immediately telling her that it was no problem and wishing her luck. His message should have brought her relief, but she'd no sooner read the words than she found herself wishing she was at the bungalow about to start an evening with Finn instead of a bar in Santa Monica figuring out how to end their marriage.

*Oh no.* This was bad. Finn had been in LA for less than forty-eight hours, and already she was not only getting used to it but enjoying it. The realization had her thinking that being away from him for a night was not only practical but necessary.

"The bathroom is covered with photos of Justin Timberlake," Julia said as she slid back into the booth. "Like every inch. The walls, the ceiling, the stall doors. It's all JT." As if on cue, "It's Gonna Be Me" started pumping through the bar's sound system.

"Did you pick this?" Cara wasn't sure why she even bothered to ask. She would have bet a million dollars—if she'd had it, that is—that Julia had used the app on her phone to hijack the bar's sound system.

"Of course," Julia said. "Oh! I wonder if Britney Spears is in the men's room?"

Jonathan was back, and the waiter was right behind him. "So much to unpack here," he said as he shoved his phone back in his pocket. "Start with Britney in the bathroom, then move on to who gets the bonus drink." He lifted a brow. "Please tell me we're going to arm wrestle for it?"

Julia laughed. "As if you could take me."

A smile curved the waiter's lips as he set the four glasses on the table. "Let me know if you need anything else," he said, never taking his eyes off Julia. He was handsome in a surfer dude kinda way: longish blond hair with sun-kissed highlights, just the right amount of scruff on his jaw, and peeking out beneath the rolled sleeves of his white shirt, Cara could see some pretty serious ink on his tanned arms. In other words, Julia was definitely going to give him her number before they left. Hell, a few more of those martinis, and she might be taking him home.

"Thanks," Julia said. But that was all. No furtive glance. No wink. Not even a smile. In fact, she hardly even looked at the guy.

"You think I'm screwed, don't you?" Cara asked as soon as the waiter left.

Julia looked up. "Me?"

Cara shifted her gaze to the bar and back. "You barely gave that guy the time of day, and he's about as close to Chris Hemsworth as you're going to get unless you date, well, Chris Hemsworth."

"I'll slip Thor my number before we leave," Julia said. "Right now, my focus is on you."

Yep, totally screwed. And if the look on Jonathan's face was any indication, he thought so too. Cara reached for her lemon drop martini and licked a bit of sugar off the rim before downing a healthy gulp. "What did Mark say?"

"Keep in mind, he's just speaking hypothetically. I only know the details you shared on the car ride over. There were a lot of questions I couldn't answer." Jonathan slid the extra blue cheese olive martini toward him, which was just as well because based on that lead-up, Cara already knew she was going to need another lemon drop. Or two.

"How bad is it?" she asked, sliding the spare drink closer.

Jonathan took deep breath. "He wasn't sure it could be handled with an annulment."

*Shit.*

"Can't she argue that she was incapacitated?" Julia asked.

Jonathan shook his head. "Only if that incapacitation continues."

"So, what, she has to stay drunk?"

"That's not the kind of incapacitation they mean," Jonathan said. "But they might be able to argue that the whiskey made her of unsound mind."

Following their conversation was like following a tennis match. "Can you guys please stop discussing me like I'm not even here?"

"Sorry," they said at the same time.

"Either way, it will be fine," Jonathan said. "Worst case, you'll just have to file for divorce."

Cara slumped back against the unforgiving wood. "Twenty-seven and already a divorcée." She spun the stem of her second glass between her fingertips. "My mom will be so proud."

"Your mom doesn't have to know," Julia said.

"Mark said he'd be happy to give you a free consult. He has an opening on Monday, if you want."

"Sure." Cara downed the rest of her drink while Jonathan texted his friend to confirm. Julia was on her phone as well, hijacking the sound system with a few more in-app purchases if the sudden blast of "Oops!... I Did It Again" was any indication.

"Subliminal messaging, Jules?"

Her head fell back on a laugh. "Not at all."

Julia might not have been trying to warn Cara, but it certainly sounded like Britney was. And she had a point. The tangy concoctions Cara had just polished off had gone down even smoother than the whiskey punch she'd had in Dublin.

"We should probably order some food," Julia said, already craning her neck for the surfer dude waiter.

Cara had lost her appetite, but Julia was right. She was taking an Uber home, but two martinis on an empty stomach wasn't a great idea either way. "Yeah, last thing I need is to roll up to the beach house drunk."

Julia paused with her glass in midair. "Could be dangerous," she said. "Considering the last time you were drunk around Finn, you married him."

Jonathan snorted. "Probably end up pregnant this time."

Both women shot him a look.

His brows shot up. "Too soon?"

"Ya think?" Julia shook her head. "Men."

Cara laughed as she opened her menu. "Screw the brussel sprouts," she said. "I'm thinking potato skins tonight," she said to redirect the conversation with small talk and carbs. But Cara didn't need to worry about making babies with Finn, or anything else for that matter, because by the time she got back to the bungalow, he was sound asleep. From the looks of him—stretched out on the sofa fully dressed and with Netflix still playing on his laptop—he'd fallen asleep waiting for her. He *was* waiting for her, wasn't he?

*Stop*, she told herself. *Not this again.*

The two martinis and her own jet lag had Cara crawling into bed without launching into her usual internal debate, but there was no amount of vodka that could keep her from thinking about him as she drifted off to sleep and no amount of fatigue that could keep her from looking forward to seeing him in the morning.

There was only one problem. When Cara woke up the next day, Finn was gone.

# CHAPTER 14

CARA WAS RETURNING FROM HER second coffee run of the day—ah, the glamorous life she led—when she saw something so shocking, she nearly dropped the entire tray of soy lattes.

Samantha was smiling.

And it wasn't the fake one she forced when what she was really thinking was "I need this B-list celebrity to stop rambling." No, this was a warm, full-face smile. The kind that reached her eyes.

She was standing in the reception area outside her office. Cara couldn't see who she was talking to, but whoever it was, she knew they had to be pretty special. She'd seen that look on her boss's face a few times before, but as far as she knew, neither Regé-Jean Page nor Ryan Reynolds were scheduled to be in the office that day. So then who was it who had her—sweet Jesus, did she just flip her hair? And was that a giggle? Holy mother of…

Forget smiling. Samantha Sherwood was flirting.

Cara rounded the fogged glass partition, expecting to find Prince Harry, Robert Downey Jr., *and* Chris Evans standing in a semicircle around her desk. But instead she saw…

"Finn?" He'd left a note for her on the kitchen counter that morning, saying he had tried to stay awake until she got home but that the jet lag had finally caught up to him. That same jet leg had apparently had him up and out before Cara was even awake, because the end of the note said he had taken Oscar for a run on the beach but would be back in time to have coffee with her before she left for work. It would have all been quite lovely if she hadn't had to leave early that day. She'd jotted a reply at the bottom of his note saying she was sorry to have missed him, but never in a million years did she think the next time she saw him would be at her office.

Finn looked at her and smiled, but it was Samantha who spoke. "Oh, there you are, Cara dear."

*Dear?* Had Cara tripped on the sidewalk and hit her head? Because that was the only way she could explain what was going on. That, or she'd somehow stumbled into a wormhole and was now in an alternate universe.

"You didn't tell me you brought a friend back from Ireland with you," Samantha said.

*Friend?* She didn't want her boss—or anyone else for that matter—to know she'd gotten drunk in Dublin and woken up married, but as Cara watched Samantha gushing over Finn, she suddenly had an overwhelming urge to claim him as her husband.

*Right, and after that, you can ask for the name of her divorce lawyer.* Not that she could afford him.

"Sorry to just drop in on you like this," Finn said. "I was at the park with Oscar." For the first time, Cara realized that Oscar was in the office as well, sitting patiently at Finn's feet. "It was the craziest thing really," he continued. "We were just there minding our own business, and then this woman came up and asked if Oscar had ever done any acting. At first, I laughed because I couldn't imagine anything more ridiculous. But then she explained she was part of a commercial that was shooting on the other side of the park and that the dog they'd hired was being a right pain in the arse. And, well, long story short—"

"Oscar has gone Hollywood," Julia said, finishing Finn's thought.

Oscar cocked his head to one side in a gesture that perfectly matched Cara's confusion. She'd been trying to make it in this town for a few years. Finn hadn't even been here for a few days and his dog had already landed a gig. Unbelievable.

"I was going to call you," Finn said. "But then Penelope said she was heading to this part of town anyways and that she'd drop me 'round." He pulled a thick stack of folded paper out of his messenger bag. "They said the contract was all pretty standard, but it reads like a foreign language to me, and since you work in the business…"

*Not exactly*, Cara thought. CTA represented people, not animals. She was about to explain that to Finn when Samantha jumped in.

"I told him I'd be happy to look it over," she said.

*What the what?* Samantha Sherwood negotiated multimillion-dollar deals, and now she was "looking over" a one-day contract for a *dog*?

"That's very nice of you," Cara stammered.

"Happy to help."

The situation had gone from absurd to insane. Samantha didn't do favors for anyone. Not unless there was something in it for her...

Cara's gaze dropped to where Samantha's hand now rested on Finn's forearm. "Have you ever thought about acting?" she asked him.

"I did a little when I was in school, but not many opportunities to pursue that where I'm from."

"Cara told me you were a mesmerizing tour guide," Julia said. Cara shot her best friend a look that very clearly said "I'm gonna kill you" but the effort was wasted seeing as how, just like Samantha, Julia couldn't seem to take her eyes off Finn.

"Oh, I don't know about that," he said. "I do try to bring a sense of drama to heighten the experience, but not sure that counts as acting."

Cara couldn't help but wonder how many times those "heightened experiences" included a near kiss in the chapel. A pang of jealousy twisted through her belly as unwelcome images flooded her mind, but then Julia said something that jolted Cara back into the conversation.

"You should go to the open call for *Mercury*," Julia said.

Had Julia lost her mind? That book had been an international phenomenon. The movie was going to be even bigger. Sure, the studio was doing an open casting call, but that was more as a gimmick than anything—a chance to get free press when local news stations filmed the line of hopeful actors that would no doubt stretch around the block.

"Those open calls are a waste of time," Samantha said,

finally sounding like herself. But then she studied Finn with her eyes narrowed as though she were squinting at the sun. Cara had worked for Samantha long enough to know what that expression meant: she was sizing him up.

"He does have the right look," she said more to herself than any of them. "He'd need a dialect coach for sure, but half the cast of the last *Star Wars* was British, so that shouldn't present a problem."

Was her boss, one of the most powerful women in Hollywood, actually considering Cara's new husband as a viable option for the most coveted role in town?

"Julia, get Finn a copy of the script."

Yes. Yes, she was.

"Sure thing," Julia said, snapping to attention.

"Finn, go over it this weekend, and then come back Monday and read for me. If your acting is half as good as your look, then I'll send you on the audition."

Cara's mouth dropped open. She was considering signing him? Was she nuts?

"Only as a hip-pocket," Samantha said, answering Cara's first unspoken question while at the same time confirming her suspicion that the answer to the second one was a resounding yes.

Finn gave Cara a confused look, but even if they could have spoken privately, she wouldn't have been much help. Cara didn't have a clue what was going on. And how could she? None of it made any sense. Not that Samantha was going to explain herself. She was far too busy firing off a list of instructions for Julia to pay any attention to Finn's confusion or Cara's shock. At least she was aware that Finn was still in the room. Cara might as well have been invisible.

"We can talk more about that on Monday," Samantha said. "Oh, and, Cara, I need a favor."

So much for invisible. And since when did she call menial tasks and errands favors?

"I have to pop down to San Diego for the weekend, and Coco has been so out of sorts, I don't want to leave her with the house-keeper. Would you mind stopping by my house after work tomor-row and taking her home with you?"

From coffee fetcher to dog-sitter. Not the career advancement she'd been hoping for when she woke up that morning. Then again, the meeting with Jeremy had gone really well. Assuming everything went according to plan, in six weeks or so, she'd be on a better path. All she had to do was bide her time…

"Actually," Samantha said to Finn. "You can bring Coco back Sunday night and read for me at my house. Two birds, one stone." Her words and tone were all business, but something about the look on Samantha's face told Cara she was definitely hoping Finn would come alone.

*Over my dead body.*

"Come, I'll walk you out." Samantha only walked A-listers to the elevator, and even that was only if she was heading that way. But after the way the past ten minutes had gone, nothing surprised Cara. Not a stroll to the elevator and certainly not the fact that Samantha had linked her arm with Finn's before leading him into the hall. They were about to turn the corner when Finn shot Cara a look over his shoulder that made it clear he had about a million questions he was dying to ask. Cara could certainly understand why—Samantha was a lot to take even if you were a Hollywood bigwig. For a guy who wasn't only new in town but the country as well, everything she'd said had to have been more than a little overwhelming. But all that would have to wait until they were back at the beach house. For now, Cara still had several hours with a woman who would have no doubt gone from Jekyll back to Hyde by the time she returned from the elevator. Joke was on her though. Because when the day was over, Cara would be the one going home to Finn, not Samantha.

Any satisfaction Cara felt was fleeting, because she'd no sooner had the thought when a dose of reality hit her so hard, it had her slumping into her chair. *Going home to Finn.* She needed to get a grip. Finn wasn't hers. The beach house wasn't their home. She needed to remember all that and more, because it was only a matter of time until he left. No sense getting used to having him around.

..................................................

Samantha was a workaholic even on a good day. Add to that the fact that she was about to go out of town for the weekend, and to put it bluntly, she was a nightmare. It was after eleven when she finally told Julia and Cara to head home, but not without first reminding them to be back at their desks by seven so she could get in a full day before she left for San Diego. Cara ended up asking Julia if she could crash at her place for the night so she could spend the hour of commute time sleeping rather than driving. It did make sense, but Julia knew Cara far too well to think the impromptu sleepover party was merely about maximizing shut-eye.

"You can't avoid him forever," Julia said as she unlocked the door to her apartment.

"I'm not avoiding Finn." Cara made a beeline for the couch and collapsed into the sea of pillows. "It's almost midnight. Driving back to Malibu would be silly." At least two of the statements Cara had made were true. It *was* almost midnight, and spending an hour in the car *was* silly when Julia lived so close to the office.

"Keep telling yourself that." Julia tossed her purse and keys on the table by the door, then flipped on the kitchen light.

"When I see him..." Cara considered her words. "It's confusing. And right now, I don't have the energy to navigate the roads let alone another night sleeping next to Finn."

"Are you hungry?" Julia yanked open the fridge. "I have leftover Chinese and the cannoli from yesterday's post." She reached for a small, white container and gave it a sniff. "Scratch that," she said with a wince. "Just the cannoli."

"Perfect." Cara was so exhausted, she hadn't been sure she could muster the strength to stand back up, but the thought of Julia's cannoli had her hauling herself out of the cushions.

Julia grabbed two pastry shells out of a plastic container and began filling them. "Mini chips or pistachios?" she asked.

"Both," Cara said as she slid onto a stool across the counter from her friend.

Julia looked up. "Both? This is worse than I thought."

Cara folded her arms and dropped her head so her forehead rested against them. "Finn is going to have so many questions," she said to the countertop beneath her face.

"Can't blame him," Julia said. From the sound of it, she'd just poured the mini chocolate chips into a bowl. "Not every day a Hollywood agent offers something like that, hip-pocket or not."

A plate clinked against the counter bedside Cara's head. She sat up to find two cannoli and one concerned friend.

"We had a lot to talk about before Samantha threw us this curveball. Finn hasn't even heard about the stuff Jonathan told us yet. And now this?" Cara's shoulders sagged. "I don't even know where to start."

Julia looked as tired as Cara felt, but it did nothing to diminish the genuine concern Cara saw in her eyes. "Start with a cannoli and some sleep. You can figure the rest out tomorrow."

That sounded like an excellent plan. Between bites, Cara checked her phone. She'd texted Finn to let him know she'd be staying at Julia's, but he never responded. Cara assumed it was because he'd fallen asleep, something he confirmed the next morning.

Sorry luv. Had crashed out. Jet lag.

No worries, she replied. Then to answer the question she knew was on his mind, she added, Don't have the script yet but they promised it will be on Samantha's desk later this morning.

Cara chewed on her lower lip for a second, debating whether to add the next part.

Which means we will have the whole weekend to work on it.

Tiny bubbles appeared on the screen almost immediately. We?

Thought you might want me to run lines with you.

That would be smashing. Thanks. A few seconds passed and then: I missed you last night.

*Whoa!*

Should be out of here by noon. Have to grab Coco on the way.

For a half day, it certainly dragged. As she finally drove home, Cara's thoughts drifted to images of her and Finn spending the afternoon lounging by the pool. Perhaps with a margarita to break the ice? Nah, too much prep time. Plus, she only wanted to break the ice, not completely melt it. Corona with a lime wedge would do just fine.

But when Cara arrived at the beach house, she found that Finn was already out by the pool.

And he wasn't alone.

# CHAPTER 15

CARA STOOD AT THE EDGE of the patio, taking in the scene on the pool deck. Finn was directly across from her, planting a rainbow of exotic-looking flowers in the long-abandoned beds that snaked around the free-form swimming pool. He was wearing a pair of faded, well-worn jeans, low-cut work boots, and a day's worth of stubble. His chest was bare and covered with a light sheen of sweat, and his hair was standing in an absolutely perfect mess.

"Cara, you're home early," Penelope said, halting Cara's imagination from conjuring a scenario in her mind that would have definitely crossed into the land of NC-17. She was poolside, stretched out on a chaise holding a martini glass in one hand and a copy of *Vogue* in the other all while wearing a lime-green head wrap, a pair of oversize sunglasses that screamed Jackie O, and a vintage bathing suit circa 1960. More than that, at eighty-two, she was totally pulling it off. "And you've brought a girlfriend for Oscar," she added.

Oscar had been napping on the lounge chair next to Penelope but raised his head when he heard his name. She didn't think it was possible for a dog to do a double take, but that was exactly what Oscar did when he saw Coco at the end of the hot-pink leash Cara held in her hand.

"Always the matchmaker, aren't you, Pippa?"

"I'd say she likes that idea," Penelope said, nodding toward the pampered pooch. Cara looked down to find Coco's tail wagging faster than she thought possible. Certainly faster than Cara had ever seen. She unclipped the dog's leash and watched as she beelined for Oscar.

"Come, have a libation," Penelope said. She looked over her shoulder as Cara made her way across the deck and added, "Finn, that goes for you as well. It's quitting time."

"Been putting him to work?" Cara asked.

"Nonsense. He offered. And he's been a doll." Penelope smiled in Finn's direction. "At the rate he's going, I'll be hosting parties again in no time."

Now that was something Cara would pay good money to see. Assuming, of course, she had any.

Finn finished patting the soil surrounding a plant that had leaves suitable for fanning Cleopatra—an image that would undoubtedly be brought to life should the previously mentioned parties come to fruition—then sauntered toward the chaises. "Hey," he said, flashing Cara the grin she'd already come to crave.

"Uber driver, musician, tour guide, and…landscaper?"

His grin widened. "Ah, you're just scratching the surface, luv."

"Soon to be adding actor to the list," Penelope said. Clearly Finn had shared the news with his temporary benefactress, and from the look on her face, she couldn't have been more pleased with the news.

"One step at a time, Ms. Parker," Finn said.

Penelope tsked in his direction. "Ms. Parker was my mother." Cara knew that wasn't true seeing as how Parker was a stage name Penelope had adopted early in her career. "Please, call me Pippa."

Finn nodded. "Yes, ma'am."

"That's even worse." Penelope rolled her eyes. "I know I'm old enough to be your..." She stopped short of saying the word *grandmother* and at the last second settled on "...favorite great-aunt, but no need to constantly remind me of that with these antiquated salutations. It's impolite."

Finn fought the smile tugging at his lips and actually managed to sound contrite. "Yes, Pippa," he said, accepting the nickname.

Penelope looked back and forth between the two of them for a few beats, then said, "I'll let you in on a little secret, Finnegan. The most successful actors know that it's not always about making an entrance. Sometimes, it's the exit that matters the most." With that, she rose from the chaise. "And on that note..." Penelope turned toward the house, waving her hand over her head as she made her way down the walkway. "Enjoy your evening, lovebirds."

Cara made a mental note to give her a bit of hell for that one—something she would no doubt dismiss with a knowing smile—then turned to Finn. "It was nice of you to help her out."

"Are you kidding? The least I can do for her hospitality," he said. "Plus, it helped take my mind off the audition." His gaze fell to Cara's messenger bag. "Did they send over the script?"

Cara nodded. "But I think we should leave it until tomorrow and start fresh then."

"Fair point," Finn said. "I'm a bit knackered from all the sun and..."

"All the Penelope?"

He laughed. "Maybe a wee bit."

Cara could relate. Penelope operated on all cylinders at all times. It could be a bit much in large doses. "Then it's settled. The script will wait until tomorrow."

"And tonight?"

"Tonight, I think we should go out."

"Yeah?"

"Yeah," she said, matching his grin with one of her own. "To celebrate."

"It's only an audition, luv. And not even for the people who could hire me."

"Doesn't matter. And it's not only an audition," she said, using her fingers as air quotes. "One of Hollywood's biggest agents wants you to read for the biggest movie of the decade. That is a *big* deal." Cara laughed at herself. "Wow, that was a lot of bigs."

"That is was." Finn grinned at her. "And it's not helping with the nerves, mind."

"All the more reason to take you out and distract you." Although, at the moment, she could think of a few ways she wouldn't mind distracting him right where they were, and all of them involved getting naked.

"Deal. As long as we don't talk about the script or the movie."

"What would you like to talk about?"

"I think I'd like to know more about my wife."

Cara both loved and hated it when he called her that. The more he said it, the more real it felt. But it wasn't real. Being Finn's wife was nothing more than a title, and even that wouldn't last for long. Still, there was no denying their connection. And it certainly felt like more than friendship.

*Wife.* That one tiny word set off an internal debate that lasted nearly the entire time Finn was in the shower. It was just as well, because she would have *really* been in trouble if she'd spent the whole time thinking about how naked he was behind that door— his body slick with soap, rivulets of water cascading over his rippled abs before finding their way lower to—

"Ready?" Finn asked.

Cara's head snapped up to find him standing in front of her wearing a pair of dark jeans and a thin, gray sweater that hugged his muscles in all the right ways. She'd also changed while he was in the shower—when she wasn't obsessing or shamelessly fanta-sizing, that is—pairing a blue sleeveless sweater with the jeans she'd worn to work that day, updating her "casual Friday" look by swapping her Adidas for a pair of heels with a decidedly more "Friday night" vibe.

"Sure." Cara started toward the door, then stopped. "Do you think the dogs will be okay here together?"

Finn looked over to where Coco and Oscar were lying side by side on a rug at the foot of the bed. "Looks like they're already best mates."

Cara might have been the one to suggest going out to dinner, but as they walked to her car, it was Finn who insisted she not only pick the restaurant but that she allow him to pay the tab as well. If his offer had been based on some antiquated male chauvinist notion, she would have told him it was Dutch or nothing, but when he explained that it was his way of thanking her in advance for running lines with him, she agreed.

Dozens of restaurants came to mind for their first night out in Los Angeles, but in the end, she settled on an open-air Mexican restaurant along the boardwalk in Santa Monica. Finn loved the place as much as she did, and the conversation flowed as easily as the beers. Cara was careful to watch how many she had, not only because she had to drive them home but because she didn't trust herself not to behave like a horny newlywed when they got there. One thing neither of them mentioned: their impending divorce.

Finn didn't ask if she'd had time to look into lawyers or even what the next step was, and Cara certainly didn't bring it up. Aside from the brief conversation at her office, she hadn't seen Finn in days. Last thing she wanted to do was launch into the steps they needed to take in order to say goodbye. And besides, it wasn't as though she was being completely selfish. Finn had had a pretty outstanding day. Regardless of what came of Samantha's offer, he should definitely be allowed to enjoy the moment.

When they were finished eating, they took a walk to the end of the pier, something Cara had never actually done before, splitting a cotton candy while watching the lights of the Ferris wheel.

"Ready to go home?" Finn asked when they were done.

Cara didn't know if four words had ever held so much promise. "Absolutely." She wasn't sure if Finn meant the question the way she hoped or if he realized the weight of her answer, but then the ocean breeze kicked up as they made their way along the beach-front, and she was fairly sure he did.

"Come here," he said, throwing his arm around her shoulders and pulling her close to his side.

"Cara?" someone said.

She looked up from where she'd been snuggled against the warmth of Finn's body. "Kyle?"

The muscles in Finn's arm tensed against her back.

"What are you doing here?" she asked.

"I live in LA, remember?" Like she could forget.

"I mean down here, by the water." Kyle hated Santa Monica in general, but he *really* hated the area by the pier. Too many tourists for his liking.

"My mom is in town." He gestured over his shoulder to a swanky hotel only steps from the sand. *That would explain the outfit*, Cara thought as she took in the sight of him: pink button-down, plaid madras shorts, boat shoes, and was that...? Yep, a Vineyard Vines quarter zip to round out the look. In other words, he looked like he'd just spent an afternoon at a New England country club.

"Oh, sorry, man, didn't see you," Kyle told Finn. Yeah, fat chance he hadn't noticed the guy standing so close to Cara that it was hard to tell where one stopped and the other began. He extended his hand toward Finn. "Kyle Banfield," he said, having totally switched to business mode as if it were autopilot.

"Finn Maguire," Finn said, keeping his own hands exactly where they were. It was only two words but enough for his accent to play on the ocean breeze. Kyle stilled but quickly recovered.

"You're Irish?" he asked, stating the obvious as he shoved his hands in the pockets of his shorts and tried to stand a little taller. His posturing was unnecessary. It wasn't his height that made Kyle come up short.

An awkward beat passed. It was Kyle who finally broke the silence. "How do you two know each other?" he asked, echoing the question his date had asked that night in the hotel lobby.

Cara was about to fumble through some totally awkward explanation that provided far more detail than necessary when Finn stepped in to save the day.

"Had the great fortune to meet this lovely lass the moment she landed."

"Fortunate indeed," Kyle said. The lack of inflection in his voice brought Cara far more satisfaction than she'd have cared to admit.

"Became her self-appointed tour guide even though I knew it was gonna bite me in the arse."

Cara looked up at him, confused. "How so?"

"Because I knew from the moment I laid eyes on ya that you were destined to break this poor bloke's heart when you left."

*Whoa.* As much as Cara was enjoying living the moment, a part of her really wished she could be writing it down, because this shit definitely belonged in a script.

Kyle's nostrils flared, and for a few seconds, he had the audacity to actually look jealous. "So you decided to follow her home instead?"

"Finn had never been to LA and…" Cara began, although for the life of her, she couldn't imagine why. What Cara did was none of Kyle's business. She was about to tell him as much when Finn jumped in with his own message for Kyle.

"I knew I couldn't let this one slip through my fingers. When you find someone like Cara…" He pressed a kiss to her temple, then leveled his stare on Kyle. "You'd be a fool to screw it up, am I right?"

Kyle didn't reply. Instead he shifted his gaze to Cara. As he did, she realized she felt nothing for him. No heartache, no anger, and certainly no love.

"If you'll excuse us," she said. "We were in a bit of a hurry to get home."

Finn kept his arm around Cara long after Kyle was out of sight. In fact, his arm was wrapped tightly around her shoulder all the way to the car. Not that she was keeping track.

The twenty-minute ride back to Malibu was spent discussing which playlist to listen to, which tacos had been better, and their love of small-batch tequila. Anything and everything except what had just taken place. And certainly nothing about what Finn had said.

By the time they reached Penelope's house, the topic of tequila had led them to the subject of celebrity-owned distilleries.

"All I'm saying is I think I'd try just about anything made by George Clooney or Ryan Reynolds," Cara said as they made their way down the now-cleared path.

Finn shook his head. "Why are women so predictable?"

"Ha! Judging by their sales, I'd say men feel the same way." She pushed open the door to the bungalow, then immediately spun around to face Finn. The change in direction was so sudden, it sent him crashing into her.

"What's wrong?" he asked.

"They are...the dogs..." Her face flamed. "We should give them a moment."

Finn leaned past her, then erupted into laughter at the site of his dog humping Coco like his life depended on it. "Oscar, man, if I've told you once, I've told you a hundred times, hang a sock on the doorknob." He looked at Cara. "Sorry, luv."

"It's fine." At least someone in the bungalow was having sex. "I mean, nature finds a way and all that, right?"

"Maybe it's not nature. Maybe 'tis true love."

Cara laughed. "Yeah, right."

"I'm serious. Sometimes even the prettiest purebred can be drawn to the rough-around-the-edges mutt." Finn held her gaze as his words hung in the air between them. It was Cara who finally spoke.

"I had a really great time tonight," she said.

"I did too. Have seen that pier in so many movies, yeah. Felt surreal to actually be there."

Mentioning the pier would have been his perfect segue into asking about Kyle, but when he moved on to the topic of Oscar's love life, it became obvious Finn wasn't going to bring up what had happened on the boardwalk.

"You're really not going to ask?" She knew she didn't have to be more specific.

Finn shrugged. "Figured you'd tell me if you wanted."

"It's not that I don't want to..." If anything, she wanted the complete opposite. Not only did Finn deserve an explanation, but Cara found herself actually wanting to share her story. Not for the reason she had in the past, but because for the first time since reading Kyle's email, she felt like their breakup had nothing to do with her and everything to do with him. "Can I ask you a question first?"

He plopped into one of the lounge chairs. "Go on, then."

"What you did back there...what you said...acting like... it was..." Cara pressed pause on her babbling and drew a deep breath. "How did you know?"

"I didn't. Not for certain." Finn said. "I recognized him from that first day when I dropped you off at the hotel. It was obvious you didn't want to see that guy then, whoever he was."

Cara came to sit in the seat beside his. "I guess hiding in your back seat was a pretty big giveaway."

"More the look on your face. I didn't know how or when, but I knew that man had hurt you." His words hung in the air between them for a beat before he added, "Then tonight, when I saw him..." Finn looked up at the full moon, then shifted his gaze to meet hers. "It had been such a grand night. I didn't want anything or anyone to spoil it, least of all a man who would be so careless with your affections."

Cara's throat felt tight, not from anything Kyle had done but from the realization that she'd let someone so unworthy of her heart occupy so much of her mind.

She cleared her throat, hoping like hell her voice would be level when she spoke. "Kyle is my ex-boyfriend."

Finn nodded. "I reckoned that much." Again, he didn't ask for details, instead letting Cara roll them out at her own pace.

There was so much she could say about Kyle, and none of it

was good. But in a surprising moment of clarity, Cara realized she didn't want to go into any of that. Finn was right. Kyle had been careless with her affections, and he'd been that way from the start. Reliving the hurt he'd caused her was only picking at a scab, not to mention giving him far more importance than he deserved. It was time to lock him away with the other ex-boyfriends collecting dust in the back of her mind, and the first step in doing that was to stop talking about him. Which was why, in the end, she decided to keep it simple. "He's the one I was supposed to go to Ireland with, but we broke up two weeks before the trip."

Finn's eyebrows rose, but he said nothing as Cara made her way to the railing that separated Penelope's property from the beach.

"I know I should have just had some sort of bonfire where I burned the ticket along with his photos, except you can't even do that anymore because no one prints photos, and it's not like you're going to burn your phone, and deleting them is so much less satisfying…"

Holy mother of god. Where was Julia when she needed her, because at the moment, she could have really used a swift kick to put a stop to the words tumbling of her mouth.

## EXT: BEACHFRONT DECK. EVENING.

FINN and CARA are enjoying a romantic moment in the moonlight while she explains how she ended up in Dublin on a trip booked by her ex-boyfriend.

>                              **FINN**
>                    (watching Cara intently)
>
>
>                              **CARA**
>                       (head held high)
>     I thought about letting the ticket expire,
>        but then I realized that if I wanted to go
>        to Dublin, I should go. I don't need a man
>        to make a trip worth taking, and there was
>        no reason to let Kyle spoil something I'd
>        been looking forward to.

Yeah, that would have been much better than rattling on about some sort of Phoebe Buffay cleansing ritual that, knowing Cara's luck, probably would have ended with an apartment fire the same way it had on that episode of *Friends*, just without the hot firemen.

Cara turned, staring out at the moon-kissed waves.

"I'm glad you didn't burn the ticket." Finn walked up behind her and placed his hands over hers where they rested on the railing, the warmth of his skin in direct contrast to the cold metal beneath her palms.

"You are?" she squeaked. So much for the level voice.

"Aye, because then I wouldn't have met you." The words were whispered against her ear. "And I meant what I said. You're not the kind of woman a man should let slip through his fingers." Then his hands were on her, the palm of one gliding over her body while the fingers of the other threaded into her hair, gently tugging her head to one side so his lips could leave a trail of kisses along her neck. "Cara…" The words vibrated against her already sensitive skin, sending a shiver rippling through her body that had nothing to do with the cool breeze. He stopped just below her earlobe, gently sucking on a spot that had her pressing back against the hard planes of his body.

"I need to kiss you," he said with all the urgency the words were meant to convey. Cara turned in his arms, and his lips found hers, slow and sweet at first, but then her fingers found their way into his hair and her lips parted, inviting him in. Finn's hand slid over her backside as he deepened their kiss in a perfect parallel to the unresolved tension that had been building between the two of them over the past few days. The realization sent a rush of adrenaline pulsing through Cara's body that left her feeling as though her skin were on fire despite the shiver that still racked her frame.

Finn pulled back to meet her questioning gaze. "I know my time here won't last forever," he said. "But while it does…"

She knew what he meant, but she needed to hear the words. "What are you saying, Finn?"

A cloud shifted, and the silver moonlight lit his face, revealing a sincerity that took her breath away. "I want to make love to my wife."

# CHAPTER 16

CARA'S HAND SLID ACROSS THE bed in search of a warm body, but all she found was more of the cool sheet. She opened her eyes, then quickly shut them against the bright light streaming in from the window.

"Morning," Finn said. She forced one eye open to find him sitting at her desk, backlit by the sun like a dream sequence in an eighties rom-com. "Sorry if I woke you. Jet lag still has me up before the sun."

"They say it's a day for every hour in the time change." Cara sat up—when had she put on one of Finn's shirts?—and rubbed the sleep from her eyes. As her favorite Irishman came into focus, she took a moment to enjoy the sight of him. He was freshly showered, wearing a pair of faded jeans and a well-worn Soundgarden T-shirt. His hair was its usual haphazard mess, and his feet were bare. Hmm, even Finn's feet were sexy. How had she never noticed that before?

"Hope you don't mind I grabbed the script out of your bag," he said, nodding to the bound papers he held in his hand. "Didn't want to wake you, but I really wanted to get a jump on these lines."

"Sure, no problem," she said on a yawn. *Wait. What?* The *Mercury* script wasn't in her bag anymore. She'd pulled it out before heading to dinner so she didn't risk losing it. Which meant the only script still in her tote was her printed draft of...*oh no, no, no.*

"Thing is," Finn said. "I can't quite figure out what part she thinks I should read for." He chuckled. "Doesn't seem like I'm a fit for either of the guys in here."

Cara threw back the covers and jumped out of the bed. No doubt her hair looked like it had been styled in a blender and her breath smelled worse than Oscar's after he'd had one those disgusting liver treats. Either of those facts should have had her dashing straight to the bathroom instead of launching herself at Finn, but at the moment, she had a far more pressing concern.

Finn wasn't reading the *Mercury* screenplay. He was reading hers. The one she never let anyone read. Ever.

"That's not the right script," she said, snatching the papers out of Finn's hand.

"Sorry, luv." Finn looked so genuinely confused, it took the wind out of her sails.

"No, I'm sorry." Cara collapsed onto the bed with a groan. "You didn't do anything wrong. It's just..." Her words trailed off as she covered her face with the script.

The bed dipped as Finn came to sit beside her. "Is that your screenplay?"

"Yes," she mumbled from underneath the stack of papers she'd obsessed over for the past three years.

He lifted the script off her face. "It's good."

She let out a laugh. "You don't have to say that. I know it's crap, which is why I still hadn't shown it to anyone." There it was, the truth she'd been dancing around in the name of perfection. Deep down, Cara knew that the script didn't need to be tweaked. It didn't even need a rewrite. It needed to be burned at the stake.

"It's not crap." Finn hesitated a moment. "Can I be honest?"

The only thing scarier than a guy asking if he could be honest was when he said *"we need to talk."*

"Sure," she said. And why not? He'd already read it. Might as well hear the review.

"It's not bad, Cara. Truly. I just didn't hear *you* when I read it. Not your actual voice, but who you are." He lay back on the bed and placed his hand on her chest. "Inside."

She'd never thought about it that way, but he was right. She'd come up with the idea when she'd first come to town. It had seemed like a surefire hit—timely, smart, and playing to all the most popular tropes. But in her heart, she'd never really connected with the characters or their journey.

"Maybe I'm not cut out for this," she said, articulating for the first time the thoughts that had rolled around in her head for months like a grenade with the pin pulled out. "When I was younger—like middle school—I was always making up stories and writing them in my journal. In high school, I tried my hand at short stories and started about a thousand different novels. It was like I had so many ideas, I didn't even know where to begin." She let out a quiet laugh. "Or end apparently."

She rolled onto her side to face him. "In college, I discovered screenwriting, and something just clicked. I wrote at least a dozen specs, and my professors loved them—"

"Specs?"

"It's like an audition for writers. How we showcase what we can do."

"And your instructors liked yours, so obviously you're good at it, yeah?"

"The ones I was writing in school were all based on long-established shows. Sort of like fan fiction. But when it came time to write something original…"

"You need a subject you're passionate about," he said. His words weren't a suggestion but rather a decision. He was right but…

"Easier said than done."

A beat of silence passed, and a crease formed between Finn's brows. "Let me ask you this," he finally said. "When was the last time you felt a fire in your belly?"

Cara didn't overthink her answer. In fact, she didn't think about it at all. She merely blurted out the thought that came immediately to mind. "In Dublin," she said. "After touring Kilmainham, I couldn't get that stuff from the chapel out of my mind."

Finn chuckled. "It was barely a kiss, luv. Hardly worth all that."

Cara gave his shoulder a shove. "Not because of that." Although she *had* spent quite a bit of time thinking about that "barely there" kiss, it wasn't what had sent her to her laptop that night. "I wanted to know more about Grace Plunkett. The story of her wedding and her husband's execution was so heartbreaking, and all I could think about was how did she feel when she left the jail that morning? What happened to her? Did she carry on with their cause, even after all she'd lost? Did she meet someone else? Was she happy?"

"And?"

"She never remarried, but she lived a long, full life. And she kept working for Ireland's freedom. I found that fascinating. I mean, the rebellion had cost her the love of her life—and it's not like women were really into activism back then—and yet she somehow found the courage and strength to kick ass."

Cara had been so busy talking, she hadn't noticed the enormous grin that had spread across Finn's face. "That's the story you should be writing," he said when she was done.

"You think?"

"I don't think, I *know*."

Cara wasn't sold, but she appreciated Finn's support. Something she was ready to return. "Definitely worth considering," she said. "But right now, we have something far more pressing."

"Indeed, we do," Finn said. The look in his eyes made his intentions clear. And they had nothing to do with the screenplay. At least not yet.

...........................................

The entire weekend was spent running lines. Penelope joined in, which was fortunate since Cara really had no idea what she was doing. One thing she *did* know was that Finn was nervous, which was why she put herself in charge of planning distracting activities whenever Penelope grew tired and needed a break. For the most part, her tactics worked. A quick trip to the Country Mart for an Ice Blended or to the Malibu Pier for tacos took Finn's mind off the audition. So did their drive up to Zuma to watch the sunset. But by Sunday morning, even a hike through Laurel Canyon wasn't enough to relieve his stress.

"You're ready," Cara said, stepping over a rock as they made their way up the steep terrain.

Finn frowned. "I hope so."

"You *are*. Granted, I'm no expert, but I've read the books, and I've certainly watched my fair share of movies. As far as I'm concerned, you're Nicholas Price brought to life."

"I don't exactly sound like a bloke from New York City."

"Don't worry about the accent. They know you'll need to work with a dialect coach. It's more about the emotion. And the look, which you've definitely got."

"I guess," he said.

"You don't have to take my word for it," Cara said. "Samantha thinks so too. I might not like working for her, but there's no denying that her instincts are always spot-on."

They hiked in silence for a few minutes. Cara didn't know what Finn was thinking, but something had been on her mind all day. "Maybe we shouldn't tell Samantha about the whole impulsive marriage thing."

Finn stopped walking. "Do you think she's only helping me because she's..."

"Trying to get in your pants?" Her words brought a smile to Finn's face, but at the moment, she was more concerned with reassuring him. "No. I mean, she was definitely flirting with you, and that's not to say she wouldn't be open to something down the road, but not now, not while you're indebted to her, so to speak. Samantha is a lot of things—the word narcissist comes to mind." Cara rolled her eyes. "But she's not stupid. I more meant she doesn't need to know about us. It doesn't affect your audition at all, but the fact that I got drunk and proposed to a man I barely knew isn't something I'd like making its way around the office. Especially when—"

"It will be over soon?"

Cara forced a smile. "Something like that," she said. Neither of them had broached the topic of ending their marriage. It made sense really. Finn needed to spend the weekend preparing to read for Samantha. Problem was, they weren't just ignoring the elephant in the room, they were acting like a happily married couple. And while the rational side of her knew that was probably going to make it a lot harder when things *did* end, another part of her argued that just because his departure was inevitable, it didn't mean she shouldn't enjoy it while it lasted. That was the side that was winning, which was why she pushed the momentary dose of reality back into the shadows.

They'd nearly reached the parking lot, providing Cara with the perfect distraction from the unwelcome ache that had settled in her chest. "Race you to the car," she said, already in motion. Then with a laugh, she upped the ante. "Loser has to clean the bathroom."

......................................................

By Sunday night, even Finn agreed he was ready. That, or he just went along so Cara would stop trying to convince him. Coco, on the other hand, wasn't ready at all. At least not when it came to leaving the beach house. It seemed Cupid's arrow had struck her pampered canine heart. In the end, the only way they could cajole her into Cara's car was by bringing Oscar with them as well.

Finn and Cara thought the two dogs' puppy love was adorable. Samantha wasn't quite so amused.

"Where's my girl?" she said in a high-pitched voice as she threw open the door. But her tone changed considerably when her gaze shifted from Coco to Oscar. "Oh, and what's-his-name is here too."

"Oscar," Cara reminded her boss.

Samantha looked at Cara and frowned. "Why did you bring—"

"That would be my fault, ma'am," Finn interrupted. "Or rather my pup's." He ran a hand back through his hair. As he did, his bicep bulged beneath the sleeve of his shirt, something Cara never failed to notice. As she turned back toward the house, she realized it wasn't lost on Samantha either. She also realized her boss was a bit overdressed for a casual Sunday at home. Unlike Cara and Finn, who had opted for jeans and T-shirts, Samantha was wearing white designer jeans, a colorful silk top—Gucci from the looks of it—and enough makeup for a red-carpet premiere. "Seems the two of them are quite taken with each other."

"It's fine," Samantha said. Her words were meant to reassure, but her smile didn't reach her eyes. "It's nice that Coco has a playmate."

*That's not all she has.* Coco's tryst would definitely not go over well with Samantha. Hopefully, Oscar could keep it in his pants. At least for the next half hour. Cara had barely finished her thought when the two dogs pushed past Samantha and into the house.

"No, really, make yourselves at home," Samantha deadpanned.

"I'm so sorry," Finn said. Cara could hear the tension in his voice. This wasn't good. He didn't need to be worrying about the dogs or anything else. The only thing that should have been on his mind was the lines he knew inside and out.

"I'll go find the dogs and get them some dinner," Cara said. "That way, you two can get to it."

Samantha looped her arm through Finn's and led him to the living room, leaving Cara alone in the foyer. She'd been to Samantha's Bel Air home several times, but it never failed to take her breath away. Even the entryway was spectacular, soaring two stories high and featuring a spiral, wrought iron staircase and an Italian marble floor. But as nice as the rest of the house was, it was the kitchen that Cara really coveted. She loved her beach bungalow, but it was a bit limiting when it came to cooking or her true love, baking. What she wouldn't have given to make Christmas cookies in a kitchen with not only every state-of-the-art appliance imaginable but an island big enough to roll out enough dough to feed everyone she'd ever met. Julia had an even bigger case of kitchen envy and in December—over a few too many holiday cocktails—had even suggested they ask Samantha if they could use her kitchen for an afternoon. Needless to say, that idea evaporated at the same time the hangover appeared. Julia was destined to build her Instagram empire in her one-bedroom apartment, and the only food Cara was ever going to prepare in Samantha's outlandish kitchen was dog food, something she was about to do again, although hopefully for the last time.

Cara found Oscar and Coco sleeping side by side in the sunroom just off the kitchen. She'd hoped focusing on the two dogs would distract her from worrying about how things were going with Samantha and Finn on the other side of the house, but no such luck. Cara was about to lose her mind by the time they joined her in the kitchen thirty minutes later.

Finn looked relieved, but Samantha gave nothing away. The three of them stood in the kitchen for a few awkward beats. "The dogs are fed and have gone out," Cara said when it became clear Samantha wasn't going to say anything about how it had gone.

"Great," was all she said in reply. No thank-you and certainly no compensation for dog-sitting over the weekend.

"So I guess we'll get going then," Cara said.

"Thank you for your time, Samantha, and for the notes. I really appreciate it."

Samantha smiled at Finn. "I'll be in touch," she said.

With that, Cara and Finn dragged a reluctant Oscar out of the house. On the ride home, Finn recounted everything that had happened in the living room. All in all, he'd read three scenes for Samantha, one of which she'd asked him to perform twice.

"I don't know," he said with a shrug. "Felt like it went well, but she didn't say much. Guess I'll just have to wait and see."

He didn't have to wait long. They'd barely gotten out of the car when alerts sounded on both their phones.

Cara's was a text from Julia, relaying the instructions she'd just received from Samantha about setting up calls on Finn's behalf. His was no doubt from the woman herself, because they both looked up from their phones with the same giddy grin.

"She's calling the casting director on Monday," Finn said.

"That's great!" Cara launched herself at him, wrapping her arms around his neck in a hug that nearly sent them both toppling to the ground. "I told you that you were amazing."

"Don't get too excited just yet," Finn said as he set her back on her feet. "She wants me to work with an acting coach first, so clearly I wasn't *that* amazing." He grinned down at her. "You might be a bit biased. Blinded by orgasm."

Cara gave his shoulder a shove. "Am not." In a haze maybe but not blinded. "The fact that Samantha is sending you to work with an acting coach is a good thing. She wouldn't bother if she didn't see potential."

"She's paying for it too."

"She's thinking of you as an investment. That says a lot."

"Can I ask you a question?" Finn said once they started to make their way back to the bungalow.

"Of course."

"And you'll promise to level with me?"

Cara reached for Finn's arm, stopping him and urging him to look at her. "Finn, I may have left out a few details about my life in LA, but aside from that, I've never been anything but honest with you."

An emotion crossed his face that Cara couldn't quite place, but then he drew a deep breath and asked the question that was obviously weighing on his mind. "Do you really think I have a shot?"

"I do. But more importantly, Samantha Sherwood does."

"She didn't say much at the house."

"Actions speak louder than words with her. Even with the biggest clients on her roster, she doesn't overpromise. But bottom line, there's no way she'd send you to an acting coach, let alone set something up with the casting director, if she didn't think you had a shot. She wouldn't jeopardize her reputation like that."

Finn's phone lit up in his hand.

"It's from Samantha." He scanned the screen. "She's messengering over a contract tomorrow."

"See," Cara said, already knowing she would be that messenger. "Forget hip-pocket. She's locking you down."

"I've been trying to enjoy this but at the same time keep some perspective. But now, I don't know, it's starting to feel real."

"Because it *is* real."

"It's a lot to process," Finn said. That might have been true, but judging by the ridiculous grin on his face, he was grasping at least the highlights just fine.

"Come on," Cara said, taking him by the hand and starting toward the main house. "Let's go tell Pippa the good news."

"Hold up," he said, tugging her back. "I hate to even say this after everything you've already done for me, but can I ask you for one more favor?"

"What is it?"

"Can we hold off on the divorce proceedings until after the audition? I don't know why, but this all feels so surreal, and I'm afraid any change might—"

"Jinx it?"

Finn winced. "Kinda, yeah. Does that sound crazy?"

"Yes, but I'm the same kind of crazy," she said, choosing not to elaborate on any of her more ridiculous superstitions. No sense in Finn knowing that she always counted as she climbed stairs or that she held her breath getting on and off an escalator. Or that, thanks to her grandmother, she still believed an itchy nose meant bad news was coming. The other thing she wouldn't admit was that shared superstitious tendencies aside, Cara wasn't ready for their marriage—real or not—to end.

# CHAPTER 17

FINN AUDITIONED FOR THE CASTING director on a Thursday. By Friday, he was a wreck.

"How long do these things usually take?" he asked Cara over dinner that night.

She paused with her fork of fried fish in midair. "Not sure. Depends on how many others they're looking at, I guess." Judging by the expression on Finn's face, her answer hadn't helped.

"Probably not a good sign if I don't hear soon, then."

Cara reached across the table for his hand. She could certainly understand why he was anxious. It had taken nearly three weeks for the casting director to bring Finn in to read for the part. Nineteen days to be exact. That wasn't a bad thing, as it gave him nineteen days to work with his acting coach, but it was a long time to be nervous and excited and then nervous again. The upside was that it also gave them nineteen more days where they didn't talk about ending their marriage, which meant nineteen more days of playing house.

There was no maybe about it anymore; Cara was *absolutely*

setting herself up for a harder fall when Finn left, but she'd deal with that when the day came. For now, her primary focus was taking Finn's mind off waiting for the phone to ring, which meant distracting him with sex, food, and laughter.

"You were great, Finn. Really great. But you don't have to take my word for it. Your coach said he thought you were ready, and don't forget Samantha. She thinks you're perfect for the role, and her instincts are almost always right."

The corner of his mouth turned up in a shy grin. "You always know exactly what to say."

Words spoken by no man ever.

"It's true," she said. "And then you'll be this big Hollywood star, and I'll have to find some other guy to cook dinner for me. I mean, cottage pie, steak and Guinness stew, and now fish and chips? A girl could get used to this." Not to mention the sex, which quite frankly was even ten times better than the food.

Finn's smile grew wider. "Oh, that's how it is, eh? Using me for my culinary skills?"

She nodded. "And your accent."

He laughed and shook his head. "You're a crazy bird, do you know that?"

"It's true," she said. "Not the using you part, but the accent."

Finn still didn't look convinced. Cara would never understand why most foreign guys didn't understand the power of their accent. Even the dude from *Love Actually* knew that. It was why he headed to Wisconsin with a bag full of condoms. Seemed like the rest of them would've clued in as well.

"Try me," she said.

"Try you?"

"Yes, talk Irish to me."

Finn raised one brow. "Is that like dirty talk?"

"It's exactly like dirty talk, but with half the effort and twice the results."

He leaned forward and dropped his voice. "Oh, I don't know. I'm pretty good at dirty talk."

That she already knew—and it was definitely a topic worth revisiting—but Cara was having far too much fun to let this line of conversation go. "Indulge me," she said, sitting back in her chair and crossing her arms.

"With dirty talk?"

"No, with Irish talk."

He cocked his head to one side. "Like what?"

"I don't know. Anything."

"Anything?"

She nodded. "Hit me with a word we don't use here."

"Gowl."

"Okay, maybe not *anything*," she said.

Finn smiled and shook his head. "Banjaxed?"

"Finn!"

"Okay, okay, no need to fret."

"There you go."

"Fret?"

Cara nodded.

"Arseways."

Not the best, but it was a start. "More."

Finn rubbed the stubble on his chin. "Bare bullocks."

Better. "Yes, more!"

He laughed. "Bloody hell."

"Now you're talking."

She saw the moment he shifted from amused to enticed. It flashed across his eyes like a billboard that read "game freaking on."

"Sucking diesel now, innit?"

"Yes... Oh god, yes."

"Best crack on, then?"

"Yes, please," Cara's hands glided up her neck and then into her hair. "Oooh, yes."

Finn fought the smile that tugged at the corner of his mouth. "You're being a real cute hoor."

"Yes, please, just like that." Her breath now came in short pants. "Right there, right there."

"Delira and excira about it, yeah."

"Yes, yes, yes," she chanted, doing her best to channel Meg Ryan in that infamous *When Harry Met Sally* restaurant scene.

Finn chuckled. "At the rate this is goin', you might need to bunk off tomorrow?"

"God, yes." Cara smacked the table as her head fell back. "YES!"

"You're a right feek," Finn said.

Cara froze because that one she knew from one of the websites she'd read before her trip. *Gorgeous girl.* But it wasn't the compliment that stopped her in her tracks. It was the way Finn said it. Like she was the only woman who mattered in the world.

She met his gaze to find the look in his eyes perfectly matched the tone of his voice.

"Glad you enjoy my accent, luv, but I can think of a lot better ways to use my mouth than talking."

"Yeah?" she asked, shifting in her seat as his tongue darted out to wet his lips. Her breath was still coming too quickly, but it had nothing to do with her fake orgasm and everything to do with the promise of what was yet to come.

Then Finn stood and, without saying a word, Irish or otherwise, scooped Cara into his arms and carried her to the bed.

..............................................

The next two weekends were spent sightseeing. At least by day. The nights and early mornings—and at least one afternoon in the restroom of a very loud restaurant on Melrose—were spent consummating their marriage again and again and again. Cara might not have remembered much of her wedding, but her honeymoon, as Finn kept referring to his time in LA, was definitely one for the books.

He'd told her that it wasn't necessary for her to cart him around to every tourist attraction in Los Angeles and that he'd have been perfectly fine spending their weekends holed up in the bungalow. But Cara argued that it would be a crime not to make the most of his time in LA. Besides, it took his mind off the audition. Not to mention the fact that if he *did* get the role in the film, it wouldn't be long before Finn would be too recognizable to play the role of a sightseeing tourist, not without a disguise at least.

Of course, she didn't tell him any of that, as it would have only made the waiting that much harder, which by weekend three had damn near pushed him to the brink.

But everything changed on the first Saturday in April.

Cara had been up to the main house helping Penelope place her online grocery order, same as she did every Saturday afternoon. But afterward, instead of finding Finn pruning the landscaping on the pool deck or throwing a tennis ball for Oscar down on the beach, he was inside the bungalow, sitting on the bed with his phone in his hand. By the look on his face, Cara knew something was either incredibly wrong or incredibly right.

He was in motion before she'd even had time to close the door.

"What's—"

"I got the part!" he said, scooping her into a hug that lifted her feet clear off the floor.

Dozens of questions popped into her head, but Cara couldn't manage a single one. Finn was squeezing her so tightly, she could barely breathe.

"Samantha just called," he said when he finally put her down. With the oxygen flowing freely, so did the questions.

"What did she say? Is she going to counter? What billing will you get? And what about box office—"

Finn laughed. "Slow down, luv. I'm still in a bit of shock."

"Sorry," Cara said. "I'm just so excited for you."

"Same. So much so that, to be honest, most of what she said went in one ear and then straight out the other."

"Are you meeting with her to discuss the details?"

He nodded. "Tuesday."

"Any idea when this will go public?" That was definitely something they'd have to prepare for.

"Naw. Right now, it's all very hush-hush."

"Of course. They'll probably want to make some big announcement at a press conference, or maybe a fan event... When is that con in Chicago? Damn, I can't remember if it's in March or April."

Finn placed his hands on Cara's shoulders. "Breathe, luv. There'll be time for all this once I know more, but for now, I want to take you out for a proper celebration. Any place you want. Nobu, Spago..."

It was Cara's turn to laugh. "Has someone been reading Trip Advisor?"

"I owe all of this to you, and since I'm about to get a paycheck for more than I thought I'd ever make in my life..."

"I don't need a fancy restaurant, Finn. I'd be happy to stay here and order delivery."

"I'd love to stay here."

"Perfect." She grabbed her phone off the kitchen counter and opened her favorite food delivery app. "What sounds good? Chinese, Italian, sushi?"

"No, I mean I want to stay *here*," he said, suddenly serious.

"In LA? Well, you won't be leaving, not for a while," she said as she scrolled through restaurant suggestions. "But I guess that depends on where they film. Might be in London or—"

Finn moved quickly, halting her train of thought as he closed the distance between them in one easy stride. Cara's mouth opened in surprise, and he took full advantage, his lips and tongue meeting hers as his arms circled her waist, hauling her against him. There was a hunger in the way he kissed her, an undeniable need, but there was also something else, something deeper, running right below the surface of his lust.

"I meant I don't want to leave *you*," he said when he finally broke their kiss. "There needs to be more."

Her head was swimming. "More what?"

"More adventures. More nights in. Or out. I don't care as long as there's more of you. More of us."

There was no denying the effect his words were having on her. The mere thought of more time with Finn sent a warm rush spiraling up from somewhere deep inside her. But Cara's instincts had been wrong before—at least when it came to men—and she reminded herself not to get too far ahead of herself. Yes, things had been going well. Okay, okay, more like extremely well. Then again, Cara and Finn never had trouble getting along. Throw in the forced proximity of their living arrangements, not to mention the heightened emotions surrounding the audition, and it was only natural they'd grown closer. Didn't mean they were anything more than two people who cared about each other and who also just happened to be married.

"Finn, I..." There were so many ways she could have finished that sentence.

*Finn, I think you're just excited about this news and are getting carried away.*

*Finn, I don't know what you mean by that, and I'm scared to ask.*

Or the one she'd been thinking for weeks but pushing aside.

*Finn, I think I'm falling for you, and I hope you feel the same.*

"And I meant it, Cara," Finn said, continuing his thoughts and saving her from her own. "I wouldn't have this role if it weren't for you."

"You really owe that to Samantha," she said, then gave a small laugh. "But wait until you see the size of her commission."

Finn shook his head. "Not the opportunity," he said. "The performance."

Her laugh grew stronger. "Now, *that* I can't take any credit for. You have a highly respected acting coach to thank for that."

"I'm talking about the reading for Samantha."

"That was Pippa. I was just in charge of fun and food, remember? You should definitely say all this to her though. It would make her day."

"I will absolutely thank Pippa. We can go see her straightaway. But that's not what I'm talking about."

"Then what?"

"You know that scene at the end?"

"The one where Nick's son dies?"

He nodded. "According to Samantha, I nailed it the day I read for her. It was what made her decide to take a chance on me."

"I'm sure you did, but I still don't understand what I had to do with that, Finn. I'm no actress, and I'm certainly not an acting coach. All I did was help you memorize a few lines."

"You did so much more than that." He took a deep breath. "I don't have any children, so I could only try to imagine how the character felt."

"And obviously you did a great job."

"Because of you, Cara." Finn stroked the side of her face. "Do you remember the conversation we had before we went to see Samantha?"

Cara tried to think back to that night. But she and Finn talked about so many things on any given day. It was hard to recall a specific conversation from a month ago.

"You said you'd rather she not know you'd gotten tipsy and proposed in Dublin."

"I was a little more than tipsy. More like—what was that word you used the other day—ossified?"

"Fair play." Finn smiled. "But the rest of what you said is what got me through that scene."

Cara frowned. As far as she could recall, that was pretty much how the conversation had ended. But Finn remembered more.

"We agreed that there was no sense mentioning a marriage that wasn't going to last much longer anyways."

Oh yeah, that. Cara looked away. "Those were your words, Finn." And even now they stung.

"You didn't contradict me, luv." He lifted her chin so she met his gaze. "I didn't realize it until that night, but a part of me was hoping all along that you would." His green eyes burned with sincerity. "The thought of never seeing you again—*that* was the emotion I channeled at Samantha's and again at the audition."

"What are you saying, Finn?" She swallowed the lump that had formed in her throat. "Do you not want a divorce?"

"I'm saying maybe we could sit with this a while."

Adrenaline coursed through her veins. She'd been dreading the day she and Finn would part ways. Now there he was, suggesting they press pause on that plan in favor of... "And then what?" she asked.

"And then we see how it goes." His mouth turned up in the shy grin that never failed to melt her heart. "All I know is, so far so good."

# CHAPTER 18

CARA WOKE UP ON SUNDAY morning with a huge smile on her face. She and Finn had indeed celebrated the fact that he'd landed the most coveted role in Hollywood, although not with a fancy dinner in Beverly Hills. Instead they'd gone up to the main house to share the news with Penelope, who proceeded to pop the cork on a bottle of champagne that was nearly as old as Cara. Several toasts and many stories later, they found themselves back at the bungalow for a more private celebration. Cara wasn't sure if they were merely celebrating Finn's success or their decision to remain married—at least for now—as well, but it didn't matter because either way, it was hands down the best night of her life, and all it involved was a few bottles of craft beer, a couple cartons of Chinese takeout, and a whole lot of naked Finn Maguire.

They'd lain in bed for hours, talking and laughing between light touches and tender kisses. The conversation about Finn's career had flowed easily, from his idea of getting Pippa a small role in the film, to the reaction his family was going to have when they heard the news, to the way his life would change once the news was made public. But the conversation about the two of them was just as natural. They'd laughed about the ridiculousness of the entire situation, how most couples dated, moved in together, and then got married, and how she and Finn had done everything in reverse. They'd made plans, not just for the next weekend but for a trip to Palm Desert the next month, all without the dark cloud of an expiration date hanging over their heads.

It made sense, really, that the two topics were intertwined, because the reality was one couldn't have existed without the other. If he hadn't gotten the role, she and Finn wouldn't have been able to "sit with it," as he said. His tourist visa was only good for ninety days, which meant the only way he could stay longer was to fully commit to the marriage. Aside from the obvious problem that it was *way* too soon for either of them to think about that level of commitment—the irony of which was not lost on her given the fact that they'd already taken that plunge—there was the practical benefit as well. No doubt there was an endless amount of paperwork, not to mention the notoriously grueling interviews, that came with a visa tied to an impulsive wedding. But now Finn didn't need to be married to remain in the country. A starring role in a major motion picture would not only provide him with a visa but also someone else to deal with the red tape.

It was kind of amazing when she thought about it.

Their marriage started the chain of events that led to Finn's audition. Landing that role was now going to allow them to take their time exploring their relationship. A true romantic would have added that the whole thing had the potential to end in a full circle moment if, in the end, the two of them decided to stay married. But that was about fifty steps further than Cara's brain could process. For now, she was beyond happy; she was euphoric.

There was only one problem. She needed to tell Samantha the truth. Regardless of the fact that Finn wasn't going to base his visa on being the husband of an American citizen, it was definitely something he'd have to reveal. Cara had no idea how their marriage would affect the process, but it was sure to make it more complicated.

Then there was the issue of what would happen after Finn exploded onto the scene. The media would dig into everything they could find on the soon-to-be star Even if, in the end, he and Cara divorced, the press would still find out about her. And if they stayed together...

For a moment, Cara indulged in the fantasy she'd flirted with the night before: her husband, the movie star. What kind of life would they have? How would it affect their privacy? Or raising children?

*Children? Jeesh!* Cara quickly pushed those thoughts away. She and Finn had decided to put a pin in their plans to annul their marriage, not plan their golden anniversary. As much as her subconscious clearly wanted to, there was no point in getting ahead of herself. Besides, there was still the matter of breaking the news to her very temperamental boss. She'd realized it the night before, and while on any other night, the thought of a confrontation with Samantha would have had Cara tossing and turning for hours, last night, she'd slept solidly in Finn's arms, something he said he'd like her to do for the foreseeable future. Nothing Samantha said or did was going to change that. Still, Cara couldn't help but wonder how she'd react to the news.

"Good morning," Finn said. He'd no sooner said the words than his sleepy smile faded. "Uh-oh, what's that look for?"

"Look? There's no look."

"I might not be privy to all your secrets, but I've come to know your worry face." He reached up and smoothed the crease that had apparently formed between Cara's brows. "What's on your mind?"

Cara didn't want to start their day talking about her boss, but it was better than having Finn worry that it was something worse. "I was just thinking about Samantha."

"You're in bed—naked as the day ya were born, I might add—and you're thinking about work?" He grinned as he shook his head. "I must be doing something wrong."

Cara rolled her eyes. Finn knew darn well he was doing *everything* right. At least when it came to the time they spent in bed. Hell, half the houses on the beach probably knew that. "I was thinking that I need to tell Samantha that—"

"You're my wife?"

She didn't know if she would ever get used to hearing Finn say that word, but judging by the warm flush that spread over her cheeks, it wasn't happening anytime soon. "Yeah."

"Do you think she'll be mad?"

Cara considered her answer. "She'll be annoyed to have been left out of the loop—something she'll get over once that commission check hits her bank account—but she'll be really pissed if the studio finds out first. The sooner I come clean, the better."

"Do you want me to tell her?"

While it was true that Samantha would never blow up at a client, it didn't change the fact that it had been Cara's idea to keep the news from her in the first place. Not to mention the fact that she'd sat outside her office for *weeks* without saying a word. Letting Finn fall on the sword wouldn't be fair. "No, I'll talk to her on Monday."

"That's still twenty-four hours away," he said as his palm slid across her hips. "Which leaves me with one question."

A shiver raced across Cara's skin as Finn's fingers dipped lower. "Which is?" she asked on a stuttering breath.

"Where is my good-morning kiss?" His words were innocent enough, but the look on his face was one Cara had come to know well. It was the one that told her she was about to get a whole lot more.

....................................................

"Julia wants to take us out to celebrate," Cara said after reading her friend's text.

"Do you want to go?" Finn walked up behind her and dropped a kiss to her shoulder.

"It might be a good idea to leave the bungalow," she said, squirming against the sensation of his tongue teasing her skin. She and Finn had been locked in her apartment for nearly twenty-four hours. Granted, they'd been getting plenty of exercise, but a little fresh air and change of scenery would probably be a good thing.

"Are you sure?"

Her head fell back on a laugh. "Not if you keep doing that." She turned in his arms. "This is huge, Finn. You deserve to celebrate."

He cocked what his countrymen would call a cheeky grin. "Isn't that what we've been doing?"

Cara pressed her hand over his mouth just as he was about to kiss her. "I'm serious. No telling how long it will be before they announce the news, and until they do, Julia is one of the few people who knows what's going on. Plus, she's my best friend. Wouldn't mind her getting to know my..." Cara paused. Finn threw the word *wife* around with ease, but until that moment, Cara wasn't sure if she'd ever referred to Finn as her husband, not out loud. Even hearing it in her head had her heart beating a little faster. "You know what I mean."

Finn pulled her hand away from his mouth and touched his lips to hers. "I do," he said, his choice of words doing nothing to calm her racing pulse. "Where and when?"

"In an hour," Cara said. "She's going to text me the address."

Finn pulled back and raised one brow. "An hour? That's not much time given the Sunday traffic on PCH," he said, sounding every bit the local if it weren't for his accent. "We better shower together to save time."

Yeah, they were definitely going to be late.

..............................................

Cara and Finn walked side by side, holding hands as they made their way down Wilshire Boulevard before finally stopping in front of an unassuming brick-faced building. The window frames were painted a dark red, and above them the name of the pub was written in simple block lettering.

"The Spotted Goat?" Cara asked.

"Aye, the best kind of goat."

Whether he was joking or not, she couldn't say, since nearly everything Finn Maguire said sounded as though he was playing.

"Be that as it may," she said. "Did my best friend really just invite an Irishman to an Irish pub?"

He shrugged. "Maybe she thought I was homesick?"

"I'll tell you right now, the Gat still won't taste like home."

Finn laughed. "Look at ya, using the right slang." He yanked open the heavy wooden door. "Don't fret, luv. This place will do just fine."

It took a minute for Cara's eyes to adjust to the dimly lit pub, but once they did, she took a long look around. The walls were covered in a dark, knotty wood, the lighting was low, and a murmur of quiet conversation hummed over music Cara couldn't name but still knew was Irish. Behind the bar, a stocky, ruddy-faced man wearing a plaid shirt and dark-green suspenders wiped his hands on a towel that looked to have been put to good use over the past few hours, and above him, a rugby game played on the television. If Cara hadn't known better, she would have sworn she walked through some sort of magical portal to Dublin. Even the beer taps were on par with the pubs there, offering Kilkenny and Smithwick's in addition to the usual suspects of Guinness and Harp.

Perhaps Julia's choice hadn't been such a bad idea after all, she thought. But then she turned and saw the smile on Finn's face, and

Cara knew with all certainty that the place was more than "just fine" as he'd said outside. It was absolutely perfect.

"I see your friend," Finn said. Between the dim lighting and the fact that he'd barely spent any time with Julia, Cara was surprised Finn recognized her. But then she turned to find her waving at them like some sort of lunatic and it all made sense.

"Julia is subtle if nothing else," Cara deadpanned.

"Why don't you join her, and I'll grab us a few a beers."

"I thought I was buying?"

The crease in his brows was in direct contrast to the grin playing on his lips. "Whatever gave you that idea?"

"Isn't that how a celebration works?" Cara said with a small laugh.

"Now there's where yer wrong. The celebration is in you joining me for a pint. I'd never allow you to pay for it. The man code prohibits it."

If a guy in LA had tried to pull something like that, she would not only have paid for the drinks but told him where he could shove his antiquated notion. But something about the way Finn was looking at her told Cara that his gesture had nothing to do with male chauvinism and everything to do with how he was raised. That, plus a hefty dose of flirtation.

Cara watched as Finn sauntered up to the bar, resting one boot on the brass footrail as he spoke to the bartender.

"Dear Lord, I would have married him too," a man said from behind her.

Cara turned. "Jonathan," she said, greeting him with a warm hug. "I didn't know you were joining us."

"Julia texted me. Said we're celebrating something that she's not allowed to discuss but that it involves your sexy Irishman."

"And that was enough to get you out on a Sunday night?"

"Who am I to say no to a celebration, even if I have no idea what we're celebrating?" He chuckled, then added, "Plus, I was dying to get a look at this guy." He exhaled a heavy sigh. "Shame he's your future ex."

"Yeah, about that," Cara began. "We decided we're gonna sit with it a while."

Jonathan's eyebrows shot up. "Sit with it?"

Cara nodded.

"As in stay married to the guy with the sexy brogue for an undetermined amount of time?"

Another nod.

"Oh, Mrs. Maguire, you are full of surprises," he said, smiling and shaking his head. "I'm gonna go grab a beer. Meet you at the table."

Cara joined Julia at the high-top table in the corner. She hadn't been seated for more than a few minutes when Finn and Jonathan wandered up, a pint of amber lager in each hand, looking like they were already the best of friends.

"I don't know what he told you to have you laughing like that," Cara said. "But whatever it was is a lie."

Finn set a beer in front of Cara, and Jonathan did the same for Julia.

"You really shouldn't be buying the drinks for your own celebration," Julia told him, echoing Cara's earlier comment.

"I didn't." Finn slid onto the open stool next to Cara. "The

bartender heard my accent and insisted these were on the house."
He lifted his pint and tipped it in the direction of the group.
"Sláinte!"

"That means cheers, right?" Julia frowned. "But in Ireland,
cheers means thank you?"

Finn smiled over the rim of his glass. "All part of our plan to
confuse the Americans."

Jonathan reached for the basket of popcorn in the center of the
table and pulled it closer. "I knew the Irish couldn't be as friendly
as they seemed."

"We're angels on the outside but devils underneath." Finn
might have been addressing the entire table, but his gaze was
locked on Cara's. The dark gleam in his eye left little doubt to the
truth of that statement, at least when it came to the charmer next
to her.

Cara broke their stare—because quite frankly, if she hadn't,
they would have been heading home without finishing the first
round—and as she did, she noticed the framed artwork hanging
on the walls behind Finn. Pastels, watercolors, charcoal sketches.
All were of Dublin landmarks and each had a small price tag in
the corner.

"The bartender said those are all by local artists," Finn said.
"The owner lets them use his walls as a gallery."

"That one looks familiar," Julia said, pointing to a pastel
drawing of a bridge.

Cara had to agree, there was something familiar about the
spot. The carpet of purple flowers, the rolling hills, the river, the
ironwork on the railings... "Is that the *P.S. I Love You* bridge?"

Finn rolled his eyes. "It's the Ballysmuttan Bridge, but yes."

"The one—"

"—they walk across?" he said, finishing Cara's question. "Yes."

"On the day they met?"

"Yes."

"You're kidding?"

Finn placed one hand over his heart. "Would I lie to you?" His words might have been sincere, but there was an undeniable smile playing on his lips.

"I need to buy that," Cara said as she slid off her stool for a better look.

"Not if I get it first," Julia piped in.

Jonathan paused with a handful of popcorn halfway to his mouth. "Oooh, a bidding war."

Finn shook his head. "No offense to Holly and Gerry," he began. "But a bridge really means that much?"

"It's not just any bridge," Julia said. "It's the bridge from one of the most heart-wrenching scenes in the movie."

"It's where one of his last letters recounts not only the day they met," Cara said, "but the way he felt about her right from the start."

Julia nodded in agreement. "The moment when he said that kissing her would be—"

"—the end of life as we know it," the two women said in unison. It was a moment that never failed to make Cara cry. Even just thinking about it now brought a tear to—

"Hey, wait a minute," she said, interrupting her own thoughts. "How did you know the character's names?"

"You said them while you were swooning," Finn said.

"I'll admit to the swooning," Julia said. "But we never said their names."

A furrow formed between Finn's brows. "Didn't ya?"

"Nope," Jonathan agreed.

"I'm sure they did." Finn shot Jonathan a look that clearly said, *Help a brother out.* It was fleeting, but not enough for Cara to miss.

Her mouth popped open in a gasp. "You knew their names!"

"I have three sisters," Finn offered as explanation. "They may have watched the film a time or two while I was in the room."

Julia narrowed her eyes. "Nice try. You like the movie."

"That's not what I said."

"You like the movie," Cara repeated.

A warmth flushed Finn's cheeks. "Okay. Maybe a little."

Cara didn't think it was possible to like Finn more than she already did, but apparently, she was wrong.

His admission seemed to have affected Julia as well. "For that," she said, sliding of the stool. "I'm definitely buying the next round."

The conversation flowed as easily as the beer, and by the third round, they'd moved to the back of the pub, where Julia and Finn turned a friendly game of darts into a serious competition. Most people would have wagered that the loser bought the drinks, but not those two. Equal parts generous and stubborn, Julia and Finn were battling for the right to pick *up* the tab.

After two games, they were locked in a tie.

"All right, you two," Jonathan said. "Let's settle this…" He held his empty pint glass in the air. "Before I die of thirst."

Finn pulled the darts out of the board. "One toss each. Highest score buys the rest of the night."

Julia raised one brow, then took a red dart out of his hand. "You're on."

"Julia went first last time," Jonathan said. He'd appointed himself the scorekeeper and judge when the wager began, a role he was taking far too seriously given the stakes. "So, Finn, you're up."

Finn drained the last of his pint, then took his position at the small, white line that had been painted on the wood floor. Raising his arm, he released the dart in a smooth motion. A wide grin spread across his face when it landed in the inner ring.

"Nice," Julia said. "Now move over and let me show you how it's done."

"Ooooh, burn," Jonathan said. The other three turned as one to look at him. "Yeah." Like the rest of them, he laughed. "I heard how that sounded too."

Julia was still smiling as she positioned her feet, but her expression shifted to steely concentration as she lifted her arm.

Cara watched as the red dart sailed through the air, landing squarely in the bull's eye. She knew it was all her friend could do not to break into a happy dance, but there was no stopping the gloating grin.

"Yes!" Julia said with a fist pump. "I'm buying."

Finn smiled and shook his head. "You're an odd lass, Julia Moretti."

Julia looked at Cara. "Smart boy you got there," she said. "Barely knows me and he's already figured that one out."

"Oh, I'm guessing he knew it day one," Jonathan teased.

"For that, you're going to come help me carry the drinks," she told him.

Jonathan followed Julia to the bar, but when he returned five minutes later, he was alone.

"I would just like to say that, for the record, I am not responsible for what's about to happen."

Cara's gaze shot to Julia, who was still standing at the bar. The look on her face was one Cara had come to know well. It was the one that said something big was about to happen. Only problem was, Cara never knew whether that something would be good or bad.

"Can I have your attention, please," the bartender said from a small stage in the back of the pub. He tapped the microphone, making it squeal, and winced. "Sorry 'bout that."

Cara grabbed Jonathan's arm. "What did she do?" she asked him, but it was the bartender who provided the answer.

"I have a fellow countryman here tonight, and I've just learned he's a fan favorite in the pubs back home. Let's see if we can't coax him into playing a song." A busboy appeared at the side of the stage with an acoustic guitar as the small crowd began to clap.

"I'm going to kill her," Cara whispered mostly to herself before turning to Finn. "You don't have to do this."

"I don't mind." He winked at Cara. "And if memory serves, you enjoyed it last time."

"I'd say she more than enjoyed it," Julia said from behind her.

"Wasn't that the night you—" Jonathan began.

Cara whirled around, stopping him midquestion. She wasn't

sure which of her friends was more deserving of her glare, but then the strum of a guitar narrowed her world to one.

She turned back toward the stage where Finn now sat on a stool, tuning the borrowed guitar.

"You'll have to forgive me if I'm a wee bit rusty," he said. A group of women near the stage let out a cheer.

"Say something in Irish," one of them said.

Finn smiled and shook his head. "It's all about the accent, innit?"

More cheering from the crowd.

"Back home, we play this song when a fella's about to propose," Finn said.

"Or a woman," Julia shouted.

"Aye, especially on Leap Day." Finn nodded as he gave one of the tuning keys a final turn. "This one's for you, Ann-am Cara," he said as he began to play the first few chords. The song sounded different than it had in the pub in Dublin all those weeks ago. Finn's acoustic version was slowed down and hauntingly beautiful, but there was no mistaking the lyrics of "Say Yes." It was a song Finn sang the night she first saw him play. The night she proposed.

The night she became his wife.

Cara watched him, mesmerized by the way his fingers glided up and down the neck of the guitar. He more than commanded the instrument, he caressed it. Somewhere in the back of her mind, Cara was aware of the crowd swaying beside her, the women near the front whispering and the bartender smiling. But all of that was secondary to what was happening on that small wooden platform.

Then he lifted his chin, and his gaze locked with hers. Even from across the bar, Cara could not only see but *feel* the sincerity in his eyes as he sang about her taking his hand and not holding back. She might not have remembered proposing, but there, in a dimly lit pub thousands of miles away, Cara remembered exactly how she felt that night. More than that, she knew in her heart that she wouldn't change a thing.

# CHAPTER 19

*IT WILL BE FINE,* CARA assured herself as she drove to work Monday morning. If it wasn't, at least the torture wouldn't last too long. She'd be moving to Jeremy's desk soon.

All that might have been true, but it didn't make her any less anxious about walking into Samantha's office, especially since the outfit of the day was solid black, which was as ominous as storm clouds rolling in during a day at the beach. And it certainly didn't stop her from putting it off as long as possible, which, while being a bit cowardly, also made good sense. Waiting until the end of the day meant that even if there was an initial storm, there was the possibility of it blowing over by morning. Of course, as with any hurricane, there was always the chance that it would pick up speed. Only time would tell.

At four thirty, Cara tapped on Samantha's doorframe. "Do you have a minute?" she asked.

Samantha looked up for a split second before refocusing her attention on her laptop screen. "One. Make it quick."

*Great,* Cara thought. Not the best mood for dropping this

kind of bombshell. She knew it would be ridiculous for Samantha to be angry with Cara for marrying Finn, but she also knew the fact that she'd been married for a few weeks and hadn't said anything wasn't going to go over well.

"I need to tell you something." Cara took a deep breath. "It's about Finn."

Samantha stilled. Now Cara had her full attention. "What about Finn?" she asked as she sat back in her chair.

Maybe it was the look on Samantha's face or the fact that Cara felt as though she could vomit at any second, but whatever the reason, her words came tumbling out in one long sentence as she recounted the details of her marriage to Finn, everything from the way they met to their decision to remain married, at least for the time being.

Samantha didn't say a word. She didn't even move. In fact, if it hadn't been for the occasional flare of her eyes, Cara would have thought her boss hadn't heard a word she'd said.

"I'm sorry I didn't tell you sooner," Cara said. "We honestly didn't think he would get the role, and if he hadn't...I know this makes things a little more complicated, so if there is anything you need me to do..."

"That will be all," Samantha said.

That was it? No questions? No yelling? She waited a beat, but when Samantha returned to her laptop, Cara returned to her desk. Business as usual. At least for the next forty-five minutes.

The fact that Samantha actually came out to the reception area instead of pressing the intercom button until Julia and Cara materialized in her office should have been the first indication that something was about to go terribly wrong. The fact that she strutted up to Cara's desk instead of Julia's should have been the second.

"Cara, I need you to get me the name of that lawyer we used for John Oliver's visa." She smoothed her hand over the twist in her platinum blond hair, knowing full well not a single strand was out of place.

"Sure thing." Confused, Cara's gaze shifted past Samantha to where Julia sat at her desk, but her friend looked just as clueless.

"Actually, just go ahead and call their office. Tell them I have a client who is going to need an O-1 visa, but make sure they know the casting news is embargoed until the official announcement." Samantha started back to her office, pausing at the doorway. "Oh, and, Cara, I'd recommend a little due diligence the next time a man tells you he's your husband. You were in Ireland after all, not Nevada."

With that, she was gone.

*What the...*

Cara shot Julia a panicked look.

"I'm already on it," Julia said. Her fingers flew across the keyboard in perfect sync with the butterfly wings flapping deep inside Cara's belly. This couldn't be true. Finn wouldn't lie to her, would he? Bile rose in her throat as she realized she didn't really know the answer to that question because she didn't really know him. Not all of him. But the part she did know didn't seem like the type of man who would deceive her. Not about something simple and certainly not about something this important.

Cara watched as Julia's eyes darted back and forth across her computer screen.

"What does it say?"

But Julia didn't tell her what she'd found. All she said was, "I'm sending you the link."

After what felt like forever, the information made its way across the cyber world to a desk that in reality was only three feet away. Cara clicked on the link the moment it popped up on her screen. It was from the official site of Ireland's Department of Justice and Equality. An entire page was devoted to foreigners seeking to marry in Ireland. Since she was fairly sure being ordained via the internet didn't earn affiliation with *any* church, she skipped the portion that pertained to religious ceremonies and scrolled directly to civil unions. She scanned the paragraphs of legal jargon, barely digesting the material as she sought the one section that would provide the answers she so desperately needed.

*...Apply to Registrar of Civil Marriages in Ireland...*

Cara's heart raced as she read through the step-by-step instructions required for noncitizens to marry in Ireland.

*...You must receive an acknowledgement from the Registrar... before you apply for a marriage visa...*

"Marriage visa?" Cara said, more to herself than anyone else.

*...the acknowledgement indicates the date that you officially notified the Registrar...*

"Maybe you don't need a visa for spontaneous weddings," Julia offered from across the room. "That's how it works here. At least I think it does."

Cara answered without giving her reply any thought. "Maybe." But then she read a line that stopped her dead in her tracks.

*…must apply to the Registrar at least three months before you intend to marry in Ireland…*

Cara looked at Julia for reassurance, but the concern she saw reflected in her friend's eyes told her she wasn't the only one assuming the worst. "It says you have to give them three months' notice."

"It's probably different if one of you is an Irish citizen," Julia said.

A voice inside her told Cara she was grasping at straws, but that didn't keep her from clicking through the site until she found the section pertaining to Irish citizens. Her throat burned as she read her findings out loud. "For a wedding to take place in Ireland, whether you are a citizen or a foreign national, you must notify the Registrar of Civil Marriages at least three months prior to your wedding."

"Shit," Julia whispered.

"I think I'm going to be sick," Cara said.

"You need to talk to Finn. I'm sure there's some reasonable explanation."

Cara's eyes darted to the clock on her desk. Five fifteen. Technically it wouldn't be leaving early but…

"Go," Julia said as if reading her mind. "She probably won't even notice, and if she does, I'll just say you're in the bathroom."

# CHAPTER 20

THE DRIVE TO MALIBU WAS a blur. The sunny California skies had given way to a steady rain that obscured Cara's view of the gray surf. Not that it mattered. She was too busy weaving through the traffic on PCH to take any notice of the view, and her mind raced even faster. Had he known all along? If so, why in the world did he let her think they were married? And more than that, why did he uproot his life to come with her to Los Angeles? The answer jolted through her body like the lightning that zigzagged through the sky. All at once, conversations from the past few weeks began playing through her head like a montage in a film.

Finn standing on the pool deck their first night in LA. *This isn't your beach house?*

The night she came clean about her job. *So you aren't a screenwriter?*

The day he turned up at her office. *I did a little acting in school, but not many opportunities where I'm from.*

Or the first time she met him, when she asked his favorite Oscar Wilde quote. *The truth is rarely pure and never simple.*

In Dublin, Cara had passed herself off as far more of a success story than she actually was. Had Finn only pursued her because he thought she was his ticket to Hollywood? If so, he must have felt like he'd hit the jackpot when she proposed.

Her shoulders sagged as the pieces of the puzzle all fell into place. She'd been a fool to think the handsome boy with the sexy brogue had fallen head over heels for an American tourist he barely knew, something she would no doubt obsess over for weeks, if not months, to come. But there was no time for that now. She had a fake husband to confront. Nursing her wounded ego would have to wait.

When Cara got to the house, she saw the lights were on in Penelope's den. Normally she would have cut through the main house on her way to the bungalow, stopping to make a bit of small talk before heading out back. But not tonight. She was too amped to chitchat about *Love Island* or to make Penelope a martini, let alone imbibe with her. Liquor was the last thing she needed on top of her already raging emotions. And besides, one look at Cara's face and Pippa would have known something was terribly wrong, and aside from confronting Finn, stressing out her elderly friend was the last thing she wanted to do.

The rain was falling harder as she reached the bungalow, but Cara still paused at the door, taking a moment to watch Finn through the window. He was sitting on the couch, reading a book with Oscar curled up at his feet. She'd come home to similar scenes before, and while the sight of him in her home still sparked a flurry of adrenaline somewhere deep inside her, this time, it was different. This time, it was more anxiety than excitement, because this time was the last time.

Cara drew a stuttering breath and reached for the doorknob, knowing full well that in a matter of minutes, everything would change.

Finn looked up, and his eyes grew wide. "Christ, you're soaked!" He dropped the book and within seconds had grabbed a towel from the bathroom. "Dry off, and I'll wet some tea."

"Stop," she said as he started toward her. Everything inside her wanted to let him wrap his arms around her and not only take away the chill that had seeped clear to her bones but to make everything in their world all right. But she knew he couldn't do that. Nothing Finn said was going to change the facts. No explanation could alter what she knew in her heart she had to do.

"What's wrong, luv?"

Cara flinched. *Luv* was an endearment Finn had used since the first night they'd met. At the time, she knew it was simply colloquial charm, but lately the word had seemed to hold more meaning. Not anymore.

"How long have you known?" she said, answering his question with one of her own.

His expression fell, but his words were steady. "Known what?"

Was he really going to make her spell it out?

"How long have you known we aren't actually married, Finn?"

He stilled. "Cara—"

"No." She squeezed her eyes shut. Hearing her name on his lips had always felt like a caress, and despite everything, it still did. If she had any hope of going through with this, she had to keep control of the conversation. "Answer the question."

But he didn't answer her. He didn't say a thing. He waited

for her to open her eyes, and when she did, she saw him looking at her as though their world were crumbling. And why wouldn't he? That was exactly what was happening. The only thing she couldn't figure out was why it mattered to him. He didn't need to continue the charade anymore. He'd used her connections, nailed the audition, and landed the most coveted part in town. Mission more than accomplished.

"Did you know that night at the pub that the ceremony was meaningless?"

"No. I promise you I didn't."

Cara raised a judgmental brow. "You actually said that with a straight face."

"Because it's true."

"So despite being born and raised in Ireland, you had no idea that you have to seek permission from some registrar three months before you can be legally married there?"

He ran a hand through his hair, then squeezed a clump of it in his fist. "It's not like I've ever been married before."

"That I know of." She wasn't giving him an inch, but Finn pressed on.

"None of my mates have gotten married—none of my sisters either—and it's not exactly something a single guy thinks about until he needs to." Finn lowered his arm and drew a deep breath. "I swear on my mam's life, I didn't know."

That one she believed.

"When did you find out?"

The look on his face told her she wasn't going to like the answer, but still he said nothing.

"When, Finn?" she repeated.

"That morning," he said, and all at once, the air rushed out of Cara's lungs. "I was going to tell you."

"When, after you'd made a few contacts? No, already did that. So yeah, maybe you decided to wait until you'd landed your first big role. Oh right, that's already happened too." Even to her own ears, Cara sounded harsh and bitter, but she was on a roll, and there was no turning back now. "So what was it going to take? What was going to make you finally man up?"

"I was waiting for the right time."

Cara's gaze shifted briefly to the bed, and her heart leapt into her throat. When she spoke, her voice was thick with the tears she struggled to keep at bay. "How many more times were you going to sleep with me before the time felt right?"

Finn straightened. "I wasn't using you," he said, looking her in the eyes. He seemed sincere, but no matter how much she wanted to, Cara knew she couldn't trust him.

"I really only have myself to blame." Her words dripped with sarcasm. "I let you think I was a big deal." She ticked the list off on her fingers. "Malibu house, Prada bag, Hollywood connections... although I guess that last part was true. Why wouldn't you want to hitch a ride with that? For a guy from Ireland who dreamed of being an actor, I must have seemed like an easy mark. All you had to do was seduce the broken-hearted American and—"

"It wasn't like that," he said, cutting her off.

"Oh, I think it was *exactly* like that."

Finn shook his head. "No. I liked you from the moment we met."

"Liked what you heard maybe. And then I got drunk and served myself up on a goddamn silver platter." She gave a harsh laugh. "Bet you couldn't believe your luck. No need for seduction. The fool actually proposed." The tears she'd fought now slipped down her cheeks.

"Cara." Finn reached for her, but she stepped back.

He dropped his hand to his side. "I wanted more time with you, which was why I asked you to stay in Dublin. You were the one who said you had to get back to LA. You were the one who asked me to come home with you."

Home. Her home. The home they now shared.

Cara shook her head. It wasn't real. This wasn't their home. They weren't husband and wife. They weren't anything at all. "I want you to leave," she said.

"Ann-am Cara, please…" His voice was barely a whisper as he called her by the nickname she'd never quite understood but had still come to love. It was more than she could bear.

Her heart was splintering into pieces.

"I'm going to go check on Penelope," she said, moving toward the door. It would have been so easy to change direction, to let Finn hold her and tell her it would be all right, that everything he'd said was real, even if the circumstances weren't. It wouldn't have been true, and deep down, Cara knew it. But that knowledge didn't ease the ache gripping her chest. It didn't quiet the voice in her head that begged her to let him at least try to make things right. And it didn't keep her from wanting, more than anything, to run into his arms. If she didn't get out of there, that was exactly what she was going to do.

She needed to go, to put one foot in front of the other until Finn was not only out of reach but out of her life.

Cara paused at the door, but she didn't turn around. "Please be out of here by the time I come back."

Once she was outside, the tears began to fall as quickly as the raindrops, and by the time she reached the main house, she could barely catch her breath. *Stop.* She had to get it together. No way she wanted Penelope to see her this upset. She paused at the door, wiped her face, and drew a deep, calming breath.

After a few more, she was ready to go inside. Or at least as ready as she was going to be.

"Good lord," Penelope said when she saw her. "You're a drowned cat."

"I, uh…"

"Let me get a towel," Penelope said. "And I'll meet you in the kitchen."

Cara had already put the teakettle on the stove by the time Penelope returned with the towel. "Aren't you having any?" she asked at the sight of only one mug on the counter.

Cara shook her head. "I'm going to have some in the bungalow—Sleepytime tea, I think—and make it an early night."

Penelope's eye narrowed. "Feeling okay?"

Cara was feeling far from okay, but she wasn't ready to talk about Finn with anyone, not even Penelope. Eventually, she'd tell her the whole story, but first she needed time to process. "I'm fine, just really tired."

"Well, if you think you're coming down with something, put a shot of whiskey in your tea tonight." A gleam lit her eye. "In fact, I think I'll add one to mine as well."

Whiskey was how this whole mess had started and was honestly the last thing Cara needed. "Thanks for the advice," she said, forcing a smile. "But I think I'll stick with a hot shower and a soft bed."

Cara made small talk with Penelope as she drank her tea. There was little doubt Penelope knew something was amiss, but as always, she didn't pry. Instead, she tried to distract Cara by telling her about the time Warren Beatty made pancakes for her in that very same spot. It almost worked too, at least enough to hold Cara's tears at bay.

As she was leaving, her phone vibrated in her pocket.

*Finn.*

She hated that he was her first thought, but there was no denying the way her heart sank when she saw Julia's name on the lock screen instead of his.

What did he say? Julia had typed.

He's known since the first morning.

There was a heavy pause before the next message appeared on the screen. Where are you?

Home, Cara replied.

And Finn?

As Cara rounded the path, she saw the bungalow was dark. He's gone, she wrote. It was what she'd wanted, what she'd demanded he do. But now...

Why did the doing the right thing have to hurt so freaking much?

*I'll be right there.*

The ocean breeze blew the cold rain against Cara's face in sharp contrast to the warm tears that once again streamed down her cheeks. *Thanks, but I just want to be alone.*

Cara was wet and tired and, more than anything, wanted to go to bed and wake up to find out the whole thing had been nothing more than a bad dream. But the truth was, she could sleep for days and that still wouldn't be the case. And that wasn't the only reality Cara had to face. As she burrowed under the covers that night, she had to admit that the pain she felt had nothing to do with her wounded ego and everything to do with her broken heart.

# CHAPTER 21

CARA WAS EARLY FOR WORK the next morning. And why not? Her personal life had gone from bad to good to worse, but if there was one thing she could count on, it was long hours at the office, which was exactly what she needed to take her mind off matters of the heart. More than that, today was the day she was going to give her two weeks' notice to Samantha. All she had to do was confirm everything with Jeremy one last time, then she'd march into Samantha's office, thank her for all the opportunities she'd given her (not), tell her how much she was going to miss working for her (definitely not), and wish her all the best. At least the last part was true. She didn't harbor any ill will against her soon-to-be ex-boss. She just didn't want to work for her anymore. How Julia had put up with Samantha for so long was beyond her. Probably had something to do with the thick skin she'd developed growing up with four older brothers. Still, for someone so tough, Julia had a heart of gold. Which was why she greeted Cara with a hug—and a box of Krispy Kreme donuts—the minute she walked in the door.

"You okay?" Julia asked, then rolled her eyes. "Sorry, stupid question. Of course you're not okay. Want to talk about it?"

"Not yet," Cara said. She still hadn't fully processed how she felt about everything that had gone down the day before. Explaining it to someone else would have been next to impossible. "If it's okay with you, I think I just want to focus on the future, at least for today."

"That sounds like an excellent plan," Julia said. "And you can start right now. Samantha had an appointment with her chiropractor first thing this morning, so she won't be in for another thirty minutes, and since I saw Jeremy's car in the lot when I pulled in…"

"No time like the present," Cara said.

"Exactly." Julia typed a quick message to Jonathan via the interoffice system. "He's got a ten-minute window in fifteen."

"Perfect." Except it was anything but. Cara knew the minute she tapped on his office door that something had gone terribly wrong.

"Cara, hey," Jeremy said. Unlike the last time, he didn't round his desk to greet her with a handshake. In fact, he didn't even stand up, and the expression on his face was far from a warm smile. More like guilt paired with a hefty dose of unease.

"Hey," Cara said. "Are you feeling okay? I can come back if this isn't a good time."

"No, no, come on in," he said. "And close the door behind you."

Cara did as she'd been told, then made her way to the chairs in front of Jeremy's desk. He didn't ask her to take a seat, but she did anyways. Something told her she was going to need to be sitting down for whatever he was about to say.

"Listen, I know I gave you the impression that moving you to my desk was just a formality," he began.

A knot formed in the pit of Cara's stomach. Jeremy had given her a whole lot more than an impression. He'd used the words "done deal." But there was no point in reminding him of that—seeing as there was little doubt he'd forgotten—which meant all Cara could do was sit there and watch her future plans fall apart at the seams.

"But some new information has come to light that prohibits me from offering you the position at this time."

His words were formal, and his tone was stiff. Nothing like the man she'd spoken to just a few weeks ago.

"I don't understand." Cara's mind raced through the events of the last month. "Did I do something wrong?"

"Not at all," Jeremy said, forcing a smile. "In fact, you've done everything right apparently."

Cara frowned. "Then why—"

"You've made yourself indispensable." The words were said quietly, but in Cara's head, they echoed like a slammed door. Jeremy didn't elaborate, not that he had to. Cara knew how to read between the lines. Samantha had blocked the move. She certainly had the power to do it, but why? What about Cara's coffee-fetching skills could be seen as indispensable? Hell, sometimes she felt as though a monkey could do her job. Unless...

"Is this about the *Mercury* casting?" The words had no sooner come out of her mouth than she regretted asking them. It was ridiculous to think her boss was keeping her chained to her desk out of fear of losing Finn as a client under normal circumstances, but considering the fact that he and Cara and weren't even on speaking terms, it was downright insane. Then again, Samantha didn't know they had split up. Sure, she knew they weren't married, but she didn't know Finn had moved out. Or did she? Cara had no idea where Finn had gone when he'd left the beach house. It wasn't like he knew many people in Los Angeles. For all Cara knew, Finn could have been staying at Samantha's house.

The thought settled like a brick in the pit of Cara's belly, but she pushed it away. Where Finn lived and what he did wasn't her concern. Not anymore. He wasn't her husband. He wasn't her anything. As for Samantha, her motivation really didn't matter because, in the end, the result was the same: her boss was blocking her attempt to move up in the world.

"Office politics can be tricky," Jeremy said. "I'm sorry, but I can't really say any more."

Now *that* Cara understood. Jeremy might have been the agency's rising star, but he wasn't immune to the office pecking order, and the fact remained that Samantha Sherwood sat at the head of the CTA table for a reason. Cara, on the other hand, was tired of begging for scraps at her feet.

"Thank you for considering me, Mr. Stone, and for your candor." Cara kept her voice even despite the tears that clogged the back of her throat. "I'm sure you will find someone who will do an excellent job."

She stood and extended her hand.

"Thank you, Cara," he said as they shook hands. "If there's ever anything else I can do for you…"

Cara nodded, then beat a hasty retreat all the way to the ladies' bathroom. But when she reached the door, she stopped short. *No more*, she thought. No more teary-eyed calming sessions in a bathroom stall, and no more wasting her time in a dead-end job. Her parents had flipped when she'd taken such a lowly position after the years—not to mention cash—spent on higher education. She'd assured them it was a means to an end, a way to get her foot in the door, a chance to pay her dues. But it didn't matter how many clichés she spouted to them or anyone else. Working for Samantha was getting her nowhere, that she already knew. But to have her block her attempt to move into a position that might actually advance her chosen career? For Cara, that was the last straw.

She stepped away from the door and drew a deep, cleansing breath through her nose. Enough was enough. The personal errands, unreasonable requests, and brutal hours were one thing—even the dog-sitting could be overlooked for the greater good—but Samantha had gone too far. If Cara didn't draw the line now, when would she? She had to make a change, and a drastic one at that, if she had any hope of chasing her dreams, because the way things were, they were dying a slow death.

With every step, her conviction grew stronger, and by the time she made it to the reception area, she knew exactly what she had to do.

"Is she back?" she asked Julia.

"Yeah, just came in, but don't worry. She doesn't realize—"

"Thanks," Cara said, interrupting her friend. It wasn't that she meant to be rude. It wasn't even that she didn't care whether or not Samantha knew she'd been gone. More that if she didn't keep moving, she would have time to think. And if she had time to think, she might chicken out. And if she chickened out, she knew she would regret it for the rest of her life.

Her first thought had been to grab her bag out of her desk drawer and just keep walking. As satisfying as it would have felt to have had her very own *Devil Wears Prada* moment, deep down, Cara knew that a dramatic exit like that only worked in the movies. In real life, all she would accomplish was trashing any hope of a decent letter of recommendation. Not to mention leaving her best friend to deal with the fallout. But as she stood in the doorway of Samantha's office, the option of running like hell suddenly sounded a lot more appealing.

Normally, a conversation like the one she was about to have would have required a significant amount of time spent writing and rewriting lines in her head followed by a mental pep talk worthy of a scene from *Rudy*. But Cara didn't do any of that. She didn't need to. Instead, she took another deep breath, then headed straight into the lion's den. Samantha looked up as she approached—undoubtedly about to make some snarky remark about knocking first—but Cara didn't give her time to say that or anything else.

"Sorry to interrupt," Cara said, even though she really wasn't. "First, I want to thank you for the opportunity you've given me over the past two years. I've learned a lot working on your desk." She really should have been thanking her for making the decision to leave so easy, but everything she said was technically true. Even the part about learning a lot was genuine, but in the end, the greatest lesson Samantha had taught Cara was to take control of her own destiny, which was exactly what she was doing now. "But I feel like it's time for me to move on to a new challenge."

Samantha's expression gave nothing away.

"I'll type up a formal letter of resignation," Cara said, filling the silence. "But please consider this my official two weeks' notice."

"No need," Samantha said.

"No need for a formal letter?"

"No need for two weeks' notice." Samantha hit the button on her phone's intercom, and a moment later, Julia was standing in the doorway. "Please let HR know they need to conduct an immediate exit interview," she told her before turning her attention back to Cara. "Gather your things, and leave your badge with security on your way out."

Cara and Julia stood side by side in stunned silence.

"That will be all," Samantha said, dismissing them with her usual indifference.

Cara didn't say a word as she packed up her personal items. She could feel Julia watching her, but she knew if she made eye contact with her friend, her carefully constructed armor would shatter. So instead, she moved quickly and efficiently through the process of leaving the only job she'd had since she moved to Los Angeles.

It wasn't until she was in the safety of her car that what she'd done began to sink in. Her decision was equal parts exhilarating and terrifying, and while her emotions were all over the place, one thing she didn't feel was regret. Not knowing what came next was *way* outside Cara's comfort zone, but she was confident that she'd made the right decision. Of course, that didn't mean she wasn't about to lose it.

She texted Julia before starting the drive to Malibu. Can you come over after work?

The reply was immediate and resolute. Absofreakinglutely.

# CHAPTER 22

THAT WAS THE THING ABOUT best friends. They gave you space when you needed it. They came when you called. And they always knew when to bring tequila.

"I'm sorry to have left you alone with her," Cara said as Julia poured them each a glass.

"No biggie." Julia shrugged. "I'm sure they'll have some poor mail room sap at your desk by morning." She waited for Cara to lick and salt the back of her hand, then passed her a shot glass and a lime wedge. "Think of how much fun I will have bossing them around."

"True," Cara said.

Leave it to Julia to find a silver lining in a thunderstorm. "To new beginnings," she said, clinking her glass against Cara's.

Cara licked the salt off her hand, downed the tequila, then sucked on the lime.

"There you go," Julia said after she'd knocked back her own shot.

Cara winced from the bite of the alcohol and lime. "It's gonna take a lot more than a shot to fix my life."

"But it's a start," Julia said, pouring them each another glass.

Cara plopped onto one of the kitchen barstools. "I'm having a serious case of déjà vu."

Julia laughed. "I'm not surprised. We've certainly had more than our fair share of tequila in this kitchen."

"Not just the tequila, but why we're drinking it." Cara resalted her hand. "Feels a lot like the night Kyle broke up with me."

Julia shook her head. "Totally different."

"But is it? Seems to me I've had quite a string of new beginnings. Would be nice if one of them would lead to a happy ending."

"You've had a rough day, so I'm gonna let that innuendo go even though it's killing me." Julia waited to see if her comment elicited any reaction, but when it failed to garner even half a smile, she changed tactics. "First of all," she said as she slid onto the stool next to Cara's, "that toast was for a new beginning in your professional life, not your personal one."

Cara snorted. "Neither one of them is anything to brag about."

"Second," Julia said, ignoring Cara's comment. "The situation with Finn is completely different than it was with Kyle."

"If that's supposed to make me feel better, it's a hard fail."

"Things with you and Finn are much more serious."

"*Were* more serious. Past tense. And again, not making me feel better. Finn was way worse. Kyle might have cheated on me, then broken up with me before a trip, but Finn pretended to be married to me."

"To be fair, he actually thought he was. For a while anyways."

"A few hours is not a while," Cara said. "Not that it makes

a difference. Doesn't matter if he knew for a few hours or a few days. He should have told me."

Julia's gaze softened. "Maybe he really liked you."

Cara's voice grew quiet. "That's what Finn said when I confronted him." It was the first time she'd talked about him since the night they broke up, if that was even what she should call it. Was there anything *to* break up if it was all just one big lie? Either way, Cara had been so busy dealing with the Jeremy/Samantha situation, she hadn't had a chance to tell Julia about the night Finn left. All she'd told her was that Finn had discovered the truth before they even left Dublin.

Julia watched her, waiting for her to speak or maybe sizing her up, Cara couldn't say for sure. "What else did he say?" she asked when Cara didn't offer more.

"That he was going to tell me but that he was waiting for the right time."

"That could be true. I mean, it's not exactly the easiest subject to bring up."

"We were together every day," Cara pointed out. "There were hundreds of opportunities to come clean. And it's not like waiting was going to make it any better. The longer he knew, the worse the truth would sound, especially after we started sleeping together." She stared at the empty shot glass she was turning in slow circles on the countertop. Long beats passed before she spoke the words that had occupied her mind since the moment she'd first discovered the truth. "It feels like he was just using me."

"Did you tell him that?"

Cara nodded. "He swore it wasn't true."

"Do you believe him?"

"Honestly? I don't know." Cara's shoulders sagged on a heavy exhale. It was true. She didn't know what to make of either Finn's words or his actions. Gestures that had once seemed so sweet—a kiss pressed to her neck as he passed by, the way he took her hand as they strolled on the beach, even the soft touches and whispered words they'd shared in bed—now felt suspect and insincere. Had anything with Finn been real? He was right about one thing though. Buying him a ticket to LA *had* been her idea.

"I *was* the one who suggested he come home with me," Cara said. "But I don't know, maybe that was his endgame all along. He said it himself, there aren't many opportunities to pursue an acting career in Ireland. Not in movies." She gave a small laugh. "If that's why he was with me, it certainly paid off."

"He didn't ask you for help," Julia said. "In fact, I was the one who suggested he audition for the *Mercury* role."

"That's true, but it doesn't change the fact that Finn has been lying to me since we left Ireland. Face it, Julia, there's no upside."

Julia poured herself another shot. "Oh, I don't know about that."

"You're not seriously going to try to convince me there's some silver lining here." Cara slid her own glass forward for a refill. "Cause that's a stretch, even for an eternal optimist like you."

Julia shrugged. "Maybe Finn was here to help you."

Cara rolled her eyes. She and Julia were different in so many ways, not the least of which was her friend's belief that people came into her life for a reason. Even the shitheads.

"Name one way my life is better for having met Finn Maguire."

"Spontaneity, for one," Julia said. "Everything in your life is always so planned out. Kyle is the perfect example of that, and look how it turned out with him."

"You suck at pep talks," Cara deadpanned.

"All I'm saying is that for the first time in your life, you were spontaneous."

Cara's head fell back on a genuine laugh. "You can't be serious?" she said. "Getting drunk and proposing to Finn was spontaneous all right. But I wouldn't call it a change for the better."

Cara had made a good point, but Julia was undeterred. "Let me ask you this," she said. "When was the last time you did one of those rewrites?"

"On my screenplay? I haven't had much time—"

"No," Julia interrupted. "That script thingy you do in your head when you're second-guessing something you've already said."

"I don't know. It's been a while." Cara hadn't realized it until that moment, but it actually had been *quite* a while.

"Since you came back here with Finn?"

"Not sure." She thought back. "It might have happened once or twice."

"Even that would be a huge improvement," Julia said. "And I think it's because you're different when he's around. I mean, sure, you get that dopey smile, but it's more than that. It's confidence."

Julia had a point. Before meeting Finn, Cara rewrote and replayed moments in her head on a daily basis. That wasn't to say she did or said everything right—far from it actually—but for some reason, it didn't bother her as much as it used to. Could Finn have had something to do with that?

"I'm not saying Finn gave you confidence. Personally, I think you've had it all along. You just let other people make you question yourself. With Finn, you didn't do that. You just *were* yourself. Maybe you need to remember that."

"Maybe."

"That's why the situations with Kyle and Finn are totally different. Kyle was a d-bag whose only purpose was to remind you, well, that men can be d-bags. But Finn…he brought a lot more to your life. He helped you to relax and be who you really are." Julia grinned, then added, "Not to mention the mind-shattering orgasms."

"There's the Julia Moretti I know and love."

"All I'm saying is I wouldn't be so quick to put Finn Maguire in the L column." She poured Cara another shot, then clinked their glasses together. "Now, let's drink until we can't remember our own names, let alone Finn's or Samantha's, and then tomorrow, we'll find you a new job."

......................................................

Tequila was just as evil as whiskey. At least this time Cara only woke up with a crushing hangover and not a tinfoil wedding band. She'd no sooner had the thought than images of Finn flooded her mind. So much for her pledge not to think about him for a solid twenty-four hours. She'd barely been awake five minutes, and she'd already blown that one.

After practically crawling to the bathroom and back, she

reached for her phone, only to remember that she no longer had a job, which meant there wouldn't be any pressing emails or urgent texts. Sure enough, the lock screen was blank. Figured. The only person who would ever text her before work was Julia, and judging by the condition she was in when her Uber picked her up the night before, she was probably doing all she could just to make it to the office without vomiting on her shoes.

On reflex, Cara launched the mail app. She was about to close it again when an email at the top of the list caught her eye. It was from Jeremy, only it wasn't from his CTA email but rather a personal Gmail account.

"I wanted to reiterate how sorry I am that things didn't work out," the email began. "But I'm sure you can understand the nuances at play."

Yeah, she understood all right. She understood so well, she'd marched her butt into Samantha's office and quit, something that hadn't fully sunk in and probably wouldn't until she'd had some water, Tylenol, and copious amounts of carbohydrates. Jeremy, however, had not only digested the news but was offering his help.

"Jonathan told me that you resigned yesterday," Jeremy wrote. "By the timing, I'm assuming it was prompted by our conversation. While I know that starting over can be daunting, knowing when it's time to move on is not only a sign of great wisdom but strength."

Cara nearly laughed out loud, and she would have if she hadn't been afraid her head might explode. Only time would tell if her decision to leave CTA was wise or not, but she certainly didn't feel strong. Exhausted, depleted, and adrift? Absolutely. But definitely not strong.

"Whatever comes next, I encourage you to continue writing," he said. "And when you do have a screenplay you think is ready for consideration, I would be happy to give it a read. It's the least I can do."

*Happy to give it a read? Least he can do?* Jeremy Stone represented some of the most successful writers in television. She'd hoped that after working for him for a year or two, he'd consider passing her spec along to one who was looking for a writer's assistant. But for him to offer to read a screenplay when she hadn't spent even a day on his desk? To say it was unexpected didn't even come close to describing how she felt.

Instinctively, Cara's gaze shifted to her small desk and, more specifically, to the drawer where her screenplay still sat unread by anyone but Finn. She'd been mortified that morning when she'd realized he'd read her script. Not that she wasn't proud of her work, but in her eyes, it was never quite to the point where she wanted anyone else to see it. There was always one more scene that need a punch-up. One more line of dialogue that needed a tweak. Was it truly because she thought it wasn't ready, or was Finn right? Was it good but not authentic and, deep down, she'd always known that?

That night, he'd asked her when the last time was she'd felt passionate about a project, and she'd answered without hesitation.

*That's the story you should be writing.*

Finn's words echoed through Cara's mind as she walked over to her laptop and opened a brand-new document. The blank page staring back at her was daunting, but naming the document took no thought at all. Cara typed "State of Grace" at the top of the page. It was only three words, but she already knew it was the start of a whole new chapter.

# CHAPTER 23

CARA WOKE UP SPRAWLED ACROSS her bed with her face smashed against the keyboard of her laptop, same as she had every morning for the past three days. Jeremy's email had lit a spark that Finn's words fanned into a flame, and before she knew it, Cara had found herself clicking through one website after another, devouring everything she could find about Grace Gifford Plunkett.

After that, everything was a blur. Her fingers had flown across the keyboard for the first few hours, making it seem as though the words appeared on the screen at the same moment they popped into her head. There were times when she'd dozed off or stopped to sift through the internet in search of more details, but for the most part, the past seventy-two hours had been an outpouring of emotion fueled in large part by coffee and gummy bears.

It was cathartic. It was a distraction. It was joy.

And then just before dawn on the third day, it was done.

For three years, Cara had obsessed over the screenplay that lived in her desk drawer, tweaking and retweaking it until it hardly resembled the story she'd first had in mind. This was different. She didn't second-guess her instincts, didn't overthink her word choices, and, more importantly, didn't hide the finished product in a drawer or anywhere else.

Her finger had hovered over the touchpad for all of ten seconds before she clicked the Send arrow. She must have fallen asleep right after that, because the "mail sent" message was still on the laptop when she woke the screen.

*Too late to second-guess now*, she thought as she crawled out of bed. Every muscle in her body ached as she stood. She stretched, then surveyed the damage: take-out containers, coffee cups, and candy wrappers were everywhere. The fact that you could get just about anything delivered at any time of the day or night was definitely a double-edged sword. But what was worse than the mess was the silence. Cara had lived alone since college. Solitude had not only never bothered her; she had craved it. But this wasn't alone time; this was loneliness.

Finn had only lived in the bungalow for six weeks, and yet in that time, he'd become not only part of her life but her home. She'd grown used to the sight of him, seated at the island as he drank coffee and pored over the day's news, lounging on the couch as he studied lines, or lying beside her in bed. But now, standing in the middle of the bungalow, all she saw were the faded remnants of those images. Her home felt quiet and still. But more than that, it felt empty.

And on top of that, for the first time in years, she had absolutely nothing to do. She was debating between going for a jog on the beach—something she'd never done—and door-dashing an order of Belgian waffles—something she'd done more times than she could count—when she heard a commotion on the pool deck.

She walked outside to find Penelope watering the flowers Finn planted.

"You're awake."

"Barely." Cara gave a weak laugh.

"I was starting to wonder if you were ever coming out." Penelope smiled.

"Yeah, sorry about that," Cara said. "I hope I didn't worry you."

"Pish, no need to apologize. I'm not your keeper. And I knew you were still alive thanks to the steady stream of deliveries."

Cara picked up the extra watering can and began to fill it from the hose. "I wrote a screenplay."

Penelope smiled in her direction. "I'm not that senile, dear. I remember your screenplay. Still waiting for you to let me read it."

"No," Cara corrected. "I wrote another one." She poured water into a large potted fern. "Over the past three days."

"Correct me if I'm wrong, but haven't you spent nearly three years on the first one?"

"Yep."

"Then I'd say that's progress," Penelope said with an emphatic nod.

"It's something, all right." This time, Cara's laugh was strong. "Let's just hope Jeremy likes it."

Penelope stilled. "The agent you're going to work for? You sent it to him?"

"I did. But I'm not going to be working for him." Cara inched her way closer to Penelope, watering flowers as she explained the events that had taken place on her last day at CTA.

"High time," Penelope said. Cara wasn't surprised. While Penelope enjoyed the gossip Cara heard at her job, her benefactress thought her time there was a waste of her talents. "And you owe it all to that trip to Ireland."

Now that one she didn't see coming. "How do you figure?"

"If you hadn't gone to Ireland, you wouldn't have met Finn. If you hadn't met Finn, you wouldn't have married him."

Cara's gaze shot to Penelope.

"Yes, I know about that. You went to Dublin over Leap Day, my dear. I may be nearly as old as that tradition, but I can still put two and two together. Plus, it was hard to miss the foil ring on the boy's finger that first day."

She had her there.

"And if you hadn't married Finn," Penelope continued. "Then you wouldn't have brought him home with you, he wouldn't have gotten that role in *Mercury*, and Samantha wouldn't have cared if you moved out from under her nose."

It took a long and winding road to get there, but she had a point. Mostly.

"Only one problem with your logic," Cara said. "Finn and I were never really married."

"Is that so?" Penelope's voice was level, but her eyebrows were high.

Cara nodded. "And he moved out." She set her watering can on the ground and collapsed onto one the chaises. "You might want to sit down for this one, Pippa."

"From the look on your face, I'm thinking we might need vodka."

"It's not even lunchtime."

"*What?*" Penelope asked, feigning offense as she stretched out on the chaise beside Cara's. "I'd put orange juice in it."

Cara smiled and shook her head, but her amusement faded as she recounted the truth she'd discovered that week. "And here I thought Kyle had done me wrong," she said on a forced laugh when she was done. "He had nothing on Finn."

"Forget Kyle," Penelope said, waving her hand through the air.

"I had. But you know how the ghosts of boyfriends past love to rise from the dead whenever there is a fresh heartache."

"Well, let's exorcise that demon right now, then."

Cara had no idea where Penelope was headed, but she was down for the ride.

"Seems to me you were so busy being upset about the fact that Kyle didn't want you anymore that you forgot to ask yourself whether *you* actually wanted Kyle."

She had a point. Cara certainly hadn't been head over heels for Kyle in the beginning. In fact, he sort of had to talk her into it. Kyle had come on strong, wooing her as though he'd read a textbook called "How to Win a Girl in Five Dates." Now that she thought about it, she kind of hated herself for falling for it even more than she hated Kyle for doing it.

"Don't beat yourself up over it, sweetie," Penelope said, demonstrating once again her uncanny knack of reading Cara's mind by studying her face. Cara often wondered if her ability to not only convey her emotions but to read those of others as well was part of what made Penelope such a fabulous actress back in her day. "He was in pursuit mode. It would be hard for any woman to withstand the charms he was laying on you, but sometimes you just have to say, 'Yeah, I know I'm that great. What else you got?' because if you ask me, the guy was a bit of a twat."

Penelope certainly had a way with words, she'd give her that, and Cara couldn't help but smile. "I didn't think of it like that at the time," she said. "I thought of it as being swept off my feet. I mean, when the guy makes some grand gesture in a rom-com starring Ryan Reynolds—or that other Ryan whose name I always forget—it doesn't seem predatory or controlling, it seems romantic and perfect." Cara groaned. "But nothing about Kyle was perfect, and yet I fell for it."

"Nothing about life is perfect," Penelope said. She sure had that part right.

"Doesn't make me feel any less foolish."

"Yes, but look how far you've come."

"Right," Cara snorted. "All the way to the altar with a man I barely knew. Except, oh wait, it wasn't legal, and he knew it. Not exactly what you'd call progress."

"That's not the way I see it," Penelope said. "With Kyle, he made all the plans and you followed along, even though I suspect something inside was telling you that it wasn't what you really wanted. But with Finn, there were no plans. Every time you saw him, it was spontaneous. Every moment was genuine. And instead of letting a man dictate your life, you grabbed your future by the balls and took what you wanted."

There was that way with words again.

"Don't roll your eyes at me, young lady. I'm nearly three times your age." Truth be told, Penelope had more than tripled Cara's age, but far be it for her to blow a woman's cover. "I know you like to blame it on the whiskey, but I suspect the truth is, you knew you'd found something special with Finn, and on your last night in Ireland, you decided not to let it slip away. Hell, I'm proud of you for proposing. I'm proud of you for marrying him. And I'm proud of you for bringing him back to LA. The only question I have for you is why the hell are you letting him go now?"

"I appreciate everything you're saying, Pippa, I really do. Not sure I agree that my drunken proposal is something to be proud of, but the part about every moment being genuine?" A lump formed in Cara's throat. "That's how it seemed at the time, but now..."

"You're looking at it all wrong," Penelope said. "Sure, some people might say marrying Finn was crazy, but others would say it was crazy romantic. And yes, some might say the fact that he may have had ulterior motives when he got here negates the fact that he's in love with you now, but others—myself included—would say it proves that his feelings are all the more genuine. And while the actual wedding might not have been legal, it doesn't mean—"

"Wait, back up. What did you just say?"

"That people might say your spur-of-the-moment Leap Day wedding was romantic?"

"No," Cara said. "The next part. You think he's in love with me?"

"Sweetie, I can barely see three feet in front of me, and even I can see that." Penelope leaned over and placed her hand on top of Cara's. "Love isn't always shown in grand gestures," she said. "Sometimes it's the simple acts that mean the most."

"What if it was *all* an act? What if he was just doing it to extend his time here?"

"The eyes don't lie, Cara. And the way that boy looked at you..." Penelope drew a deep breath. "I've been around a long time, dear, and I know love when I see it. But you don't have to take my word for it." She pulled an envelope out of the pocket of her caftan and handed it to Cara. "I suspect the young man makes it pretty clear in this."

"Where did you get this?"

"Finn dropped it off first thing this morning," Penelope said.

"He did?"

She nodded. "He asked me to give it to you tonight and not a minute sooner. Made me promise, as a matter of fact, but we both know I've never been very good at keeping promises." She stood and started toward the house. "Now, if you'll excuse me, I'm going to see about that drink."

Cara's fingers shook as she opened the envelope and unfolded the paper.

*Cara,*

*You never asked me what I wished for that day you saw the ladybug. The answer is simple: more of you. When we woke up together in my bed that last morning in Dublin, my first thought wasn't regret but relief because those tinfoil rings meant we weren't saying goodbye. Not yet at least. I wasn't ready for you to walk out of my life. It was why I asked you to stay and why I flew back with you. I didn't come to LA looking for a career. I came because I wanted to spend more time with you.*

*You've told me how embarrassed you were when we first met—doused in water and hiding behind the seat of my car. I believe your exact words were that you wanted the ground to swallow you up. The truth is, you captured my heart that day, and it's been yours ever since. I love you, Cara, which is why I'm leaving. By the time you read this, I'll be on my way home. I've told Samantha to turn down the role because as much as I want it, I could never be part of something that had caused you pain. If an acting career is meant to be, then it will happen without involving you in any way.*

*I'm so sorry for not telling you the truth from the start, and while it doesn't change the fact that I deceived you, I want to assure you that my motives were never about anything but you.*

*Always,*
*Finn*

Penelope strolled onto the deck just as Cara finished reading the note. Sure enough, she'd made herself a screwdriver. Light on the orange juice, if the color was any indication. "Oh dear," Penelope said when she saw the tears in Cara's eyes. "For once, I wish I was the kind of old lady who carried Kleenex in her pocket."

Cara wiped her face with the back of her hand. "The stupid part is, it's not even the letter that made me cry."

"What was it then?"

"There's this nickname Finn had for me and reading this…" She looked down at the letter she held in her hands. "I know it sounds crazy, but it was like I could hear him saying it again now."

"What did he call you?"

Cara was almost too embarrassed to say it out loud. "Ann-am Cara." She shrugged. "Just some silly version of my name." She shrugged. "It doesn't even make sense and yet…"

"*Anamchara*," Penelope said in an accent nearly the same as Finn's. "It's not a silly version of your name. It's an Irish term of endearment. It means soul mate."

Cara's breath caught. "What? Are you sure?" Had Finn been telling Cara how he felt about her all along?

Penelope nodded.

Still, she needed to be sure. "How do you know that?"

"I was engaged once," Penelope said with as little fanfare as if she'd merely commented on the weather. "To an Irishman in fact." If Penelope had dropped that little bomb at any other time, Cara would have had a million questions for her. But coming on the heels of the whole soul mate thing, the second revelation rendered her speechless.

"He was an actor as well." Penelope took a seat on the chaise beside Cara. "In those days, the studios liked to pair us up. You know, for publicity. Eamon—that was his real name, but they made him change to something that sounded more American— had been matched with a sweet young thing from Oklahoma about six months before we met. When we did…" She stared out at the ocean. "It was love at first sight."

A few silent beats passed, and for a moment, Cara thought that might be all Penelope said on the subject.

"After he proposed, he went to the studio and told them he wanted to stage a fake breakup for his fake relationship," Penelope added. "But the suits weren't having it. They were afraid it would be worse than the Eddie Fisher situation." She didn't need to explain any further. Even Cara knew of the fiasco that had erupted when the singer had left Debbie Reynolds for Liz Taylor.

"What happened between the two of you?"

Penelope shrugged. "We parted ways and focused on our careers. At the time, we thought it would be temporary." Tears pooled in the old woman's eyes. "We were so busy filming love stories, we let our own slip away." She took a sip from her drink, then straightened. "And now you're doing the same thing, Cara. You've been so busy waiting for your life to turn into one of the rom-coms you're always watching that you haven't even realized you're living one right now."

"He's leaving, Pippa. He told Samantha to turn down the role, and he's flying back to Dublin. Today. That's why he didn't want you to give this to me until tonight. He didn't want me to know how he felt until after he was gone."

"So I was right. He *is* in love with you."

"That's what he said." Although his words hadn't really sunk in.

"And he's leaving because he wants to prove that his love is real and not tied to his career," Penelope said. It wasn't a question. "Call him."

"Right now?"

"Right now."

Cara pulled her cell phone out of the pocket of her sweatshirt, opened the call log, and hit Finn's number. She had no idea what she was going to say to him, but in the end, it didn't matter. "It went straight to voicemail." Made sense, seeing as how Samantha had no doubt been blowing up his phone.

"Then I only have one question for you," Penelope said. "What the hell are you doing here talking to me? I didn't get my Hollywood ending, but it's not too late for yours."

"What do you want me to do, race to the airport and try to stop him?" Cara was only joking, but the look on Penelope's face told her that was exactly what she wanted her to do. "You can't be serious."

"I know in the movies it's usually the other way around, and nine times out of ten, it's the male lead who makes the over-the-top romantic gesture, but this isn't someone else's story, Cara. It's yours. So go. Walk into that airport and tell the guy with the accent that you're just a woman asking a man to love her."

Cara would have taken a moment to explain that the scene Penelope described actually *was* from someone else's story, but that was beside the point. Penelope was right. It didn't matter how their relationship started. Cara loved Finn and she needed to tell him before he left the country.

"Thank you, Pippa," Cara said, pressing a kiss to her cheek. "Wish me luck."

Penelope pulled a small, leather box out of the pocket of her caftan. "Open it at the airport." She smiled. "You'll know what to do."

Normally, curiosity would have gotten the better of her, but at the moment, Cara had a bigger issue on her mind. She needed to stop her husband from getting on that plane.

# CHAPTER 24

CARA NEEDED TO FOCUS ON what she was going to say to Finn, but before she could do that, there was one item that was nearly as pressing as stopping him from boarding that flight.

She pulled up her contacts as soon as she was in the car but stopped short of dialing Samantha's cell. If she had any hope of her former boss answering the call, she needed to block her number from showing up in caller ID. Besides, nothing said "potential client" quite like a private caller.

Samantha answered on the first ring. "Samantha Sherwood."

"Don't hang up," Cara said. Might as well get right to the point, because once Samantha heard Cara's voice, there was little doubt that would have been her next move. "It's about Finn."

"You mean the man you married but didn't really marry? I'm not interested."

"No, the man who is going to be the biggest client you've had in a decade."

Samantha made a most unladylike sound on the other end of the line. "You really should get your facts straight."

"I know the facts, Samantha. I know he told you to turn down the role. But I also know that there's no way you would have done that just yet. Not without trying to convince him to stay."

A dog barked in the background.

"Is that Oscar?"

"Yes," she said. "Bad enough Finn left me with this contract mess, but apparently he expects me to sort getting his dog back to Ireland as well."

"With any luck, you won't have to do either one."

Samantha exhaled a heavy breath. "Look, I tried, but he wouldn't budge. And now his cell is going straight to voicemail, and I have no idea where he is."

"I do," Cara said. "And I'm hoping I can change his mind. Do me—no, do yourself and Finn a favor, and sit on this news as long as you can."

"The press conference is Monday. I can't very well let them announce the star of the biggest franchise since *Star Wars* and have the spotlight fall on an empty chair."

Samantha was right. That kind of stunt would burn more than a few bridges. But if Cara knew Finn half as well as she thought she did—she glanced at the letter sitting on the passenger seat—and if he meant half of what he'd written, then as long as she got to him, everything would be fine. All she needed was a little time.

"Three hours," Cara said. "Hold off on making the call for three hours. If you haven't heard from me by then, do what you have to."

No response.

"Please, Samantha, you owe me this much. And if you won't do it for me, then do it for Finn and the fifteen percent he's going to pay you."

A few tense moments of silence passed, but when Samantha spoke, the edge to her voice had softened. Not that the woman could ever manage warm and fuzzy, but for her, it was a major about-face. "Fine," she said. "But I'm calling the producer in three hours and not a minute later."

Now all Cara had to do was get to Finn before he boarded that plane.

........................................

Cara had only flown first class once in her life, and while she wouldn't have minded doing it again sometime if for no other reason than to experience the wonders known as the First-Class Lounge, at the moment, all she really wanted was a shorter line at the Emerald Air ticket counter. She inched forward, then checked her phone. Finn's flight—or what she assumed was Finn's flight seeing as how it was the only nonstop of the day—was due to depart in just over an hour. If she didn't get through the security line in the next thirty minutes, she was screwed.

While she waited, she snuck a peek inside the small box Penelope had placed in her hand. When she did, she smiled. Penelope was right; Cara knew exactly what to do. Assuming she got to Finn in time.

A door opened behind the counter, and a woman in a green blazer emerged. Within minutes, she was opening a new station at the ticket counter. Only problem was, it was yet another for first-class passengers. In for a penny, in for three grand, Cara thought as she ducked under the rope to the empty priority line.

The desk agent greeted her with a warm smile that reached her bright-blue eyes. "Good afternoon," she said with a hint of an Irish brogue. "Passport and itinerary?"

"Actually, I need to buy a ticket," Cara said as she handed over her passport. "Flight 1207 to Dublin."

"I'm sorry, but that flight is sold out."

"Even first class?"

The woman nodded. "And we're under the required time for international bag check."

"I don't have any bags," Cara said. "I don't even really want to go to Dublin. Not that it wasn't wonderful. I mean, I met my future husband while I was in Ireland—married him then too—which is crazy considering I flew there nursing a broken heart." She frowned. "Or at least I thought I had a broken heart. But it's nothing compared to the way I feel now."

The woman's eyes grew wide. "You flew to Dublin with a broken heart and flew back with a husband?"

Cara nodded.

An internal struggle flashed across the agent's face. One she ultimately lost, or won, depending on her perspective. "It's none of my business but... How did that happen?" It was a fair question. One Cara couldn't really blame her for asking.

"Leap Day," Cara said.

"Ahh. Caught up in the spirit, were ya?"

"More like caught up in the whiskey," Cara said. "But yes, I saw a woman propose in the pub where Finn's band was playing, and one thing led to another, and next thing I knew—"

"You were down on one knee?"

"Exactly. I woke up with a wedding ring on my finger, which is why he came back here with me. Except it turns out we were never really married. Well, we were married, or rather we had a wedding, but it wasn't legal because the priest wasn't really a priest, he was a minister of the internet, which might have been okay, but we hadn't asked permission of the Registry."

"Registrar?"

"Yes, that, which is why the wedding wasn't legal, but that doesn't change anything as far as I'm concerned. I thought it did. I was so angry when I found out he'd known it wasn't real pretty much all along. I told him I never wanted to see him again, and the look on his face..." Tears welled in Cara's eyes. Not for herself but for how she'd hurt Finn. "That's why he's about to get on that flight. I have to stop him. I have to tell him how I feel."

For a moment, the woman looked as though she might cry as well, but then she straightened and drew a deep breath. "Let's get you to that gate," she said as her fingers flew across her keyboard. "Okay, yes, this is good."

"What?" Cara said. Good was definitely a good start, but she was running out of time.

"The flight is leaving from the domestic terminal, which means you don't need a ticket to Dublin after all. I'll just book you on a flight out of that same terminal." She tapped a few more keys. "There's one to Las Vegas. Oh, and an even cheaper one to Dallas."

An idea began to take shape in Cara's head. "Let's go with Vegas," she said as she handed over her credit card.

The woman gave her a knowing smile, then got right to work. When she was done, she handed Cara the boarding pass. "I'll call the gate and ask them to stall, but hurry because there's only so much they can do."

The woman didn't need to tell her twice. Cara thanked her, then raced to TSA, where she shamelessly begged passengers to let her to the front of the line. She'd always hated when people did that—they shouldn't have cut it so close and all that—but desperate times called for asshole measures, and while a few people gave her dirty looks, most were quite supportive when she frantically explained it was a matter of the heart. Still, even with the kindness of strangers, Cara found herself sprinting through the terminal.

Hopefully she wasn't too late.

# CHAPTER 25

FLIGHT 1207 WAS BOARDING AT the end of the concourse. Cara really shouldn't have expected anything less. No way she was going to stroll up calm, cool, and collected like Julia Roberts when she walked into that bookstore in *Notting Hill*. Nope, in Cara's version of a romantic gesture, the heroine was a sweaty, out-of-breath mess.

She scanned the seats while fighting the urge to collapse into one herself.

"Cara," Finn said from behind her.

She spun around so quickly, she nearly passed out.

"What are you doing here?" He seemed genuinely surprised.

"I came to tell you off." Her breath was coming in short, sharp pants. Damn, she really should have taken up jogging when she moved to the beach. Lot of good that yoga app was doing her now.

"You have every right to be angry," Finn said. "But—"

"You're damn right I'm angry," she said, cutting him off. "How dare you try to skip town?"

"I deserve whatever you want to throw at me. But I didn't think you wanted to see—"

"After everything we've been through," she said, interrupting him once again, "you leave me a letter, telling me everything I wanted to hear, but tell Pippa to wait and give it to me *after* you've left town. That's low, Finn, really low."

"The letter wasn't meant to upset you. And I wasn't trying to tell you what you wanted to hear. It's how I really feel."

"It doesn't change the fact that you're a jerk."

Finn nodded. "I know. I never should have—"

Cara would have thought by this point, Finn would have just shut up and let her say her piece. "A woman doesn't want to hear that kind of stuff in writing. In a way, it's even worse than a breakup email." Part of her knew she could have really benefited from a few scripted lines, but Cara was on a roll. The words that spewed from her heart to her mouth were the truth, and eloquent or not, he needed to hear them. He needed to know how she felt. "When a woman is in love with a man, she deserves to hear how he feels face-to-face. Not in some letter that gets delivered after it's too late to stop him from getting on the plane."

His eyes darted to hers. "Did you just say…"

"That I love you?"

He nodded again.

"Yes," Cara said. "I love you. I don't know exactly when—"

This time, it was Finn who did the interrupting, silencing Cara with a kiss that made it clear he was a man who'd more than just had his wish granted. He had everything he'd ever wanted. "I love you too," he said when he finally broke their kiss. The adrenaline coursing through her veins had slowed to a steady hum, but it was his words that sent a shiver racing across her skin.

"Did you really think it would make me happy to never see you again?" she asked.

"I knew I'd hurt you." Finn's arms tightened around her as he pulled her against his chest. "And as much as I wished it weren't the case, I didn't think you'd want to be with me again after that."

"You do have a point," she said.

The muscles in Finns arms tensed.

Cara leaned back to meet his furrowed brows with a raised one of her own. "You realize it's going to be a colossal pain in the ass hanging out with Hollywood's hottest leading man," she said.

Reality dawned. "You're—"

"Taking the piss." She smiled. "Although there will be *some* downsides. Women are going to be throwing themselves at you left and right."

"I don't want to be with any woman but you."

"And then there's the paparazzi."

"I don't want to be with them either," he teased.

Cara laughed. "No, but they will be there anyway. Which means I'm going to have to stop wearing my pajamas on our Sunday-morning coffee run."

"I love your pajamas. Especially the ones with the flying pigs." He leaned closer and whispered. "I like them on the floor even better."

Cara rolled her eyes at his cheesy line. "Well, they won't look great on TMZ."

"You won't have to worry about any of that, luv. I turned

down the role. I didn't come to LA to become a movie star. I came to spend more time with you."

"Hmm, that's a shame, because there's a script I think you would really love. No one has picked it up yet, but with the right star attached, it would probably get a green light—as a small indie, but still."

"What's it about?"

Cara tried her best to keep a straight face but failed. "Ireland's Easter Rising," she said.

The dots connected, and Finn broke out in a smile that matched her own. "You wrote Grace's story?"

"Yes."

"Now *that* sounds like a film I'd like to make."

"You'd be perfect for the role of Joseph. You'll have to shoot *Mercury* first though."

"Is that so?"

"Definitely. For starters, it's the smart thing for your career. And the high profile of a blockbuster film would all but ensure that the indie one gets made. Of course, we're going to want to lock you in before the success of that film drives your price up. Nothing personal," she added. "It's just good business."

"Understandable." Finn was trying his best to sound professional, but the light in his eyes was *all* mischief.

"Still, some will say we only got you for the role because you're the screenwriter's husband, but nepotism is rampant in Hollywood—I mean, *hello*, half of *Schitt's Creek* was related—so screw them. Haters gonna hate."

Finn's head fell back on a laugh.

"I'm serious."

"I know you are, luv. One problem though. Actually two."

"And those are?"

"Like I said, I told Samantha to turn down the role."

"Then lucky for you I called her on the way to the airport and asked her to sit on the news."

"And she agreed?"

Cara nodded. "Until the end of the day. You just have to call her."

"There's still the other matter."

"Which is?"

"I'm not the screenwriter's husband."

"Already thought of that." And so had Penelope.

Cara pulled out the leather box Penelope had given her and dropped to one knee. A woman beside Finn gasped and, in the distance, Cara heard a man with a heavy brogue say something about how Leap Day had already come and gone. He had a point. Not that it mattered. Cara didn't need a holiday to go after what she wanted. And what she wanted was to marry Finn.

She flipped open the top of the box to reveal a pair of gold Claddagh rings. "Finn Maguire, will you marry me?"

Finn's eyes grew wide at the sight of the Irish wedding bands. "Where did you get these?"

"Pippa gave them to me," Cara said. "It's a long story that I will be happy to share with you later, but right now..." She glanced at the crowd that had formed a circle around them. "I'm kind of on my knees here with a question pending."

Finn cracked her favorite lopsided grin. "Of course I will

marry you," he said. "Every day of the week and twice on Sunday."
He pulled Cara to her feet and into a kiss that had the crowd
around them cheering.

"We have an audience." He'd broken their kiss but not their
contact, resting his forehead sweetly against hers.

"Guess we better get used to that."

"Mm-hmm." He hummed his agreement as he stole yet
another kiss. "What now?"

"Now," Cara said, rearing back to look at him. "There's the
matter of our flight."

Instinctively, Finn glanced over his shoulder to where the
Jetway door remained closed. "I was thinking I'd skip the trip
across the ocean and just stay here with my fiancée." The words
had no sooner left his mouth than his eyes narrowed. "Wait, did
you say *our*?"

This time, the warm flush that crept over Cara's face had
nothing to do with her airport sprint and everything to do with
hearing Finn refer to her as his fiancée. "Yes," she said.

Finn's brows knit together. "You're going to Dublin?"

"No." She shook her head. "And neither are you."

Finn looked thoroughly confused. It was downright adorable.
"Sorry, luv, but you've lost me."

"We are *both* going to Vegas." Cara took her boarding pass
out of her bag. "We need to have them pull your luggage and go
see my new friend at the counter about getting you a ticket, but
then—"

"Why Vegas?" Finn interrupted.

She cocked her head to one side. "To get married, of course."

His eyes grew wide. "You want to marry me *today*?"

Cara nodded. "Does that sound okay?"

"Sounds smashing." The words weren't really necessary. Finn's feelings on the matter were written all over his face.

"Come on," she said, taking his hand. "Let's go get hitched."

Which was exactly what they did.

And the next morning, both of them remembered it.

# EPILOGUE

MY HUMAN GOT MARRIED. AGAIN.

I thought he'd been hitched since we left Ireland, but I found out differently about six months ago when he and Cara were sitting on the couch looking at photos from a ceremony that had taken place the year before in some town they referred to as Sin City. No idea why it's called that, but they looked really happy in the pictures, so I guess it's a good thing. In a few of them, they were posing with some guy wearing sunglasses and a sparkly jumpsuit, but for the most part, it was just Finn and Cara, smiling and slobbering all over each other.

They didn't take me with them on that trip, which was fine, but I was pretty pissed—and let them know by, well, pissing— that they didn't take me to Dublin last summer for the wedding reception Finn's family threw at the pub where the wedding-that-wasn't-a-wedding took place. Everyone knows I like a party as much as the next canine, plus it had been ages since I'd snatched a decent sausage off someone's plate. But Finn said if he took me with him, I would have to quarantine in something he called doggie jail, which did not sound like fun. Instead I stayed with Coco and our offspring at her Bel Air home. Her human was livid when she found out I'd knocked up her precious poodle, but she came around after the puppies arrived. She and Cara actually get along now, something Cara says was made possible by the "wad of cash" Finn made her, but personally I think it has more to do with the pups. I've never seen a woman lose her mind like that. Baby talk is one thing—"who's a good boy" and all that—but Samantha takes it to a new level. She insisted on keeping the entire litter—three boys and a girl—which was fine with me and made Coco so happy, she ran in circles for a solid ten minutes. So now we have something called a custody arrangement. Don't know what that is, but it must be funny judging by the way the humans laugh when they talk about it. All I know for sure is that it means I get to spend half my time in Bel Air with Coco and the kids, and the five of them spend the other half with me in Malibu.

Not tonight though. Tonight, I'm flying solo with Finn and Cara to something called a premiere. According to them, I was invited because I'm now a movie star. Not sure how that happened, but best I can tell, I did such a good job eating a bowl of food that day in the park that they wanted me to do tricks with Finn while he was dressed up in some strange clothes. That was all fine because every time I did a trick, I got a treat, but I never understood why there were so many people watching us or why some woman would come over every now and then to paint stuff on Finn's face. He didn't seem to mind though. In fact, he seemed really happy.

"Ten minutes out," the man in the front seat said. The car he brought to pick us up was longer than any I'd ever seen before. It stretched the entire length of the driveway, and inside it had long bench seats and bottles of water, plus a few of the ones that make me bark when the cork pops. There's been a lot of popping corks in our lives lately—for the anniversary and the arrival of the puppies but also for the script Cara sold and at some party for our movie where a very large man yelled, "That's a wrap."

Not tonight though. Tonight, the bottles with the foil tops sat untouched, although they did let me eat a few of the ice cubes from the bucket.

"Come here, boy," Finn said. He patted the seat next to him, and I moved to join him and Cara on the other bench. He was holding her hand with one of his, like he always does, but with the other, he stroked my head, paying special attention to the spot right behind my ear that always makes my leg twitch. "It's gonna be loud out there, Oscar, and there will be lots of cameras."

Great. Cameras meant flashing lights, and lately it also meant people rushing up to my humans. Sometimes they're nice folks who do to Finn what he does to me when he sticks his hand out to shake my paw. It's harmless enough, and they usually leave us alone after they pose with their phones held out in front of them. But other times it's people who push and shove and get way too close to my humans, all just to take a picture of them eating at a restaurant or walking down the street. One time, an intruder was using a long camera down on the beach, but I took care of him with a lot of barking and a chase that ended with my teeth in his hind quarters. It had made Finn laugh so hard, he'd had water coming out of his eyes, but afterward he told me not to do that again. Something about big trouble had I broken the skin.

"These photographers are good. They are supposed to be there, and we don't mind them taking our picture." Finn wrapped his fingers around my jaw and turned my head so we were eye to eye. "I need you to be on your best behavior, okay, mate?"

I licked his nose, and he smiled.

"That's my boy," he said. Then he looked at Cara, and his smile got even bigger. His face always did that when he looked at her, but tonight he also kept telling her how pretty she was. Probably because she was wearing a long dress and the kind of sparkly collar that Coco wears, only Cara's was delivered by a security guard who said he would be back to pick it up as soon as she was done.

When the car finally rolled to a stop, Cara reached up and placed her hand on Finn's face. I knew she was trying to show him affection, but in my own experience, a belly rub was far more effective than a head pat. Still, Finn seemed to enjoy it. He leaned into her touch, then turned and kissed her palm.

"You're going to do great," Cara told him.

"It's a lot to take in," he said.

She smiled, and when she did, Finn's shoulders relaxed. "Enjoy this. You earned it."

Finn leaned over to kiss her lips. "We earned this, luv. None of this would have been possible if it weren't for you."

"Ready?"

He nodded. "Let's do this." With that, he opened the door to the sounds of people screaming and clapping and shouting Finn's name as though they wanted him to do a trick or something. Except none of them were offering treats. All they had were sticks they wanted to put in front of his mouth while he spoke. Seemed to me they would have wanted him to fetch, but they were happy just talking. Most of the people asked him the same questions. They wanted to know who made his and Cara's clothes, where Cara got her collar, and if he did his own tricks when we were making the movie. Then one man asked Finn what he was going to do next. I was secretly hoping his answer would be that he was taking me for a long hike in the mountains behind the beach house, but apparently the guy didn't want to know what Finn was going to do tomorrow. He wanted to know what his next movie was going to be.

"I'm not sure if I'm supposed to talk about this yet but..." Finn turned to look at Cara, who gave him a smile and a nod. "It appears the boss has given me the go-ahead." He grinned. "Not a bad place to break the news."

Finn wrapped his arm around Cara's waist and pulled her closer. "My next project is an indie film about a brave young woman who, after losing the love of her life, carried on the work he and so many others died for during the Irish Rebellion." He looked at Cara, then back to the man with the stick. "But the person you really want to ask is Ms. Cara Kennedy. She's the film's screenwriter and executive producer."

"Co-executive producer," Cara was quick to clarify.

Finn stepped back, letting Cara move in front of the stick, and squatted down beside me. "She's something, isn't she?" he asked. I licked the side of his face. Of course I knew that Cara was special.

It was why I had jumped in her lap the first night they met. She and Finn were meant to be together. It just took a little longer for the humans to figure it out.

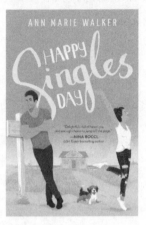
# CHAPTER 1

PAIGE PARKER DID NOT NEED a man.

She'd just told her assistant as much, but that didn't stop him from swiping through the photos he'd prescreened for her on some app that promised to find a date for even the loneliest of spinsters. Okay, maybe they didn't word it *exactly* like that. But the home page featured a slightly overweight woman, typing on her computer while a cat sat perched on her lap. If Paige hadn't known better, she'd have thought they snuck into her apartment to take the photo. Even the woman's hair color was the same shade of auburn as hers. Of course, she would never have seen the site if it weren't for her assistant, let alone opened an account. One of the hazards of having an employee with access to your driver's license and credit card who also happened to be your meddling, though well-intentioned, best friend.

*Speak of the devil...*

He said nothing in reply to her proclamation. Instead, he merely pursed his lips into a frown.

"Present company excluded," she added. And it was true. If there was anything or anyone Paige couldn't live without, it was Samuel Lee, her assistant since the first day she'd opened Chaos Control. Although she hated to admit it, her dream of running a successful life-organization company would never have been possible without his hard work and dedication. If only he would stop trying to apply those same skills to resuscitating her long-dead social life.

Sammy sat a little taller in his chair.

"While I appreciate the exception, what if you wanted a man with more to offer than an uncanny ability to anticipate your every need? What if you wanted a little S-E-X?" He cocked his head to one side so dramatically, his jet-black hair would have fallen across his forehead had it not been gelled to perfection. "Come to think of it, that talent would be quite handy in the bedroom. But don't be getting any ideas." He waved his hand in the air as if to wipe the thought from her head. "This handsome exception plays for the other team." He tapped a few images, then swiped right. "Which leaves Mr. Rochester as the only other long-term relationship in your life, and last time I checked, dating your cat is frowned upon in most states."

"Thanks for clarifying." Paige rolled her eyes even though she knew he wouldn't see. He was far too busy humming over the next batch of men who had appeared on the screen.

"Well?" he said without looking up.

"I can have meaningless sex without being in a relationship.

Men do it all the time." Except she wasn't. And she hadn't. Not for a long time.

He laughed a little too hard for her liking. "Right. And how's that working out for you?"

She straightened. "Fine."

"Fine?" Sammy knew the long hours she put in at the office, which didn't leave much time for life's more, um, carnal pleasures. Not unless she wanted a quickie at midnight, and to be honest, most nights she just wanted her fuzzy slippers and a glass of wine. Still, she didn't need him to shine a light on it.

Paige picked a nonexistent piece of lint off the sleeve of her ivory silk blouse. "Yes. Fine."

"What if you want more than fine? What if instead of a glass of wine and a tub of ice cream, you wanted a big O?"

She felt a warm flush creep across her cheeks. What in the world was wrong with her? It wasn't like she was a teenager. She was thirty flipping years old, and her assistant had made her blush just referencing an orgasm.

He grew serious, and all at once she knew what was coming.

"What if you wanted a family?"

"I don't," she said matter-of-factly. Why was it that people assumed every woman in her thirties was pining for kids? Was it so hard to believe that someone was happy with her work and her friends? Not that she had time for many of those, come to think of it. But she had her career and Mr. Rochester, and he was always happy to see her. Well, mostly. In fact, usually only if he was hungry, but still.

"Hypothetically, what if you did? Those eggs aren't getting any younger, you know."

She frowned. Lack of desire to trade in her pencil skirts for mom jeans aside, no woman liked to be reminded of her ticking clock. Ever since her birthday, it had rolled around in her brain like a grenade with the pin pulled out. Even if she felt no urge to use her ovaries, the thought of them shriveling up into prunes wasn't a pleasant one. There was still plenty of time to change her mind, and if she *was* suddenly hit with an inexplicable change of heart, she didn't need a man to procreate. Well, she did, but not in the way Sammy was implying. "Hypothetically," she said, leveling the full weight of her I'm-a-badass-businesswoman stare at him, "I could go to a sperm bank."

He raised one brow. "Uptight much?"

"I just don't need to be harassed into a dating life I neither want nor need." It wasn't like she didn't know what she was missing. She'd had all that and more. Hell, three years ago she'd even had a ring and a wedding date. But then she came home early one night to find her boss/best friend riding her betrothed like a bronco at the state fair. It was one of those moments in life where you can either wither up and die or come out swinging. Paige chose the latter. She tossed him out, quit her job, opened her own company, and never looked back. Problem was, she never slowed down either.

"What you *need* is a vacation. Someplace where you can let your hair down out of that supertight bun and cut loose a little."

Cutting loose was not in Paige's vocabulary. Order and control were the keys to happiness. They were the principles that had guided her through life and the ones that led her to becoming a certified organization professional.

"You do realize my entire existence is about the opposite?" She glanced around her immaculate office. From the bleached oak floors to the white, midcentury-modern sofa to the glossy white filing cabinets lining the wall beneath rows of glass shelves, everything was clean lines and clean space. Not that she didn't enjoy color and texture. Colorful blown glass dotted the shelves, and strategically placed throw pillows in various hues of red flanked both ends of the couch. But the overall look was simple. She had certainly worked with clients who preferred things a bit more shabby chic, but when it came to her own personal taste, the expression "Less is more" fit her to a T. Less clutter, less hoarding, less crap.

She reached for the mug of tea sitting on a coaster atop her desk. Like the rest of her furniture, the desk was minimalist in design, comprised only of a single piece of beveled-edge glass supported by polished chrome legs. Some might say it was impractical, but it suited her just fine. Drawers served as a means to stash items that really didn't need to be that accessible. Her desk was a place for action items, not to stockpile Post-it notes and paper clips.

"Oh!" Sammy's exuberance should have served as a warning, but to be honest, nothing could have prepared Paige for what came out of his mouth next. "I once read this book where a woman went to a secret sex island."

Paige sputtered and coughed. "You're joking?" she said as she wiped tea from her chin. But even as she asked the question, she knew he wasn't. The glimmer in his eyes told her he absolutely had read a book about some erotic version of *Fantasy Island*, and what's more, he'd loved every minute of it.

"Total anonymity for three days." The tone of his voice was

half that of someone revealing a dark secret and half of someone hatching a fabulous plan. "*Anything* goes." His fingers flew across the tablet screen. "I wonder if a place like that actually exists."

"Let me save you some time. No way."

His shoulders sagged. "How about Vegas then? It's a bit of a cliché—what happens there stays there and all that—but desperate times call for mediocre measures."

"You've lost your mind." Paige rounded the desk and tugged his shirtsleeve. "Now get out of my office so one of us can actually get some work done."

His sad-puppy eyes nearly broke through her resolve, but Paige held her ground, hitting him with a compliment she knew would ease the pain of being thrown out. "Nice scarf, by the way."

"Isn't it fabulous? I got it in France last year." His wide grin faded. "I know what you're up to, and don't think for a minute that you can distract me with flattery," he said as she herded him toward the door. "I'm not letting this go. You need a vacation, Boss Lady. I've worked for you for nearly three years, and you've never taken one. Time to take off those Jimmy Choos and walk barefoot in the sand."

Paige scowled at him as she shut the door, but her confident strut slowed with each step, and by the time she'd made it back to her desk, she could do nothing but collapse into a chair that was designed for anything but lounging. Sammy was right. She needed a vacation. The days and nights had started to blur together to the point that she was seriously considering an investment in day-of-the-week underpants if for no other reason than to keep track of her personal hygiene.

But there was work to be done: new clients to meet with, existing clients to satisfy, and an entire file of new promotional ideas that had been on the back burner so long they were no doubt starting to congeal. Not that it mattered much. Business was good. Really good. So good, in fact, that she really didn't need to spend much time on marketing. Word of mouth was taking care of that just fine. Of course, that was only going to continue if she stopped thinking about vacations on sandy beaches where she'd have time to actually read a whole book and not just the Goodreads summary.

She shook her head to clear it of the thoughts that, thanks to her assistant, had begun taking root, and booted up her laptop. But when she launched the browser, a headline caught her eye that completely distracted her from the hunt for the perfect shoe cubes.

Couples Have Valentine's Day, Single People Have SAD

The unfortunate acronym was like her own personal catnip, eliciting a curiosity that was a mixture of defensive amusement, and before she knew it, Paige had read the entire article. In the end she'd learned this: Singles Appreciation Day began as a protest to a holiday many saw as nothing more than a nod to consumerism, raking in money for jewelry stores, candymakers, and greeting-card companies, while also serving as an affront to those who were alone, whether out of choice or circumstance. The article went on to say that millions of people have begun celebrating February 15th instead, opting for shopping sprees, spa days, and even solo getaways.

The author also noted that the number of divorced or

never-married adults in the United States now exceeded those in wedlock. Paige would have taken a moment to ponder that last bit of information—not to mention how the word *lock* came to be synonymous with eternal love—if it weren't for an ad promising to find her "the perfect Singles Day vacation destination" if she answered a mere three-question survey.

For the most part, Paige hated the targeted marketing that popped up whenever she was online, but she had to admit, this one intrigued her. And while she doubted a rental site would know what she needed more than she did, her curiosity about what questions they would ask outweighed her disdain for falling prey to clickbait. Besides, if she was going to take a vacation, emphasis on *if*, what better holiday to celebrate than Singles Day, which—she glanced at the date displayed on her desk phone—was only a week away.

She tapped the "Find your dream vacation now" button, which took her to the three-question survey. The first one nearly had her closing out the tab.

What is your astrological sign?

Paige never understood how the date of someone's birth was supposed to offer insight into their personality. She knew plenty of people who shared birthdays and yet couldn't be more different if they tried. And while she did have many of the characteristics of a Capricorn—practical, stable, loyal—her ex-fiancé had been born under the same earth sign and was none of the above, especially when it came to loyalty.

Still, *in for a penny, in for pound,* she thought, clicking the picture of the sea goat. She took a sip of her tea as the next question loaded.

Which Disney character do you most identify with?

Paige groaned, already wondering if this meant all quiz results led to Orlando, when she suddenly realized that all of the options were female. And more than that, all of them were princesses. And not even the complete set! She scrolled through the choices in search of the fierce, gender-defying Mulan, but when she couldn't find her on the list, had to settle for the Little Mermaid. At least she and Ariel both had red hair and loved the ocean, which was a lot more than she had in common with Snow White or Cinderella.

The final question was the most difficult to answer.

What annoys you the most?

The options were varied and yet, in Paige's opinion, each and every one deserved a click: waiting in line, slow internet, screaming children, crowds, group texts, traffic. She'd finally decided on traffic when she reached another conclusion as well: she was way too uptight. Sammy's words from not ten minutes before played through her head just as her "dream destination" loaded.

"The Copper Lantern Inn" was printed in intricate scroll across the top of the screen with a quote from a magazine she'd never heard of that described it as having "one of the best beaches on the Outer Banks."

She snorted quietly to herself. Must have been quite the algorithm, she thought, sending her to North Carolina in the middle of February. Not exactly prime beach weather. Then again, with her alabaster skin, she wasn't really much of a sun worshipper. Plus, the beaches would be quite empty this time of year. No crowds, no kids kicking sand or screaming because they didn't want to come out of the water to have more sunscreen applied. Maybe it would be the ideal place for her because, aside from chilly temperatures, the place looked absolutely perfect.

Cedar shingles covered what could only be described as a cross between a Victorian home and a European castle. The lawn in the front looked like something out of an old black-and-white TV show, impeccably manicured right down to the freshly painted white picket fence. But it was the photo of the rear of the house that took Paige's breath away. Rocking chairs faced tall seagrass that swelled and dipped atop dunes that stretched along white-capped waves for as far as the eye could see.

For a moment, she imagined herself wrapped up in a cashmere blanket, reading a book that had nothing to do with maximizing floor space and everything to do with escapism romance. Not that she believed in those types of happy endings, not anymore at least. But there was something about getting lost in a fictional world where love conquered all—and where the girl always came first— that she still found appealing if not a little comforting.

A barefoot paradise awaits you at the Copper Lantern Inn, a quaint, castle-like beach home fit for a queen. Featuring three unique guest rooms, a common room, and a porch overlooking a mile of secluded beach, the Inn offers one of the best views on Aurelia Island while still being only a short bike ride from town.

Normally, the mention of self-powered transportation would have given Paige a moment's pause, but she was far too focused on the name of the island to give much thought to the coordination it would take to maneuver a bicycle after a dinner that would undoubtedly be accompanied by a bottle of chardonnay.

*Aurelia.* Her grandmother's name. The woman who taught her how to play, and cheat, at Rummy 500, who reminded her to stand up straight and put her shoulders back because "If you got it, flaunt it," and who always told her that having no man was better than the wrong man.

It was a sign. It had to be. As if Granny was still looking out for her from the great, big kitchen in the sky.

Paige scrolled through the room options, settling on the one in the inn's turret, then clicked the tab that read "extras."

Champagne and roses

Nope.

Romantic beachfront fire

Nope.

Special occasion cake

She was about to scroll past that one as well, then paused, a devious smile curving her lips as she imagined placing an order for a cake that read "Happy Singles Day."

Paige hit a button on her desk phone, and a moment later Sammy was standing in the doorway. "You rang?"

"You could have just answered the intercom," she said.

"And miss out on a chance to add a few steps?" He held up his arm to reveal the ever-present Fitbit he wore wrapped around his left wrist. He was always on her to purchase one, telling her how they could have challenges. And while a part of her feared her competitive streak would have her walking laps around the office building, another part of her knew she spent far too much time in front of her computer. Maybe she would add one of the blasted devices to her packing list. Beaches were a great place to walk and think and kick your assistant's ass in a virtual race.

"Do me a favor and pick me up one of those tracking devices while you're at lunch today." She delighted in the look of utter shock that crossed Sammy's face, knowing full well that what she was about to say next would have his jaw hitting the floor.

Paige leaned back in her chair. "And clear my schedule for next week," she said as her assistant's mouth popped open. "I'm taking a vacation."

# CHAPTER 2

LUCAS CROFT KNEW WHEN HE was being played, which was why he would have bet his last dollar on the fact that the woman sitting across from him was about to hit him with a whopper. Lucky for her, they shared the same DNA.

"Are you going to get to the point, or will there be more chitchat first?" he said.

His little sister's hazel eyes grew wide, but her feigned shock was no match for experience. Ever since they were kids, she'd been roping him into her crazy plans. He'd figured she would eventually outgrow it, but seeing as she'd just celebrated what she referred to as her twenty-ninth trip around the sun, that was looking less and less likely.

He leaned back in his chair and crossed his arms over his chest. "I know you're up to something, Smalls. Why don't you save us both the warm-up and just spit it out."

Her face scrunched up like she'd just sucked on the lemon dangling off the side of her herbal tea. "You know I hate that nickname."

"And you know I hate being dragged into your plans." Despite his best efforts to the contrary, Lucas couldn't help the smirk of amusement that tugged at the corner of his mouth. His sister might have been a complete pain in the ass, but her heart was always in the right place. Still, her ideas were usually a little eccentric and, if they involved him, often downright wacko. Like the time when she was seven and he was ten and she hatched a plan for them to run off to Antarctica to save some rare breed of penguin. He'd been grounded for a month over that one! Or when she convinced him to help her turn the old fire station into a used bookstore. The long nights painting the walls had been bad enough, but lugging all those books was worse than even the most punishing day in the gym. Although to be fair, that idea had actually turned out fairly well. After five years, Blazing Books was staying afloat, which was more than he could say for his own business venture.

Sophie lifted her chin in defiance. "Maybe I just wanted to see my big brother. Ever think of that, Mr. Smarty Pants?" Between her size—five foot two on a good day—and her pixie haircut, his sister was always being mistaken for a college student. Her insults, on the other hand, were one hundred percent middle school.

Lucas's smirk widened into a full-on grin. "You expect me to believe you closed the bookstore for an hour in the middle of the day just because you felt the overwhelming urge to buy your brother a blueberry muffin and a shot of espresso?"

She squirmed in her seat, a surefire tell if there ever was one. "I know they're your favorite. Besides, Maddie loves this place."

On instinct, Lucas's gaze shifted to where his four-year-old daughter was busy drawing rainbows on a pint-sized chalkboard.

As usual, she'd assembled the three stuffed animals that accompanied her most everywhere into a makeshift classroom. Lord only knew what she was teaching them today, but whatever it was had her smiling, and that was all that mattered despite the fact that they were a motley crew of fluff. There was Floppy, a long-eared rabbit from her very first Easter basket who was now missing his cotton tail; Stanley, half an avocado with a smiley face that was a gift from who else but the dork currently seated across from him; and a well-loved, pink-and-white teddy bear named Stinky. His name wasn't actually Stinky, but that's what Lucas had vowed to call him until Maddie relented and allowed the bear to take a bath in the "spinning machine."

"No fair using the kid to get you off the hot seat." He leaned forward and placed his elbows on the table. "Now spill. What are you up to?"

"Okay, fine." Sophie looked down, fiddling with the spoon, the napkin, the lemon—anything to keep from meeting his stare. "I *may* have reactivated the listing on the rental site."

Cute little sister or not, she had no right to reactivate the listing on his now-dormant bed-and-breakfast. It might have been his business, at least at one point, but it was also his home. This was crossing the line, even for her.

"Take it down."

She winced. "I already booked one of the rooms for next week."

If his daughter hadn't been within earshot, Lucas would have let Sophie have it. As it was, he was in danger of grinding his molars into dust.

"Look, I know you haven't hosted guests in a while, but it will be like riding a bike. Once you get going, it will all come back to you."

There was a litany of reasons why this was a bad idea, the most glaring of which was the fact that the place wasn't even close to being ready for guests, but he chose to focus on the most immediate one.

"Maddie won't like it."

"You don't know that."

"She was two the last time a guest stayed in the house. She doesn't even remember that lifestyle."

"She was almost three," Sophie corrected. "Your daughter is a lot more open to new experiences than you give her credit for, and unlike her dad, she actually likes meeting new people." Her words came quickly, no doubt an attempt to cut off his protests. "Besides, you don't have to worry about Maddie. She can stay with me."

"For a whole week?" He shook his head. "No way."

His sister looked genuinely hurt. "Maddie loves spending time with me."

"Yeah, for an afternoon, maybe a day here or there, but she's never been away from me that long." He tried to soften his objection with a little levity. "Plus, a whole week of glitter nail polish and ice cream before dinner?"

"It's not like you won't be seeing her every day. It's just so you can have the flexibility to get stuff done. And you should be thanking me. If it weren't for me, the poor thing wouldn't have even known what a skirt was, let alone tights."

"And that would have been a bad thing?" As far as he was

concerned, Maddie could stay a little girl in blue jeans and pigtails forever.

"I'm serious, Luc. I love spending time with my niece. Plus, it's good for her to have a female in her life, and since apparently the idea of actually asking a woman on a date is out of the question..."

He shot her a look he knew could freeze lava in hell. "Not this again." They'd been over the topic so many times he'd lost count. There weren't many women on the island to begin with, and by the time you weeded out the ones who were too old or too young, there wasn't much left. Not that he was in the market. *Love* was a four-letter word as far as he was concerned. "So help me, if you're about to tell me yet again how much Susan at the bank thinks I look like Ryan Reynolds—"

"Settle down, Cujo." Sophie held up her hands in innocence. "I wasn't even going to mention Susan." She stuck her tongue out. "Personally, I think you look more like Ryan Reynolds in *Deadpool*, but hey, to each their own. All I'm saying is that Maddie could benefit from a week of frills and glitter."

"She's fine. We both are." His voice lowered. "Plus, what if she has a nightmare?" It had been months since the last time Maddie had woken screaming his name, but the sound of her little voice quivering in fear was permanently ingrained in his mind, not to mention his heart. If she woke up looking for him and he wasn't there...

"Then you can FaceTime and sing that silly song she loves, and if that doesn't work, you could be at my place in less than ten."

Ten minutes away from a frightened four-year-old was ten minutes too long. The doctor said she would outgrow it, that as the memories of losing her mom faded, so would the nightmares she'd been having about losing her dad. It was a double-edged sword really. As much as he wanted his daughter to have a peaceful night's sleep, the thought of her mother fading from her memories was almost harder to bear than Maddie's screams.

"Or I could skip the late-night ride and she can just stay home and we can forget this whole thing." Lucas began to stand, but Sophie's next words stopped him in his tracks.

"I got double the summer rate."

"What did you just say?"

"You heard me."

"How the hell did you manage that?" No one paid double the summer rate in summer, let alone the dead of winter.

"I may have told her there was a man from Louisiana who came back every year to see the sea turtles."

"You spoke to her?" He wasn't sure what made him ask because at the moment, the fact that his sister was chatting with potential customers was the least of his concerns.

"We messaged through the site."

Lucas ran his hand through his hair. "Turtle season ends in August."

Her ears turned pink. Tell number two. "I may have fudged the dates a bit."

"And the place doesn't look at all like the website photos anymore." That was the understatement of the century. It wasn't like he'd meant for it to get so out of hand, but after the funeral, he'd focused all his attention on Maddie. Then one day slipped into the next, and before he knew it, even he had to admit it was a mess.

"Yeah, I may not have mentioned that either."

"What *did* you tell her?"

"That it was tranquil."

More like deserted.

"Good news is she booked the turret room," Sophie said as if reading his mind. Not that it mattered. There was only one guest room left. The others had been...repurposed.

"You know I haven't had a booking since..." A profound sadness crept into his heart like ink seeping into parchment.

"I know." Her voice had grown softer. "But the last thing she would want is for you to lose the inn. It meant so much to both of you. And with the taxes coming due..."

There it was, the truth he couldn't deny. Death and taxes, the two inevitabilities in life. One had rocked his world, and the other was threatening to clear away the rubble.

The cash from Jenny's life insurance policy had covered their mortgage and living expenses for the last two years, but that account was dwindling quickly. He had enough for about three more months—which, if he *was* going to reopen, would get him to the summer season—but not for the full tax bill as well. He and Jenny had poured their hearts and souls, not to mention every dime they had, into their little beachfront castle. The thought of running it without her brought the emotions he tried his best to bury right up to the surface. But the thought of selling it—or even worse, having it taken away by the county—would be like losing her all over again.

A week's rental at double the summer rate would certainly buy him the time he needed to figure out his next steps, not to mention get his little sister off his back.

Lucas pressed his lips into a thin line, then let out an exaggerated breath. "Fine. I'll take the booking."

Sophie clapped her hands together. "That's great!"

"What's great?" Maddie asked. Her dark-brown curls swayed as she skipped toward the table.

"Your dad just agreed to let you sleep over at my house for a few nights."

His little girl's eyes grew wide. "Like a slumber party?"

Sophie smiled. "Exactly like a slumber party." She cocked her head to one side. "Except it's not much of a party if it's only the two of us. Can you think of anyone else we can invite?"

"Stanley would love to come," Maddie said. "So would Floppy and Raymond," she added, referring to Stinky by his given name.

Shocker, Lucas thought. But there was no denying the warmth that spread through his chest at the sight of his daughter so happy.

"Then definitely bring them." Sophie pulled her niece into her lap, then turned her attention back to Lucas. "Want me to come by tonight to help you tidy the place up a bit?"

It would take a hell of a lot more than a little "tidying" to make the place presentable. For a moment, he almost felt guilty about that. But then he thought about the kind of uptight woman who would pay double just to beat out some imaginary schmuck looking for turtles in winter, and all thoughts of Southern hospitality left him. "No thanks," he said. "I am who I am. If my guest doesn't like it"—he narrowed his eyes at his sister—"she can message her host."

# CHAPTER 3

PAIGE REALIZED SHE'D MADE A terrible mistake the moment she stepped off the ferry. The tiny hairs on the back of her neck stood at attention the way they always did when she was making the wrong move, but that wasn't even the most obvious sign that disaster loomed ahead of her. No, it was the enormous dark clouds that had suddenly shrouded the whole marina like a blanket of doom and gloom.

She should have hightailed it back to the mainland right then and there, but the room at the inn was prepaid and she'd flown all the way to North Carolina. Last thing she wanted was more time in an airport. Besides, snuggling up on a rocking chair, watching the storm move across the ocean while wrapped in a blanket and sipping herbal tea—or even better, a glass of chardonnay—might be just as nice as walking the beach. But first, she needed to get to the inn.

She pulled out her smartphone and opened the Uber app. Nothing. Not a single car anywhere on the digital grid.

*What the...*

She glanced around for a taxi stand. Again, nothing.

"Excuse me," she called out to a man loading the last of his fishing gear into a wagon-like device he had hitched to his bicycle. "Can you tell me where I can grab a cab?"

The man looked around and chuckled. "Raleigh maybe?"

Paige frowned, and the man's laugh grew deeper. "Just come in on the ferry?" he asked as he sauntered closer. He had a kind face, weathered from lack of sunscreen but in a way that made his eyes crinkle when he smiled.

She nodded toward the suitcase at her feet. "Pretty obvious, huh?"

"Not too many tourists this time of year." He took off his red cap and wiped his brow with the back of his hand before shoving the hat squarely back on his head. "But the ones we do get usually know there's no cars on the island."

Paige's mouth dropped open. "No cars?" Guess that's what she got for choosing traffic as the thing that annoyed her the most.

"Nope. That's the charm of Aurelia." His deep voice switched into a singsong. "Trade the hustle and bustle for the charm of a simpler time." No doubt he'd just recounted some sort of Department of Tourism slogan. Too bad Paige was only just now hearing it for the first time.

"In season, the bike rental shop is open," he continued. "They usually have a stand set up to greet the ferry. But in February..."

*Good to know.* Even her unspoken words were dripping with sarcasm because none of that information did anything to help her immediate predicament.

"Where ya headed?" the man asked.

"Copper Lantern Inn."

His brows shot up so high they were practically under his cap.

Paige was about to ask him about his reaction when he caught her off guard with an offer she wanted to refuse but couldn't.

"Tell you what," he said. "Load that bag of yours on top of my gear, and I'll drop you by on my way home."

For a moment, she thought he planned to pedal her to the inn on his handlebars like they were a couple of ten-year-olds, but then he wheeled the bike toward her, revealing a sidecar. On a bike. This day really couldn't get any worse, she thought as she used a bungee cord to strap her Louis Vuitton bag on top of a rusty tackle box.

But when she reached the inn, she knew her assessment had been premature. She also knew why her chauffeur had reacted the way he did when she told him where she was staying. To put it bluntly, the place was a dump.

From a distance, the outside of the inn looked pretty much the same as it had on the website. Aside from the fact that the bright-yellow shingles now looked a bit faded and two shutters hung slightly askew, it was still the epitome of beachfront charm. But as she drew closer, she noted that the manicured lawn was comprised of more weeds than grass and the white picket fence was now a shade of dingy beige, thanks to being weathered to nearly bare wood.

Paige took a deep breath. She wasn't planning to be out front much anyway. As long as the back porch still had rocking chairs and a view of the ocean, she'd be just fine.

Famous last words.

Determined, she made her way up the porch steps, careful to avoid a nearly rotted tread. But when she reached the front door, she hesitated. Do you knock at a bed-and-breakfast? Granted, it was a type of hotel, but it was also someone's home. What was the protocol?

"Go on in," her chauffeur called out as if reading her mind. "Lucas is probably out back."

She walked through the leaded-glass door and came to an abrupt halt. The website had used words like *quaint, charming,* and *picturesque,* but the adjectives ricocheting around Paige's head as she took in the sight of the front room were more along the lines of *cluttered, disgusting,* and *unsightly.*

Clothes were strewn about on every piece of upholstered furniture, while dirty plates and cups sat piled on the flat surfaces. And dear Lord, was that peanut butter on the banister? Her eyes were drawn to the back of the house, where a wall of French doors revealed the seagrass swells that led to the white-capped waves. At least the ocean was as advertised, because the rest of the place certainly wasn't. With the exception of being quiet, nothing was as she expected, but even that would have more appropriately been described as desolate.

"Can I help you?"

She turned around, ready to give her would-be host a piece of her mind, but at the sight of him, all thoughts of the pigpen left her because holy macaroni, the pig himself looked more like a freaking movie star than a swine. And there he stood, barely a foot in front of her, wearing nothing but a pair of faded jeans and a few days' worth of stubble. With his chiseled jaw, light-brown hair, and warm hazel eyes, he was a dead ringer for... What was that guy's name? Damn, she should have paid more attention to Sammy's screen savers because whoever this guy's doppelgänger was, he'd definitely been featured as Mr. October. But unlike the hot dude on Sammy's tablet, the man before her didn't have eyes that sparkled when he smiled. Well, maybe they did, but it was impossible to tell, because at the moment Mr. Look-Alike was sporting a brooding frown.

"I'm looking for Mr. Croft."

"I'm Lucas Croft."

Paige wasn't sure what she had been expecting an innkeeper to look like, but this guy wasn't it. He looked more like the hot-as-hell neighborhood handyman on some sort of *Desperate Housewives* reboot. Sammy was right. She really needed to watch less television and spend more time with actual humans.

"Paige Parker." She stuck out her hand. "From Chicago." When her introduction drew no reaction, let alone an extended hand, she added, "I have a reservation."

He yanked a T-shirt out of the back pocket of his jeans and pulled it over his head. "Guess that would explain why you just let yourself into my house," he said as his face poked through the neck hole.

"The man on the bike said..."

"It's fine." He let out a sigh that was about as far from welcoming as she could imagine. "You're paying enough to waltz in like you own the joint."

So much for Southern hospitality. Lucas Croft was crusty with a capital C.

"Your room is at the top of the stairs, first door on the right. Don't even think about going into any of the others. You're the only guest, but that doesn't mean you have the run of the whole place."

Forget crusty, this guy was downright rude. He sounded more like a drill sergeant giving her a tour of the barracks than the owner of a bed-and-breakfast greeting a guest. And not just any guest either, but the *only* guest apparently. *No surprise there*, she thought, nearly snorting out loud. She could hardly imagine people were beating down the door to get in. Well, not people who'd taken a minute to do their due diligence anyway.

"The bathroom is first come, first served, but keep the hot-water use to under ten minutes or I'll turn it off from down here."

She'd barely processed his threat when he motioned for her to follow him down the short hallway to the kitchen. "Dinner is served at six. If you miss it, you're on your own. Tonight will be pizza and salad." He opened the fridge door and pulled out a bag of what had once been mixed field greens, but was now more of a liquid, and wrinkled his nose. "Make that just pizza."

He launched the bag toward a trash can with a mildly impressive hook shot that would no doubt have been a three-pointer had the can not already been overflowing.

Frozen pizza served in a pigsty by a guy who made even her dirtbag ex-fiancé look like a pretty friendly guy? No thanks.

"You know, I think I'll pass. In fact, I'm going to take a hard pass on all of this." Her eyes darted around the room. "Nothing is the way it looked online."

# ACKNOWLEDGMENTS

This book was written in 2020, a year that brought difficulties in many forms. Writing was no exception, and this book would not have been possible without the love and support of my family and friends.

As always, I thank my agent, Pamela Harty, first and foremost. Your faith in me never fails, and I thank you not only for that but for the "okay, now tell me what else is going on" portions of our phone calls.

To everyone at Sourcebooks—Deb, Susie, Stefani, Katie, Margaret, Jessica—you guys worked tirelessly under the most challenging circumstances, and I appreciate all you have done to make sure these words reach readers.

To my fellow authors who I am proud to call friends, you are always there with exactly what I need, whether an encouraging text or a wine-fueled Zoom, and for that I will be forever grateful.

To the readers, bloggers, and bookstagrammers who have hosted events, posted reviews, and sent messages that kept me in front of my laptop even on the toughest days, thank you from the bottom of my heart. You are the ones who make this possible.

And finally, to my family. To my parents, thank you for always telling me that I could do anything I set my mind to, and to my kids—Jack, Kiley, Maggie, and Ryan—you inspire me on a daily basis, not only with your achievements but with the way you treat each other and the world. You are my proudest accomplishment, and I will be forever grateful to be your mom.

# ABOUT THE AUTHOR

Ann Marie Walker is the author of nine novels, ranging from romantic suspense to romantic comedy. She's a fan of fancy cocktails, anything chocolate, and '80s rom-coms, her superpower is connecting any situation to an episode of *Friends*, and she thinks all coffee cups should be the size of a bowl. You can find her at annmariewalker.com, where she would be happy to talk to you about alpha males, lemon drop martinis, or Chewbacca, the Morkie who is kind enough to let her sit on his couch. Ann Marie attended the University of Notre Dame and currently lives in Chicago.